A ROOM FULL OF NIGHT

A ROOM FULL OF NIGHT

A THRILLER

TR KENNETH

OCEANVIEW PUBLISHING
SARASOTA, FLORIDA

ISBN 978-1-60809-385-4

Cover Design by Christian Fuenfhausen

Published in the United States of America by Oceanview Publishing

Sarasota, Florida

www.oceanviewpub.com

10 9 8 7 6 5 4 3 2

For Tommy and Johnnie—with love always and forever

A ROOM FULL OF NIGHT

PART ONE

If you set a horse's tail on fire, he will take the fire with him when he runs.

ROBERT RUTHVEN

CHAPTER ONE

He was a determined gimp.

Stag Maguire possessed a hitch in his walk, even in the massive Sorel snow boots he used to plod through the rubble of ice on the curb. Past midnight, the sidewalks mirrored with black ice, he traversed his way toward Gerde's Biergarten as if headed toward the Holy Grail instead of a forlorn drinking establishment that had in truth died years ago. All around him, the wind hammered off Lake Michigan, whomping whatever wasn't battened down. It sent tiny ice shards into his stinging eyes. Like micro-knives, the ice and wind shredded the tattered highway-stripe yellow banner in front of Gerde's.

Going Out Of Businesss, it said, the misspelling a spit on an already-cold corpse.

He should have been home, nursing his bad leg with whiskey. It was reasonable and sane that he should shrug and tell himself that he had problems, too. That there was no need to get involved in people's crap. Others were nothing but an inconvenience. They were all a pain in the ass, and he'd not been rewarded well for his concern. Ever.

But, above all, Stag Maguire was an unreasonable man.

He should have stayed home. Stayed home and reenacted the family tradition by slipping a needle in his arm and sink into sweet oblivion. It was insanity to continue this life of few rewards. By all that was holy, he should have just jawed the end of a revolver long ago.

But no.

Instead, he trudged onward. Because his friend was in peril. Because the night was dark and treacherous, and he was an unreasonable man.

Against the screaming current, he arrived at the huge Black Forest doors of Gerde's. A sheriff's notice to keep out had been stapled over the seam where the two doors met, but the notice was ripped now. The entrance had been breached. The two halves tenuously flapped in the ferocious wind.

"God dammit, Harry," he said under his breath.

He clutched the door handle and crashed into the establishment with all the grace of a bear tearing through a dumpster.

The interior was lit with one sad light bulb. It haloed a figure; overweight and lumped over the bar like a lonely, forlorn toad. In front of him were a dozen opened bottles of beer, none of which particularly grabbed his attention. Looking down on the whole tableau was a humorless, smoke-dimmed portrait of a man in clichéd Bavarian attire who sported a ridiculous wooly orange beard.

Stag broke the thick rime of ice that coated his balaclava. It made a magical noise of tinkling glass.

In the darkness, it was more like the notes of a music box in a horror film.

The fat man did not look up, and Stag caught the eyes of the portrait. They stared at him, those eyes. They were the kind that followed the viewer wherever he stood in the room. It took talent to make eyes like that, but the artist's work was undone by the ridiculous clothes and beard. Stag pulled off his balaclava. Shaking the ice from his hair, he got a good look at the painting now. It was strange how the world was in those eyes: two-dimensional, deep-set. And like the world, they were too close together, and too cold to care.

"Harry." Stag's expression worked up the permanent knot of tension between his eyebrows. It was his usual stance now. To view everything as phantasmagoria.

Dragging up a bar stool, Stag sat down next to him and silently commiserated for a long moment.

Finally, in the sole acknowledgement that he was no longer alone, Harry said in a drunken voice, "How the hell did this happen?"

"I don't know. You worked like a dog."

"I ran the numbers. I had the same number of customers that my dad had in his day. And my grandfather's. They both made it. How come I couldn't?"

Stag put a hand on his shoulder. "You'll start again." The words sounded limped dick, even to him.

Both men settled back into the silence, each staring ahead to a dark, imaginary horizon.

"Why?" Harry said miserably.

"Ah, the *why*," Stag said.

"The numbers should have worked. I should have been able to make a go of it. Now Julie's divorcing me and taking the kids. I've got nothing."

"I don't know how to answer the *why*."

"All I ever wanted was to run this lousy place. Like my father and his father and his father. Now, fuck!"

Stag didn't say anything at first. He just looked at him, concern tight on his face. He finally said, "The elusive *why*. I mean, what-the-fuck? WHY? It's endless."

Harry slid him a gimlet-eyed glance.

"It haunts me." Stag released a sigh. "The eternal why."

"I used to think the facts would add up. But the facts," Harry said, slightly slurring his *s*, "they don't add up." He turned to Stag. "You're the journalist. Look at my books and tell me why."

Stag knew even as a journalist, the *why* left nothing but a constant craving for more facts. Until you found yourself in a spider web of facts, sometimes none of it making any more sense than it did at the beginning.

"People want absolutes. It's not always about absolutes. Sometimes it's about night and fog."

Harry pondered this while the shrill scream of the wind fled across the roof. Finally, he said, "You know what my father always told me? He'd say, 'When the wolf comes to the door, feed it. Or it will feed on you.'"

Stag commiserated. The only thing he could think to do was let Harry get it off his chest. Even if he made no sense.

"That was the problem, see? I didn't feed the wolf. I didn't feed the blood-sucking wolf, and now look." Harry gestured around in grief, finishing off one of the many half-empty beers in front of him. "My great-grandfather started this place. It's been here since 1934. I'm the fourth generation of Gerdes and I lost it—I fucking lost it. Because I didn't feed the wolf." Harry looked like he either wanted to break the beer bottle or burst into tears.

Stag didn't know what to say. Gerde's had been around a long time. He remembered the long nights of drunkenly dancing around the subject of whether Gerde's had been sympathetic to the National Socialist cause in the thirties. Shit, there'd been long nights ruminating over the portrait alone. The rumor was that the painting had hung in the Berghof and had been given to Gerde's by a marauding G.I. Joe after the war.

But drunken speculation didn't make things true. And crying when you were fucked, didn't unfuck yourself. The wolf metaphor escaped him, but if the money added up then and didn't today, the business was going under. Facts could be cruel foes.

"This is all I ever wanted. To run the family biz and be happy with Julie and the kids. So why?"

"There's chaos even in math," Stag said. "And 'therein lies the rub.'"

"A plus B equals C. Why'd that work then but not now?"

Stag twisted his mouth in something like a grimace. He toyed with one of the half-empty beer bottles, and took a sip. It was warm and flat, but he didn't care. "I don't think I ever told you this, but, you know, I had a really good childhood. Really. That probably surprises you."

Harry looked at him suspiciously.

Stag shrugged it off. "I mean, yeah, I had no dad—but I never really cared. You don't miss what you never had. And I had the nicest mom in the world. Nothing ever scared her, nothing ever made her angry. I always believed she loved me a lot. She was always gentle, always patient. Always smiling."

He took the beer and downed it. "I lost her when I was thirteen, and I wanted to know why. If she loved me so much, why did she do it? But the fact was she loved that needle more." He released a deep breath. "That's when I knew I wanted to become a journalist. I wanted to know why. And you know what?"

Harry shook his head.

"I still don't know fucking why."

Both men grunted their agreement like two prisoners greeting the noose. The only rational response was to say, *Hello, old friend.*

Harry began peeling off the label to his beer. "Here we are. Broken." He reached for a fresh bottle. "Both of us."

"The hell." It was all Stag could think of to say.

The men continued their vanishing point stares. Then Harry said, "I should just burn this place around me. Fuck the sheriff and his spoils. Just burn it and let it take me down too. I got nothing."

"No, you've been with me through all my wars, and there was one thing you learned in a war: You never leave a brother behind." Stag tightened his hand on Harry's meaty shoulder. "C'mon, brother, let's get out of here."

Harry raised his bleary, drunken gaze to the portrait on the wall. "Hear that, man? They're coming to take it all away—to take you away. I got nothing left—"

Stag took the beer bottle out of Harry's grasp. "You can crash at my place—your shit's back there anyway since Julie left. No point in staying here another minute."

"I don't think I can leave. This is my home. I've been living here one way or another all my life."

"Time to get a new life. C'mon. You can do it." Stag gave him an encouraging slap on the back.

"I'm not your real brother. Fuck, I wish I was. You're the brains. The journalist. Of course, I'm not." Harry waved his hand at the portrait. "No, these are my people."

"Hell, losing this place hurts me, too." Stag looked over the bar made of substantial blackened oak. "I proposed to Holly here. Right here at the bar by the portrait."

"You never told me."

"Yep. I brought out the ring and got down on one knee—the whole works."

"Who'd have thought you were a romantic?"

Stag snorted a laugh. "Too bad Holly didn't think so."

"You mean she turned you down?" For a second, Harry snapped out of his misery.

"One of my all-time stellar moments. She didn't want to marry a broke writer. I mean, who-the-fuck would?"

"Really? She turned you down?"

Stag gave a quirk of his mouth. "Yeah, well, I'm not a quitter. It took another five months and sore knees, but she finally accepted."

"How'd you convince her?"

"Right time, right circumstances. Her father had died and she was undone by it, in free fall. I told her I would take care of her for the rest of her life." Stag nodded. Then he nodded again, as if to re-assure himself. "And she damned straight knew I would keep pro-posing. She was the only answer to why."

Harry absorbed this new information. Then he said, "We're al-most brothers, aren't we?" He looked at Stag with a drunk's new-found sentimentality. "I got your back. You know it, man."

"Goddamn right. If it hadn't been for you convincing your par-ents to take me in, I'd have been ass-raped in foster care at thirteen. We're better than brothers. Brothers by choice." Stag stood. "C'mon. That's what I'm here for. Let's go."

Harry slowly conceded the barstool. His eyes were red from un-shed tears. He was drunk and dazed. He looked around, while Stag grabbed the parkas.

"My people... my people..." Harry's voice descended into misery again. "Fuck the sheriff! I'm taking my people with me—" Harry clambered onto a bar stool and reached over the bar. He put his hands on either side of the portrait's frame.

"You're supposed to leave everything—"

"I've spent my whole life with this fucker. I'm not leaving him now." Harry forcibly ripped the picture off the wall. A clean rect-angle was left behind it, where it had hung for decades in the smoke-filled bar.

Stag shrugged. "Okay, it's a shitty painting. The sheriff won't miss it. Let's go."

Harry pulled the portrait from his chest and gazed at it. "Yeah, it is a shitty painting. And you know why? The guy doesn't match.

From his outfit he should be all friendly and doing the chicken dance, but instead, he looks kinda . . . kinda . . . well, kinda scary."

"Frankly, he looks like a bastard. Always has."

Harry clutched the portrait to him again, stumbling. "Yeah, but we go way back."

"Who is he anyway?" Stag asked, shrugging into his parka.

"Don't know—everybody always called him 'Our Reini'."

"'Our Reini'? You're right. He doesn't match. With that name he should be doing the chicken dance."

"What am I gonna do?" Harry whispered in misery, staring down at the painted face.

"You're going to come home with me and sleep it off. Then tomorrow you'll start again." Stag grabbed him by the shoulders. Painting and all, he plowed him toward the door.

"I can't do it." The beer and the stress had caught up to Harry, and the belligerent was coming out.

"I'm not going to let that sheriff arrest you." Stag used even more force to keep the momentum toward the door.

"Fuck that cock-sucking sheriff!" Harry stood still, rebelling. "Let him try to make me leave—"

"You do not want to be the local kook on FOX News."

"Still. Fuck 'em. I should burn the place down. Burn it right down to the ground. Take a stand. Be a man!"

"Be a man some other way," Stag said, urging him along with his balled-up parka.

"That's what I'm gonna do—burn it to the ground!"

"Do not do that." Stag struggled with him as Harry tried to turn back to the bar.

"Who'll have the last laugh then!" Harry wrestled with the parka, the painting, and Stag's grasp. "I'll make FOX News all right!"

"Harry, you're the only family I've got. I can't let you burn this place. Not even if I have to cold-cock you and drag you out of here."

"I'm gonna do it—I'm gonna make my stand!"

"You are *not*!" Stag shoved him against the wall, his fist in Harry's face.

They struggled with each other until something dreamy and white floated down beside them, detaching itself from the lining of the portrait. As if watching a falling angel, both men stopped and stared as the long strip of white silk slid to the floor and came to a halt.

"What—" Harry loosened his grip on Stag.

"It must've been stuck in the back of the painting." Stag shoved Harry away and picked it up. "There's writing on it."

"Does it tell us who the guy is in the painting?"

"It's in German."

Harry took the strip of silk, holding it up in one hammy fist.

Stag watched his reaction go from curiosity to creeping horror. Unexpectedly the hair raised on the back of his own neck.

"What's it say?"

Harry didn't answer. He looked as if he were working something out in his head.

"What's it say?" Stag grabbed at the white strip. The German words crept into his bloodstream.

Harry's voice was stone cold sober. "It says, 'Help me.'"

CHAPTER TWO

"THERE'S A BUNCH of other writing on this—you're the one with the master's in German, so you tell me. Look—that's definitely a street address—106 Wilhelmstrasse—apartment 12A." Harry lifted a drunken hand to the mug of coffee Stag offered and took a deep gulp. "There's a lot of stuff on here I can't make out at all. Looks like it's written in code."

They were back at Stag's, the painting propped on a chair while they studied it and the strange piece of silk. The cheap furnished apartment was a temporary landing spot Stag had managed to find in the miasma of his return to Wuttke. It was now official. He hadn't written a word for over three years. He'd come limping home and plopped aimlessly into a monthly rental. The place was now filled to the ceiling with cardboard boxes—some his, some Harry's— and piles of clothes. A Salvation Army futon groaned under the big man's weight.

Stag looked down at the fluttery white silk strip, incongruous in Harry's freckled paw. It had already been a long evening just getting Harry out of the bar. He was exhausted, his gimp leg pounded with pain. At least there was this small mystery to distract them.

He got his own cup of coffee. Walking to the futon, a glint of metal next to one of the painting's stretcher bars caught his eye.

"What you got?" asked Harry.

"Something's here. Something—" Stag edged it out with a fingernail. It was the tip of a key. He could see that from the cuts on the side.

He went to the kitchen and got a knife. Slowly, so as not to damage the painting, he slid the key out from between the stretcher and canvas.

"I guess this is the key to the address." Stag held it out in his palm. It was the brown color of worn brass. Definitely not modern.

"Fuck. I can't believe all this time it was in there." Harry rubbed his jaw. "I wonder what this means."

"The note's on parachute silk," Stag said almost subconsciously.

"Parachute silk?"

"Back in World War II, they used this thin white silk for parachutes and spies used it for writing codes just like the one here." Stag ran his finger down the fabric's smooth surface. "You could slip it underneath the lining of a coat or a suitcase, and no one could detect it in a cursory search."

"Huh. But that doesn't answer who wrote the note and why it was stuck in the back of this guy."

Harry smoothed the strip out against the futon and began translating the faded peacock-blue writing. "The first part is definitely some kind of code. Total gibberish. The rest of it says something about—I don't know—something's in a truck—the handwriting's not too legible, but something's in a truck—at the bottom of the lake. And there's a shape drawn on here. A rune? A map? It looks like a long scraggly finger with a string tied on it. Maybe that's where the truck is. It might be the outline of a lake. But what lake?" He gulped his coffee and held out for more.

Stag went to get the coffeepot, but then Harry shot out, "Fuck me! I can't be sure but I swear the word's diamonds. The diamonds are in a truck at the bottom of the lake."

As if this were an everyday conversation, Stag poured the fat man another cup of coffee and replaced the pot. "I wish your dad was still around. He could tell us more about this."

"Yeah." Harry ran his thick finger over the writing. "I mean, he never really talked about the painting. The rumor of it coming from the Berghof was just bullshit he liked to spread around." He shook his head. "Holy shit—do you think—I mean—is this some kind of clue to—"

"Nazi treasure?"

"Is it? Is this a fucking Nazi treasure map?"

"It's decades old. And completely without provenance and context. If it was some kind of clue to finding hidden Nazi diamonds, trust me, they're long gone." Stag held up the key. "No, what we've got here is a historical curiosity."

"The diamonds are in a truck at the bottom of the lake!" Harry smoothed out the silk again. "If that's not talking about Nazi diamonds—"

"We don't even know for sure if the word is diamonds, it's kind of hard to make out." Stag eyed Harry with extreme skepticism, then picked up the long strip of silk again and contemplated it. "Sure. It looks like the word diamonds. I agree this is something out of the ordinary, but again with no context . . . Did your dad keep any files or anything we could look through?"

Harry was sobering quickly. "Files? No, there aren't any files. He got rid of all the files. The only thing he left was the accounting books. That's all. Nothing more. No files."

Okay, Stag thought. Really, really no files. "We should Google the address. It might be current—it's a possibility—"

Harry snorted. "This note's been in that picture for decades. I can guarantee nobody's touched that guy since he was hung on the wall." Tapping into his phone, Harry put the screen in Stag's face. "It's an address, all right. In Berlin. It's still there."

"We should call it. Maybe we'll find out something that way."

"Good idea." Harry found a phone number for the address. It was an apartment building called the Dresdenhof. He entered it into his phone, and then promptly handed it over to Stag.

"You're the one with the master's in German, for Christ's sake."

Stag reluctantly took the phone and introduced himself. The connection seemed to falter and he said his name again. "Yes, Stag Maguire. Calling from Wisconsin. USA." He began a dialogue with whoever was at the other end. After a lengthy back-and-forth, he then said, "*Danke.*"

Stag shrugged, handing Harry his phone back. He was unsure what the conversation meant. "Apparently it's a high security building for diplomats. No one needs help in 12A, they said. The apartment's been unoccupied since 1942. And they said even if someone did need help, there would be no point in calling the police because the Dresdenhof is out of their jurisdiction and has been since the war."

"For how long?"

"That's what the guy said."

"What the fuck does that mean?"

"That's what I wondered. Something about diplomatic immunity, the Swedish embassy." Stag turned his attention to the window. Dawn was just seeping in. Propped up against a chair, the painting stared back as if daring him to blink.

"You know, in this light, the paint looks..." Stag gazed at the painting. The first sunbeam had just lain across it.

He walked over to it, and scratched at a peeling flake of paint on the portrait's beard. He took off another, then another, flake of alligatored paint. "Look at this. I think it's been painted over. That's why the guy looks funny."

"Nothing is funny about that bastard. Seriously. Not even a mother could love that evil-eyed turd."

"This has been over-painted." Stag tilted the painting to better catch the sunlight, and with it, the outline of paint beneath the surface. "I think he's wearing a uniform. Maybe we should see if we can scrape this top layer off. Get me a pen knife. If he's wearing a uniform, maybe we can find out who the guy is."

Harry suddenly looked like the kid ready to barf on the Tilt-A-Whirl. "Shit, if he's wearing a uniform then he's probably a—" His expression turned dark and unsettled.

Stag gave him an unsure glance. "They did that, you know. Painted over uniforms to make the figure more politically correct. But that doesn't mean anyone in your family knew there was anything underneath this guy. I mean, how could they? The bar was dark and they hardly paid it any attention."

Harry still looked reluctant.

"Look, get me something to scrape with. It's the only way."

"If he's in a uniform, then that means, fuck, we've had a Nazi hanging in the bar for my entire life."

Stag put the painting back on the chair. Both men stared at it.

"You know, maybe I've always known. Fuck!" Harry wearily palmed his face. "Fuck this. And fuck me!"

"I'll get a knife," Stag said.

Forty minutes later, an entirely new portrait was propped back on the chair. The beard was gone, and the Bavarian peasant garb. After making a drift of paint chips, Stag stepped back, strangely repulsed by his accomplishment. There was no mistaking the German field gray uniform. Nor the Death's Head on his cap. Furthermore, he had a pretty good idea who it was, but he didn't want to freak Harry out even more.

"This is bullshit. What the hell were they doing hanging a Nazi on the wall?" Harry muttered to himself.

"Maybe they didn't know who he was."

"Sure," Harry answered miserably. "That's why they called him 'our Reini.' *Our!* Reini!"

"I'll take it to Jake this afternoon." Stag wiped a few chips of paint stuck to his cheek. "Maybe he can identify him."

"No," Harry said. "I don't want you to take it to Jake. I want the motherfucker gone. Let's burn it."

"But the note—"

"Seriously, it's my painting. I don't care about it. I want it gone. Burn it!"

"What about the diamonds?"

Harry rubbed his bleary eyes. "Fuck! I don't like this! Nor this guy!" He began to come down from his rage. "But maybe if there are diamonds, I could get Julie and the kids—"

"Let's take it to Jake. We'll find out what this is all about." Someone had to remain sane, and it sure as hell wasn't going to be Harry. "It's highly unlikely this is about diamonds, nor that they're still around after all this time," Stag said.

"Look at this bastard's fancy-ass medals on his uniform. Sure, there are diamonds. Maybe a whole truck full of them. In the lake," Harry said, miserably.

"First we need to stick to finding out who this guy is and maybe who wrote that note before we go—"

"I could get Julie back."

Stag gave Harry a worried look. There was no yearning in the world like wanting to turn back the clock and get back all you'd lost. Knowing him as well as Stag did, he could see the insane path of Harry's thoughts. Sure, it all sounded good. Harry could win Julie back, and he himself could become the famous journalist who found the lost Nazi diamonds in the lake. All would be righted and ennobled almost by the hand of divine providence.

And unicorns would fart rainbows.

"First things first. Let's get a bead on this guy." Stag forced Harry's attention back to the portrait. There the lizard eyes stared back at them, and Stag felt a queasy sink in his stomach.

It was crazy. Far-fetched in the extreme, and he had a duty to get Harry's grief-stricken thinking back down to earth. It didn't help Harry's current emotional state to be trying to win Julie back with the lottery of spurious Nazi treasure. Whatever had been written on the strip of silk was decades old. What the hell were they going to do with that information in Wisconsin, at this date and time? Not much, was the answer.

And there was only one thing he was sure of even if there were diamonds.

A whole truckful of them.

In a lake somewhere.

The cocksucker in front of him probably stole them.

And there was no need to speculate from whom.

CHAPTER THREE

EINHAR KRONBAUER SLOWLY replaced the phone and stared at it for a long time. His tea was growing cold in its Meissen cup, and outside it had begun to snow on the Wilhelmstrasse, but he didn't notice either of these events.

A watershed moment had just occurred. He found himself paralyzed. He'd been concierge at the Dresdenhof for forty years; his father had run the building before that, his grandfather before that. There had never been a call about apartment 12A. Not one time. Not on anybody's watch. In that time, bombing rubble had been cleared away, a wall had been erected bisecting the city and finally torn down, diplomats had come and gone, but 12A remained intact. A time capsule. They might have even made jokes about it being the Nazi equivalent of King Tut's tomb, if his grandfather hadn't taught them that speaking of 12A was absolutely *verboten*.

Now someone had called about it.

His stare bore a hole into the ivory-colored phone receiver.

He would have to make his own phone call now. Report the inquiry.

He picked up his pad and tapped into his contacts. The number was in there in case of emergency. His father had handed it down to him like a scepter. There were only three things to remember about

12A, he'd told him: Have it cleaned once a week by the maintenance company that had been managing the building since the
Weimar Republic, and call the special number if anyone else showed
up connected to it. The third thing was don't worry about calling
the special number because no one was going to show up.

Now someone had made an inquiry.

Kronbauer adjusted his yellow Hermès tie, his shirt collar con-
stricting strangely on its own. There had always been something
ominous about apartment 12A, just as there'd been something ominous about his grandfather's uniform in the war. He suspected it
was that trifle of embroidery on the left sleeve. The diamond outline
embedded with the letters *SD*. His grandfather didn't tell, and
Einhar, even as his grandson, knew better than to ask. So the family
stuffed the uniform full of mothballs and cedar, stuck it in the
trunk with the old photos, and went on with life. After all, it was a
very long time ago, and people had had to do what they'd had to do
during the war to get by. Berlin was whole again. Germany was
thriving. The past was in the past.

But some things just wouldn't stay buried.

He looked out the window all the way down to the corner of
Neiderkirchnerstrasse, where the ruins had been discovered. The
notorious address used to be 8 Prinz-Albrecht-Strasse. The Gestapo.
The city had been bombed to kingdom come and then rebuilt in
modern international style, and yet there were those who insisted
the ruins be dug up all over again and put on display—insisted there
be yet another awful reminder made of Germany's past.

He watched the snow start to stick to the steel arcade that protected the ruins. The bricks no doubt echoed like conch shells with
the screams of the tortured and dying. That the old foundation was
still there surprised everyone. It had been uncovered when a postwar
building was torn down. Now no new building could be erected

because the infamous Gestapo basement ruins had to be preserved for posterity. To show again and again how very horrible the Germans were, *ad nauseum.*

Taking a deep breath, he punched in the number on the phone. He was shocked at the mundane-sounding ring on the other end. In his imagination he'd always thought the number would ring up someplace unearthly—patched through a satellite circling Mars to an overlord of the ice planet Hoth. Normalcy or not, he was still not sure how to approach the strange subject of an inquiry on an apartment that hadn't had a visitor since 1942.

"Herr Kronbauer calling," he said in German to the harsh *"allo,"* murmured through the receiver.

He explained the inquiry and gave the name of the man who called. Stag Maguire. Yes, that was correct. Stag Maguire.

Then it was over. The voice on the other end thanked him and hung up.

No more to do now. The instructions had been followed. The weekly cleaning of 12A would continue, the illustrious and diplomatically immune tenants would continue to need him to hold open their Mercedes' doors, and he would remain on call should reservations be needed for the restaurant Borchardt. His duties were exacting and methodical, and he performed them just the way he'd been taught to by his father.

He took a sip of cold tea and grimaced. His routine was going to fall back into place again, just like before. But he couldn't shake the idea that his phone call had been like a tiny fissure in the bottom of the ocean, one that would give birth to a devouring tsunami once it was felt onshore.

CHAPTER FOUR

STAG WOKE WITH a lurch. Through the stickiness of sleep, he knew he'd been shouting. He was having the nightmares again. Not only did they mess up his sleep, they'd managed to scare every potential girlfriend into a one-night-stand for the past year. He'd taken all the prescribed cures: Xanax, psychoanalysis, EMDR—Eye Movement Desensitization and Reprocessing—but the night terrors still hung on as tenacious as a starving tick.

He rolled onto his back and stared at the ceiling. In the other room, Harry snored on the futon, deaf to the shouting. Stag rubbed his leg. It ached as it always did, a dull thumping pain that left him exhausted. When he walked, the thrum moved from the titanium rods in his ankle, pounding its way up to his hip. At thirty-five, he was already an old man, weak and limping. Every day it was just another drop of water that comprised his own personal ocean of fury.

PTSD was a bitch. He was thankful he'd only had one blackout. He'd come out of it in the middle of Walmart. As if waking from a dream, he'd looked down and saw he had a cartful of items he would only buy for Holly: popsicles and animal crackers, tampons and champagne. It had scared the piss out of him. There was no rational motive for what he'd done, no context, no *why*. He stood staring at the items in the cart for such a long time that a little tattooed Goth queen asked him if he was all right. He'd looked up at her blankly, wanted to knee-jerk the words he was fine, but he wasn't fine. He was terrified. There was no answer for him being at Walmart with a cart full of inexplicables. He was lost again without the *why*. He looked at the black-clad girl, and then he fled as fast as his lame leg would take him.

Rubbing his face, he sat up in bed and made up his mind. He couldn't save Harry from the flood that had washed away his marriage; nor could he save himself from the landslide that was burying him little by little every day. The only thing they could do was get out of the way of the reminders.

"Wake up," Stag barked to Harry. "Let's go see Jake."

"Meh?" Harry slurred.

"Yeah. Get up."

Harry rolled out of bed and righted his huge form on the edge of the futon, still groggy. "If the sheriff's taken the bar, I gotta find some work or shit."

"You don't have to today."

"I don't have any money."

"You don't need money. I got this," Stag replied.

Harry opened his eyes wider.

"I've got the Fucking Settlement, remember? I can afford to prop you up a while. Let's go talk to Jake."

Stag went to the kitchen and began a pot of coffee.

*　*　*

"Look at the detail. Superb. Even the underlay on the shoulder straps. That's good ol' SS toxic green." Dr. Jake Bratch, retired head of the University of Wisconsin Center for World War II Studies,

leaned back in the leather swivel chair in his den. He peered at both
men from above his reading glasses. The seventy-year-old man's
khakis and blue oxford shirt were as wrinkled as used Kleenex. Stag
knew from all the late-night, beer-laden discourse at Gerde's that
Jake was brilliant, but his obsession for knowledge made him un-
aware of many of the social graces. Since his wife passed away—a
Wuttke girl—Stag doubted the guy'd ever washed his clothes.

"Where did you get this?"

Stag and Harry seemed unable to move.

Jake continued, not making note of the sudden discomfort. "This
is really remarkable. You know, I don't think I've ever seen an oil
portrait of him. Very rare."

"Him?" Harry had grown more and more tense while Jake
studied the portrait.

"Yes, there's no mistaking him. He's got the Honor Chevron for the
Old Guard, first- and second-class Iron Cross, the *Frontflugspange*,
for aircraft reconnaissance work; it's all there in detail."

"Who is it?" Stag asked.

"Look at his eyes. There's only one man who looks like this. They
used to call him the Green Basilisk, eyes like a dragon. Yes, it's
Heydrich. This is Heydrich."

Stag felt a coldness work down his spine. He'd been right in his
suspicions. Now that they were confirmed, he could see. It was
Heydrich. "*Our Reini.*"

"Sorry, I'm not up on my Nazi stuff. Who the hell is that?" Harry
blurted defensively.

But Stag knew who it was.

He stared back at the unfeeling expression, the awful realization
that behind the bad overpaint, this face had been hanging in Gerde's
all the years he'd been going there. Heydrich. The one and only. The
Hangman. The Blond Beast. The Nazi Aryan ideal all wrapped up

in the Gestapo, the SS, and, worst of all, the SD, the Nazi security agency. He had so much information on people, even Hitler and Himmler got nervous around him. Sure, they gave him a nice SS funeral when he was assassinated in Prague, but no one was really sorry to see him go.

No one.

Jake placed his fingertips together, forming a chapel-roof with his hands. His expression steeled as he looked at the face in the painting. The light in his eyes stilled. "Harry, I hate to have to introduce you to Reinhard Tristan Eugen Heydrich, Reichsprotecktor of Bohemia and Moravia, Chief of the Gestapo and the SD."

Harry looked like his mouth had gone dry and it was difficult to speak. "I thought Heinrich Himmler was head of the SS."

"Yes. But within the SS was the much-more feared SD. The *Sicherheitsdienst*."

"*Sicherheitsdienst?*" Harry wore a vaguely nauseated expression. "Doesn't that mean—"

"Exactly. Security service," Jake interrupted. "These were the ultimate men of the Reich. They literally determined who lived or died." Jake took another study of the portrait. "The provenance of this piece must be researched. I hate to say it, but it would bring a fortune on the Nazi memorabilia market. Anything Heydrich-related is very rare. But, in truth, I'd rather see it's handled properly and donated. We don't want this to form the centerpiece of some neo-Nazi cult. Now tell me where you got this again?"

"Look, I don't understand. I'm of German heritage but that doesn't make me an expert on *Mein Kampf*!" Harry crossed his arms as best he could, almost in an act of defiance.

Jake released an ironic smile. "Very few are. Even back in Germany in the thirties, *Mein Kampf* sold to every household and illiteratti, and made Hitler millions, but no one cracked it open. Oh, they loved his ideas, but even Hitler regretted writing such a crappy book. However, it was a required purchase, if you didn't want guys like this snooping around." He nodded to the painting.

"Never heard of him." Harry was adamant.

Jake nodded. "Czech patriots assassinated Heydrich in '42, which is partly why he's not a household Nazi name, so to speak, but had he lived—many were fully expecting him to take over the entire SS from Himmler. Perhaps even take over from Hitler. They had a saying, *'Himmler's Hirn heisst Heydrich.'* 'Himmler's brain is called Heydrich.'"

Harry shook his head. "He was under Himmler then? He was some kind of SS?"

"You don't understand." Jake clasped his hands as if in prayer. "This man founded the SD, the *Sipo*—SS Security Police—and the *Einsatzgruppen*, the mobile killing squads that murdered all in their path behind the Wehrmacht as the German army drove east. Heydrich had been instructed to develop the death camps of Treblinka, Belzec, Sobibor, and Auschwitz-Birkenau—as a kindness, believe it or not. Gassing was a way to relieve the *Einsatzgruppen* of their emotional burden of shooting women and children. But quite frankly, I don't think Heydrich himself ever thought about the emotional burden."

Jake finished, his voice dropping. "Heydrich was the reason the Third Reich kept their secrets. He was the one behind the horror of our first enlisted men stumbling unawares into Buchenwald. Heydrich was bad. Ground Zero bad. He could make Himmler look like a philanthropist."

"Weren't they all bad?" Harry blurted out, a creeping revulsion tightening his expression. "I mean we're talking about Nazis here."

"You've heard the saying, 'Three men can keep a secret as long as two of them are dead'? I'd be surprised if Heydrich didn't make that quote up. He was good at his job because no one talked. No one dared. So they put him in charge of the Wannsee Conference." Jake took a long hard look at the painting. Suddenly the old man's shabby clothes were overwhelmed by the intelligence and fierceness in his eyes. "This is the man who organized the Final Solution."

"Fuck me," Harry whispered, a strange emotion in his eyes.

Stag glanced at the painting. Heydrich's stare frosted up even more.

"Seriously, where did you get this?" Jake asked. "You know, there's something familiar about it—more than just Heydrich himself. I feel I've seen this before."

Harry said nothing; he simply looked at Stag as if for help.

For some strange reason, evasion seemed to be in order right now. The idea they'd all been drinking beer for years beneath the painted gaze of Harry's family's "Reini" wasn't quite appetizing, and Harry's revulsion over that fact was palpable.

"I found it in a junk shop," Stag interjected. "I figured you'd know who he was."

"If you can find out where this came from, it might really be worth looking into. Like I said, Heydrich died young. His reign was short but notorious." Jake pointed to the canvas. "This didn't come out of a vacuum. There's a story behind it. Without a doubt."

"Without a doubt . . ." Stag's words drifted off.

The men sat in silence for a moment before Jake said gently, "You should write a piece on this for the paper, Stag. Get back in the swing of things again."

"Maybe I will," he answered noncommittally.

Jake turned to Harry. "Sorry about Gerde's. No place like that one. I can even remember my father going there after the war."

Harry nodded, his eyes worried.

"This portrait may be important to Holocaust studies. If you'd care to donate it, I can have that arranged. We'd have professors and students lining up to research it."

"I want to get some more info on it before I do anything like that," Stag said.

"Where are you boys going to do your drinking from now on? With Ruthie dead and gone, I can't bear the evenings alone. I confess Gerde's filled them for me for a long time."

Harry took another miserable glance at the painting. "This guy was involved in all that?"

"Not just involved," Jake said. "A main architect. It's believed the operations of the death camps were named *Aktion Reinhard* in his honor after his assassination. Heydrich was able to do things others could not bring themselves to do." He grew sober. "We've got to find the history behind this. It is that important."

Stag stared at Harry. Harry looked like a drowning man.

A moment of silence followed before Jake said in a harsh voice, "At Heydrich's funeral, Reichsfurer-SS Himmler referred to him as, 'The Man with the Iron Heart.'" He gave both younger men an ominous stare. "Gentlemen, you have a helluva portrait on your hands."

CHAPTER FIVE

HE WAS ABLE to do things others could not bring themselves to do.

Things others could not bring themselves to do.

His stomach fell every time Stag thought of Heydrich. Harry's reaction was worse. A weight seemed to have settled on Harry since they left Jake's.

"Our Reini. *Our*." Harry stared down at the beer mug in his hand. They'd stopped off at the first tavern on Wuttke Avenue, another sad, run-down bar frequented by bikers.

Stag was at a loss. "You didn't know," was all he could think of.

Harry's face was pale, and he'd grown quiet since they'd left Jake's office.

Stag thumbed the moisture forming on his beer glass. "I mean, shit, the guy was painted over. After the war, someone could have sold it to your grandfather for a loaf of bread, and the name stuck. No damnation in that coincidence."

"Nobody in my family had to fight for the USA. My grandfather was too old, my father wasn't born yet."

"Just because they didn't fight the Nazis doesn't mean they sympathized with them."

"Yeah," Harry said, unconvincingly.

"Your family was the best there ever was." Stag had to pull the words from the cold place in his soul. The spot had frozen over since Holly had been standing by his side. And then wasn't anymore.

"You and your family, out of the goodness of your hearts, took on a fucked-up, rebellious, completely charmless, thirteen-year-old. Your folks were all right. You can't question that just because they had a creepy painting in their bar. They probably didn't even know about it."

"But what about the SD. The *Sicherheitsdienst*?"

"What about it? It was a security service. Every government has one. If we knew everything the NSA has done, we'd never sleep at night. Are we responsible for them?"

Harry seemed unconvinced. If anything, he got even paler.

"They were good people, Harry. Good people." Stag swallowed a sudden feeling of helplessness with a swig of beer.

A long silence followed before Harry began to murmur his thoughts. "Back in high school I did a paper on Birkenau, the death camp at Auschwitz. Ever tell you that?" He emptied his glass and motioned for another. "One guy—he worked in Birkenau as a guard—he'd oversee gassing people all day long. Men. Women. Children. Men would cram them into the chambers until they could barely shut the door because the gas worked more efficiently that way. Here were all these naked and shaved people, families, mothers and babies. Total chaos and terror. One day the guard wrote about an incident. A little boy about five years old tried to stop in this mass of screaming humanity because a little girl ahead of him had dropped some kind of trinket she'd managed to keep. The little boy picked it up off the ground and chased after her, until he was crammed into the death chamber with all the rest.

"At night the guard would go home after seeing all this, and he'd have dinner with his family. In his journal, he would write about how excited he was to take his children to the movies in town. Yeah, all day he would gas other people's children, nice children, sweet children trying to return trinkets, and then go home, and do something completely normal with his own, like he was the god-damned postman."

His next beer arrived, and he took a deep thirsty gulp. "And that was the worst part about doing that paper, see? Not what the guy actually did in Birkenau, but that I had to explain the unexplain-able. Here was a guy just like my dad, hardworking, responsible. He would go home at the end of a long day, and have dinner, and plan fun times with his kids, never thinking at all about what he was doing all day."

He frowned, the shadows on his full face deepening into fur-rows. "We're all capable of that, you know. We don't want to admit it, but it's really easy to just go along with things, and not think about them, not question what we're doing until we've become monsters. We detach ourselves. Pretend what we're doing is okay. We can do really bad things. Then go on, normal as pie."

"'Those who can make you believe absurdities can make you commit atrocities,'" Stag said, quoting Voltaire.

The chiming of glassware as the bartender stacked it was the only sound breaking the ensuing silence.

"There's always worse though."

Stag raised an eyebrow.

Harry took a long swig. "Worse are the ones that do give it a lot of thought. 'Cause they're convinced they're right."

* * *

The cell number had been listed in the name of Harold Gerde. 4EVER did his research. It had taken another nanosecond to find the address. But there was nothing at the listing except a defunct bar with civil sheriff's tape across the door. He moved on to the other name: Stag Maguire, the one they'd talked to. That name came up in research as both Stag and the fucked-up name of Hyortur Maguire. But it eventually made sense. Hyortur was an Old Norse name for deer or stag. Maguire, it turned out, was Icelandic-American; probably—as 4EVER's research told him—from people who farmed in North Dakota or Minnesota. All that was easy. What wasn't easy would be getting information directly.

There was the obese Mr. Gerde who owned the phone they'd called the Dresdenhof on, and the goddamned Viking, Stag Maguire, who'd done the talking. The employer wanted information and for that they needed Maguire to tell them what he knew and why he had called. 4EVER'd been on the phone to Zug, Switzerland, for ten minutes. Fear was one method of getting people to talk. It wasn't the only method, and there was debate whether it was the most effective. But it was certainly an effective way to start.

And that was how he was told to start.

He parked the Infiniti in the parking lot of Hyortur Maguire's apartment complex.

4EVER didn't understand what all the Nazi shit was about, but ultimately, he didn't care. Nazis were other people's scourges. His ancestors came out of the plantation system of the Old South. He was born to a welfare-mom crackhead on Livernois Avenue. If his IQ hadn't been off the charts, there was no way a kid like him would have been offered a free ride through Harvard. Now he was one of the highest-paid independent contractors in the world. And he gave the Ivy League full credit for that.

Along with his thug life in Detroit. And a healthy dose of training by independent military contractors like Tarnhelm. They loved him in Zug. He was a rarity. He bought vertical auctions of rare wine, and he came with a genuine street cred and name. 4EVER.

Because when he did his job, you were "Deyah-d fo'evah."

From the scrupulously clean windshield of the Infiniti, he watched a fat man in a dingy blue parka leave Maguire's ground-floor apartment. It was Harry Gerde. He matched the mug shot from a DWI he'd gotten just last year. Now it looked like the guy was either having a stroke or drunk. 4EVER figured the latter because the hog staggered across the parking lot, skidding on the ice patches and righting himself as only a drunk can.

4EVER waited and watched, poised like a Zegna-clad bird on a wire. A bird of prey.

Rummaging through his pockets, Gerde found keys to the car in front of him. He opened it and retrieved three six-packs of Beck's. Juggling them, he shoved the car door closed, and turned toward the apartment.

"Excuse me," 4EVER said, getting out of his car. "Excuse me, sir." He hoped the camel topcoat and the swank white car would keep the guy disarmed. Nothing like an impeccable white middle-class accent to generate trust in a black man.

"I'm looking for Mr. Maguire. Do you know where Mr. Maguire lives?"

Gerde looked a bit startled. "Yeah. He's right over there." He pointed to the door of the apartment.

"I'm with a law firm trying to reach him to settle an estate. We have some money for him."

"Some money?" The guy's triple chin went slack.

"Could you do me a favor and give him my card, Mr. . . . . uh?"

"Gerde."

"Where can I reach you, Mr. Gerde?"

"I'm right-the-fuck here."

4EVER smiled. He didn't know if the guy was being honest, or sarcastic, or stupid. Nonetheless, he gave him a trademark warm smile, letting his lip curl boyishly. It was amazing how much information people gave you when you just asked. He extended his Hermès-gloved hand. "Here is my card. Would you please convince him to call the number on it?"

4EVER watched Gerde's reaction to his creamy, expensive engraved card. It was a fraud; of course, a beautiful luscious fraud of a card, but Gerde would never know.

"Okay. C'mon." The fat fuck turned toward the apartment from which he came.

"Actually, I'm not the one who needs to speak to him. I'm really just here to deliver a message."

Gerde sloshed around and stared at him with dull, alcohol-fueled eyes. "He's right here, dude. Jus' c'mon."

"No. When he's ready to talk, have him call this number. You got that?" 4EVER stepped closer to the guy. Gerde took an unconscious step back.

"Yeah, I got it, but why don't you—" Gerde's chins went slack again, this time in fear.

4EVER took out his gun.

He shot him, and casually stepped away as if he'd just waved goodbye.

Gerde screamed and watched him walk away, his eyes popped with abject terror.

CHAPTER SIX

STAG HEARD HARRY'S screams and instinctively bolted for the front door. He was expecting to find him fallen on the ice. Maybe a broken arm. It was unnerving to see him upright, just standing and screaming for no apparent reason. Screaming at the dirty drifts of snow edging the parking lot.

"What the fuck, man?" Stag shouted over him. "What the fuck?"

"He shot me! He shot me!" Harry screamed, his features screwed up with fear. "I've been shot!"

Several other tenants rushed to their balconies to assess the situation. Sliding along the ice, Stag raced to Harry. "Where?"

"Call 911!" someone shouted around them.

"Lean on me," Stag ordered, pulling and half-carrying Harry across the parking lot to his front door. "Can you walk? Think I can get you inside?"

"I'll get there. I can get there," Harry stammered, his face ghost white.

Stag left the front door open and pulled Harry to the futon. He then ran for a towel.

"What the fuck happened!" he shouted, pulling open Harry's parka.

He was braced for the sight of blood, but there was nothing. He couldn't find anything, and yet, Harry was still whimpering like a baby.

"Where'd you get hurt, buddy?" he coaxed.

"In the chest. He got me in the chest." Harry looked down dumbly at his polar fleece. No blood in sight.

"Where?" Stag demanded frantically.

"Right here," Harry whimpered, patting his chest. "He took out this black handgun and shot me. I can still feel it going in!"

Stag pulled up the shirt and polar fleece. There was nothing. Just rolls of pasty belly flesh and a galaxy of freckles.

"The police are coming," announced the old hippy that lived upstairs. He stood in the doorway like an aging Jesus, his face lined with concern. "They're sending an ambulance. What the hell happened?"

"Checking him now," Stag said. "Look, Harry, you saw the gun and maybe just thought—"

"He shot me, I'm telling you! I can still feel it! Right here!" He pointed to a reddish freckle. It pretty much looked like all the rest.

Stag nodded and stood. He could hear the faint beginnings of sirens. "Not long now," he offered. "Did the guy steal your wallet?"

Harry had begun to sweat. "He said they wanted to talk to you. Ask you some questions, then he pulled out this gun! This really strange gun!" Harry looked to be panicking all over again. "He left this card. Man, if he wanted to scare me, he sure as fuck did!"

"Calm down. They're almost here. Just hold on." Stag ground his teeth. He didn't know what to make of this. It was bizarre.

"I think he's killed me somehow, man. I really do," Harry shot out.

"You'll be fine as soon as the paramedics check you out," Stag said, but for some strange reason, even he wasn't sure about that.

* * *

"I'm telling you, the black guy shot me," Harry said once the paramedics were gone.

The police had questioned them and filed a report. Stag didn't mention to Harry the cop who'd taken him aside and asked if his friend had been popping any hallucinogens.

"The gun must've misfired, thank God." Stag stared at him, his face filled with concern. The whole episode was crazy. Wearily, he took a long pull on his Beck's. It had been another long, long day.

"He fucking pulled out this really strange gun and just shot me." Harry stared down at his bare chest. "You going to call?"

Stag looked down at the card. He'd given the police the information but he bet they didn't even write it down. Harry looked like just another drug-crazed loser wasting the authorities' time with paranoid delusions. He'd bet that the number on the card was linked by the internet to another number, this one probably overseas. A sickening feeling overtook him. The phone might even be in Berlin, where that apartment was.

Harry got up and began pacing. He rubbed his chest. "Man, they got me. Maybe I'm being poisoned. Should probably get some blood work."

"Then let's run you to the emergency room."

"What do they want? You better call them first."

"Let's head to the emergency room first for the blood work."

"No, call them—then they can tell you what the hell they did to me!"

Hesitantly, Stag punched the number into his phone. It took a while for the connection to be made. It only rang once before the phone was answered.

"*Allo.*"

"What the fuck did you do to my friend?" Stag didn't bother to hide his animosity. Behind him, Harry paced, his face getting paler.

"What is your interest in apartment 12A?" The voice had an accent, but Stag couldn't place it. He didn't know if it was German, French, or Swedish.

"First you tell me my friend's okay."

"Your friend will die."

Stag barely comprehended the words.

"That is not a warning. That is a fact. You will die too if you don't tell us your interest."

Stag felt the blood run backward in his veins. After the first wave of shock hit him, he wanted to punch something, but with nothing but a voice on the other end of the phone, he was fighting a shadow.

Slowly, he said in a low rumble to not freak out Harry anymore, "What's this all about?"

"We need to know what is your interest?"

"We found a note."

"Who gave it to you?"

"Reinhard Heydrich." The silence at the end of the line didn't surprise Stag. The shock was palpable. "So you think you can tell me what's going on here?"

"You are a journalist, are you not, Mr. Maguire? You wrote quite a reputable series about corrupt politicians taking money from the NRA."

He was stunned at hearing his name. It made the breath go tight in his chest. "I was a journalist."

"We don't want attention."

"Well, you got it now, you motherfucker. I want to know what you did to my friend."

"He has perhaps fifteen minutes to live. You may go to the authorities, but his death will be from a heart attack. He is an

overweight man, is he not? You Americans and your constant desire
to feed—"

"What the hell did you do?"

"We do not like inquiries. We have your cell number and your
name. Now as you watch your friend die, you see we are serious. We
want the information you have. How did you find out about 12A?"

"Heydrich told us, you fucktard. And I'm going to goddamn
make something of this! You tell me what to do for my friend!"
Stag's anger became rage.

"Heydrich has been dead since '42."

"Maybe," Stag baited. "But he sent the note anyway."

"What did the note say?"

"It talks about diamonds." He snorted. "And you'll never fucking
see any of them if anything happens to Harry."

"We will pay for your information. Any amount you require."

"Go fuck yourself." He lowered his voice to a growl. "Now tell me
what you did to my friend—"

He felt the connection terminate before he heard the click.

"Whh . . . what-the-fuck?" Harry stammered, paler still than a
moment ago.

"Let's get you to a hospital." Stag stabbed through his jeans
pockets for the car keys.

"What did he say? What did they do to me?" There was real fear
edging Harry's voice. Stag had a hard time meeting his eye.

"I don't know. Let's go get you tested. Now."

"Yeah. " Harry's hand shook when he ran it through his hair. His
face was drained of color, but he was sweating profusely as if he was
overheated. He unconsciously rubbed his chest.

"C'mon." Stag held the door.

Harry nodded, took a step, and then paused, as if surprised.
He gasped.

"What is it?" Stag demanded.

"I swear, I think I'm having a heart attack. "

"Look, let's get you—"

Harry doubled over, groaning.

Stag instinctively punched 911 into his phone. "Get me an ambulance," he barked into the phone.

The furniture shook when Harry slumped to the floor. Stag bit out the remaining information for the ambulance, then went over to him.

"They're coming, bud. Hang in there," he said softly.

"I think I'm having a heart—" Harry began vomiting copious amounts of beer and pizza. It ran down his chin and puddled on the front of his polar fleece. "Fuck."

"It's cool. It's cool." Stag ran for another towel. When he came back from the bathroom, Harry was nearly unconscious. The whine of a siren began in the distance like a refrain. "Hold on. Here they are," he said, bending down to him.

"Tell Julie and the kids . . . love 'em . . ." Harry took Stag's hand. He squeezed it weakly. "Tell them I'm sorry about being a shitty husband and father."

"Chill, man. Relax. You weren't."

"Don't tell them about the *Sicherheitsdienst*."

"Don't worry about that now. Seriously, the ambulance is almost here."

"I don't want them to know about Heydrich."

"Fuck Heydrich." The anger in Stag's voice even surprised him.

"No, man. You don't understand."

"It's okay, Harry. Don't worry about that now."

"I . . . I just figured it out. I keep thinking of all those gatherings my dad held at Gerde's. I mean—"

"Really, don't worry about that now, man. The ambulance is almost here. Everything's gonna be all right."

Harry clutched at Stag's shirt. "No. There was always talk. You understand? *Talk.* I never paid much attention because when my dad died, Gerde's fell on me, and I was too crazy trying to make a living out of it to wonder what all those meetings were about."

"Hang on there, man. You don't need to be worrying about this." Stag was relieved to hear the siren get closer.

"Don't you understand?" Harry insisted. "Don't you see? We're all Heydrich. That's the problem. We've been Heydrich all the time."

"You are from the best people I know, Harry. No way you're from a bunch of Nazis." Every nerve in Stag's body was taut, waiting for that ambulance.

"But my grandfather . . . I mean, I didn't understand at the time. My grandfather talked about it, and. my God, my father too . . . He and my father had these strange meetings with strange characters. Then when Dad died, a bunch of men came to get his files. And Mom just let them in and they took everything. After the war, you see? *After* the war—" He moaned loudly and squeezed his eyes shut. Tears streamed down his round cheeks. Gritting his teeth through the pain, he ground out the words, "That's how they kept Gerde's going, during the down times, see? That's why I couldn't make it. When the wolf came knocking, I didn't feed it like they told me to. I didn't want to. I didn't want anything to do with them."

"It doesn't matter," Stag commanded, kneeling in the vomit to support his flagging body. "That's long over."

"But it does. It does matter, don't you see?" Harry whispered. He doubled over once more. "The *Sicherheitsdienst*, the SD. It's still out there. It still exists. *And if you don't feed the wolf, the wolf feeds on you.*"

Then he collapsed. Dead.

CHAPTER SEVEN

Numb, Stag let Harry's body slip to the ground. The useless siren grew louder in the distance. The shock of Harry's last words repeated over and over through his brain, but it was eclipsed by the horrific reality of Harry's dead eyes, staring out at him.

For a long moment, Stag stood paralyzed. Unsure. Terror and rage began to build, slowly at first, then gaining traction with every whine of the siren. The phone call to Berlin had been on Harry's number, but Stag had been the one to talk to them. They'd killed Harry because they'd identified him from his phone. They'd killed him solely to get Stag to talk about what he knew. Now the horrific possibilities that some entity was around, and focused on him, began to ignite the fight or flight instinct. It didn't seem real that Harry was lying dead right in front of him, but fear told him only one thing right now: whoever had gotten Harry was outside somewhere waiting for him.

He stood clutching the towel stained with Harry's vomit and tears. He looked down at his dead friend, his insides balled up in knots. Yeah, people thought of Harry as a loser and a drunk. But the guy had extended more kindness to Stag than he could ever repay. Harry was his last friend on earth. Now everyone was dead that he'd ever had a connection to. All of them now. Gone. And he was left behind in an acid bath of grief.

He glanced up at his apartment, seeing it no longer familiar, now finding the cardboard boxes, the ugly futon, hostile and foreign.

Almost against his will, he walked up to the portrait. The cold, unsympathetic eyes still followed him. A surge of anger welled up, and with it, a strange momentary clarity. He opened the front door wide for the ambulance team just pulling into the parking lot. With a deliberation he didn't quite comprehend, he picked up the white silk note and old-fashioned key laid out next to the portrait. He gingerly placed the business card the black man had given Harry into a Ziploc bag on the slim chance they might get a fingerprint off of it. Then he took his wallet and his shabby pile of personal documents and stuffed them into his parka.

He felt the portrait's frigid eyes on him as he went to the back of his apartment. Then, pure instinct kicked in. He crawled out his bathroom window, limping quickly through the garbage-blackened snow of the service alley.

And disappeared.

*　*　*

A couple days ago, Stag was retrieving Harry from the empty shell of Gerde's Biergarten. Now he was pulling a rental car up to the Investigations Division in Green Bay, hunted and on the run. From what or whom, he didn't quite have a grip yet.

Sitting in the hotel room by the interstate, he'd recalled a Detective Bruce James. He'd done an article on Green Bay's spectacularly low homicide rate as compared to Milwaukee's, and James was the point man. He didn't know if Detective James would be able to help him, but he was going to give it a try.

It was also a big plus that Green Bay was an entirely different jurisdiction as Milwaukee. Just as a precaution.

He was shown into the office while the detective was still on the phone. James waved him forward and motioned to a chair in front of his desk.

"I don't know why she doesn't listen. Maybe it's because she's fifteen." He nodded to Stag and made a jabbering motion with his hand. "Yeah. Maybe. But maybe she just thinks you're a bitch. I mean, I don't think you're one, but she—"

He paused to listen. "Yeah. Okay. Tell her I said so. I'm okay with being the bad guy."

While the detective talked on the phone, Stag was struck with the normalcy of the conversation. Particularly amid the strange backdrop of lurid color photos of a recent murder-suicide that formed one wall of the office.

Just regular people doing extraordinarily awful jobs. For better, as in this case, or for worse, as in the case of the guard in Harry's paper on Birkenau. It was crazy how easy it was to make insane look normal.

"Thanks for seeing me," Stag said when James hung up.

"Hey, any time. Your article was great. The Captain's still crowing about it and it's been three years." James took a sip from a stained Starbucks cup. "You doing a sequel?"

Stag shook his head. Unsure how to begin, he said, "I've got a strange situation. My friend in Wuttke, well, he died unexpectedly. I was hoping you might have the autopsy results in and could give them to me."

"Oh geez, sorry about that. His name?"

"Harold Gerde."

James began typing in his computer. "Yep. Here it is. Didn't take long. SCD. Sudden Cardiac Death." He kept reading. "Due to . . . pulmonary embolism." He looked up at Stag.

"Anything else?" Stag prompted.

James scrolled down a bit. "No. Cut and dried. Looks like he was pretty overweight, huh?"

"Yeah." Stag ruminated, unsure how to approach the questions, let alone the answers.

"Ah . . ." James continued to read the screen, his expression growing sad. "Says here there's no investigation opened but they'd like to talk to you. It seems you abandoned the body." The detective looked at Stag. "I know you had a hard knock with your wife. It was all over the papers here. If you'd like, I'd be happy to go with you down to Wuttke to talk to them. I mean, it's understandable you'd freak out with your buddy dropping dead in front of you."

Stag just nodded slowly.

"You're not under arrest or anything. They'd just like to talk to you about the circumstances."

"The circumstances, yes," Stag offered, his mind whirling.

"You okay?"

There was that question again. But why wouldn't he be okay? Why? The eternal why.

"There's a building in Berlin. Harry and I, we called about it, you see. They wanted to talk to me. To ask me what I knew about the message in the painting . . ."

The detective only looked at Stag with pity and concern seeping into his eyes.

"I've begun some research into the building," Stag continued. "The building's owned by an international corporation with a thousand entities. I don't know how to figure which one got Harry—"

"*Got Harry?* There's no foul play here. He had a heart attack. Like fat guys do."

"No. They shot him. With something, I think. Maybe a poison—"

"No bullets, no poison mentioned in the lab reports. Hey, can I get you some coffee or something?" The detective was beginning to look worried.

Stag knew he appeared off his rocker. Maybe there was some PTSD going on inside his head with the shock of Harry's death.

Fuck, maybe he was just dreaming. He'd drive to Wuttke and find Harry behind the bar like always, talking to that horrible painting. Maybe even find Holly was looking for him back in Milwaukee. Wondering what he'd bought for her at Walmart.

"I couldn't answer the why on Holly's death, you know? Some questions just don't have answers. But . . ." Stag took a moment to find the words. "But I think there is a *why* on Harry's death. I think I can find out the why on this one, but I'm going to need some help."

"Yes." James stared back, his eyes cooling with wariness.

Stag's senses came back to him. He stood abruptly. It was clear no one was going to worry about Harry's strange death because it was only strange to Stag. And they weren't going to believe talk about a building in Berlin and a phone call and a strange gun that fired invisible bullets.

His head began to pound. He realized he was sweating. The best thing to do would be to research it himself. No one could do it as well as he could anyway. Besides, drowning beneath the caution and pity on James's face, he realized he was entirely on his own.

"I'll head home now," Stag assured the detective and held out his hand.

James stood and shook it. "You sure? You don't look too well. I could—"

"I'm sure," Stag answered, a half-second too quick.

He turned to look back at the detective only once. Bruce James was on the phone, dialing a number that he would bet was the Wuttke police.

CHAPTER EIGHT

THE SILK STRIP was wadded in his jeans' pocket; the brass key, he'd thrown casually into the plastic X-ray tray alongside his wallet and iPhone. Stag stepped through the imaging machine, raising his hands like he'd just robbed a liquor store. He was in Chicago O'Hare for the flight to Berlin. He looked around, warily wondering if he'd caught a tail, wondering if some entity had already managed to track him through the new iPhone he'd just bought at the Apple kiosk.

The newspapers had said nothing about a man found dead in an apartment in Wuttke or wanting to talk to Stag, but paranoia burrowed deep. Two days at the hotel in Green Bay doing research, and now one evading the police who wanted to talk to him if just out of concern for his PTSD. After all, who calls an ambulance, then ditches their dead friend in their own apartment? Strange circumstances indeed. But he wasn't sticking around to assuage curiosity. Harry didn't die of a heart attack. He was murdered. He couldn't prove it yet. But he was going to prove it. He couldn't explain what had happened to his mother, nor Holly. But there was an explanation for Harry's death. Someone was walking around that had all the answers to the *why* on Harry's death. He was going to find that person even if it killed him.

Whoever had given Harry that card was dangerous as hell, and the entity that employed the monster was worse. And he didn't feel like trying to convince the cops that Harry had indeed been shot by some high-tech, unseen bullet. He'd be sent home like a confused child, a ripe target for his own assassination in the parking lot.

"Sir, would you please step over there?"

He met the eye of the TSA agent. A shot of fear and paranoia surged through him. Numbly, he walked to the right where two more TSA agents were waiting for him.

He again held out his arms while they ran the wand over him. Another agent took his bag off the conveyor and stepped to a table nearby.

Were they looking for him already? The US authorities had a long reach. They'd be able to stop him pretty much anywhere. They'd ask him questions for which he would have no answers. Until he could do some research and get to that apartment in Berlin, he had nothing. Just the phantom of a man in the parking lot and Harry's insistence that he'd been shot before he died.

Then there was that other person, the man who had said, "*Allo,*" tersely at the end of the line. The one who'd promised Harry would die.

Stag had felt something snap inside of him after he'd left his apartment. He'd hit the wall. His oblivion of grief had been overwhelming before, but Harry, loser though he may have appeared, had been his last lifeline. Now Stag was no longer willing to accept his demise. Harry's death put him on a mission. His talk of the SD left his journalist's brain on fire. He was going to find the motherfuckers who had killed Harry. He was going to find out who they were and why they'd done it. And expose them all.

"Sir."

The TSA agent handed him his bag. There'd been nothing in it but new clothes from Walmart, their tags still attached, and some toiletries hurriedly stuffed into Ziploc bags because he hadn't wanted to take the time to search the store for a dop kit.

The agents nodded his go-ahead. He took his bag and walked down the long concourse to the flight.

By Gate 34, he was over the paranoia of the TSA search; by Gate 42, his mind was fully working on Harry's death.

The first improbability was the SD. How could something like that still exist? The Allies were thorough in dismantling the Third Reich. But there was one enormous loophole. Corporations were largely exempt from punishment for their complicity in Germany's war and Nazi Party. He thought of Bayer and their friendly little orange baby aspirin. They were still ubiquitous. Not so much the information that Bayer had made Zyklon B. Krupp made the guns and the steel for the Reich. ThyssenKrupp AG, still around. Bertelsmann, the giant publisher, was found not to have been shut down by the Nazis as they had claimed, but rather was entirely along for the Nazi ride, making a fortune along the way. Stag was shocked, shocked Bertelsmann hadn't just been publishing Bibles, as they'd claimed.

But the real story was the slap on the hand when all came to light. These corporations hung their heads, made a heartfelt apology, and continued to function as before, only now complicit with their new Lord and Savior, the US. Was it possible the SD could still be around in corporate form, specializing in private security and private paramilitary? It was possible. What was more possible was the ability to maintain secrecy at which the SD was so brilliant. It became a conundrum. If the SD was so good at secrecy, how could anyone ever be certain they still existed?

He wondered about Harry's family. Harry's mention of his father's files kept coming back to him. Those files probably told more truths than any of them could stomach, but they were long gone, purloined by the shadowy associates who cleaned them out after Harry's father died. If Harry's father was feeding the SD information on his various clients at Gerde's, that could very well be construed as "feeding the wolf," as Harry mentioned. If Harry had been unwilling to spy, it all seemed painfully obvious. Gerde's had never been a moneymaker. Sure, it had been a gathering place for locals, but locals in an economy like Wuttke's didn't pay their tabs all that well. Harry's father and grandfather supplemented their incomes by covertly working for a leftover from the Nazi SD. It explained Harry's failure to make a go at Gerde's. How could he make the same living as his father and grandfather if he was uncomfortable getting in bed with the resurrected SD? That explained Harry: honest and kind to a fault—not the sort of man to work at a concentration camp and then head home to take the kids to a movie. No, it all made sense now. Harry eschewed the added income because of his conscience, and in the end, Gerde's folded because it wasn't profitable as a bar alone. The thought cracked the pond ice of Stag's emotions. Harry had been set up as a victim, but, yet, Stag was suddenly, overwhelmingly proud of his friend's resistance. Harry, it turned out, wasn't a loser at all.

His thoughts went back to his research on the SD. De-Nazification was thorough. Still, Stag knew there were Nazis who, after the war, had made it out of Germany on what was then known as the ratline. Their fellow SS helped secrete their wanted brethren out of Germany to South America and Switzerland. Many got out with the full knowledge and help of unlikely third parties. The priest, Alois Hudal, with the blessing of the Vatican Secretary of State, had Nazis in a continual march down the ratline. Some even took the salvation the Allies offered. There was no denying the US's role in cherry-picking forgiveness when one had a Wernher von Braun on the hook. Was it possible that the thought process of the SD was still around? All one had to do was come upon an alt-right internet troll on Twitter to see the garbage still being fed to people.

He found his gate. They were boarding and he got in line, still deep in thought.

In what form was this other SD? Where was it? It seemed doubtful it was government sponsored—Germany had a few right-wing nutjobs and always would, but Germany's actions, particularly with refugees, proved that the guilt associated with the war was real and still influencing policy. If this new SD was now privatized, who ran it? And what exactly did this new entity do? This was the 21st century, the age of information. There were too many crazy people spouting off on the internet to believe in hidden conspiracies, but the SD was able to keep a pretty good lid on the Holocaust until the Allies walked into their first concentration camp. It seemed entirely possible for them to keep a lid on themselves after the war.

Selling secrets would be a lucrative business, particularly when one no longer was constricted by an allegiance to a country or a people, but only to the bottom line of profit.

He handed the Lufthansa attendant his boarding pass. He took the stub and entered the jetway. He didn't know what the answers might be, but he had nothing left in his life but to find out. There was no doubt what happened to Harry. He'd been murdered by that man with the strange gun in the parking lot. Stag was going to find who had sent him. And if there was any justice at all, he would see someone rot in hell for it.

He found his seat and put his bag in the overhead compart-ment. He looked forward to the long flight, hoping the calm would fuel clarity. Even though he'd been panicked, he'd had the forethought to buy some underwear and a new jacket and stuff them in a bag. Now he was thankful he had. There was no traveling internationally without luggage. Too much attention. The last thing he wanted now. He'd ditched his phone also. If these people knew his number, they sure as hell might have the ability to track him with it. He was unused to paranoia, unused to watching his back to see if he'd caught a tail. But the world was different now. Sure, a lunatic could come up and blow you and yours to kingdom come. There was no preventing that. But these people were out to get him. He would have to think ahead. Always.

He sat back in his seat and briefly closed his eyes. In that strip of silk, he had information no one else had, something they were willing to kill to get their hands on. He was going to try to dodge their bullets and dig deeper. He'd made it this far. He was safe on the plane and he would have time to think about his next move. He was traveling to Germany with a new phone, a bag of new clothes—none of which might even fit—and not sure where to begin. But he'd work all that out before he got to Berlin.

He'd figure out a lot of things during the flight.

Where to stay. Whom to trust. Whom to question.

He had eight hours and thirty-five minutes, and he would need every minute of it.

* * *

A long stone-paved lane wound through the skeletal elms that sentineled the drive. Zug was quiet this time of year. *Eisschloss* particularly with his wife in Gstaad and the mistress in Rio for Carnivale. Luc Portier wished he could have joined Maria in Rio. After his prostate surgery, he had nothing left but wealth and treachery with which to get his sexual thrills, but she was still a hot piece of ass and he enjoyed looking at her.

But there was no jetting down to South America now. With the latest news, he couldn't do more than sit in his Louis XIV tapestried armchair and stare out the window at the frozen lake. Who was this Maguire? Why had he appeared now? What did he want?

By all intelligence, Maguire was a peon who should have been swatted like a fly. A trifling journalist from that mecca of world information, Wuttke, Wisconsin. But Maguire's interest in 12A made him loom like an Amazon. He knew about it, therefore, he had to have information about its secrets, information even Luc Portier did not possess. And that made Maguire dangerous.

12A. The very idea of someone inquiring...

The place had been cleaned, researched, catalogued, and maintained for decades. It had never revealed its secrets. That had allowed Portier to lie back on a silken bed of false security. The silence seemed to prove that the rumors were untrue. That the danger was only a myth. The wispy stuff of legends.

But tickling at the back of Portier's mind was the real worry that Maguire would turn out to be trouble. If the man was asking about 12A, then he knew something. But what? Despite all their efforts to conceal and solve the riddle of 12A themselves, this American had found something out—something intrinsic to the hallowed ground of 12A. Something they had missed. Now they had to get that information before all else. If they didn't find out what he knew and neutralize the danger immediately, Maguire might instead prove to be a long parasitic worm that ate them all from the inside out.

Luc Portier placed his well-manicured hands on the arms of the chair and serenely allowed the long white fingers to drape over each side. It wasn't that he was better than others. On the contrary, there were others much more gifted than he. With more handsome faces, more brilliantly educated, certainly bigger—and more workable— manhoods. He'd come up the ranks of the organization, but like fate or destiny or simply the triumph of the will, he'd endured and flourished at a job that was made for him. He'd taken the organization from floundering to ubiquitous in less than a decade. It was all running to plan, on schedule, like clockwork. His life's work. His life's apotheosis. He did not need any wrinkles.

So he canceled the drop-in to his private compound in Gstaad; cancelled his jet's flight plan to Rio after that. And now he sat. Waiting personally for the news that the wrinkle had at last been flattened beneath a hot iron.

CHAPTER NINE

STAG YEARNED FOR sleep. He stared at the luxuriously made bed in his room at the Hotel Adlon but knew it would have to wait. He was in a hurry. Much to his anxiety, he'd had to register in his own name because the Adlon required ID. He didn't know how much time he would have before someone got a bead on him. Now, curiosity and rage demanded he go right away to scout out the Dresdenhof. Harry was dead. Someone had murdered him. He wanted to know what was waiting there.

All the impotent fury with his wife's killing, his frustration over the three years of senseless bullshit over the Settlement—the depositions of who was at fault when Clarence the Nut Job at Starbucks went postal, shot him, Holly, five others, and then ultimately himself; and then the endless back-and-forth over the monetary worth of his entire world—it all now bubbled over with Harry's killing. He'd crawled back, wounded, to Wuttke to be with the only family he'd had left in the world: Harry. The kid who'd insisted his parents foster his friend when the juvenile authorities were getting ready to take him away. With Harry murdered, he had no one. No one. So he was willing to shove aside his weariness and fear. Unlike Holly and the bad choices of his parents, there was a target this time.

Harry's death couldn't be shrugged off as fate, or the sad case of an undiagnosed mental disorder. Now, for the first time in what was forever, he had a focus, a purpose. The enemy would be a ghost no longer. He would find out about the circumstances that got Harry murdered, if it took his final breath. He was an unreasonable man with absolutely nothing to lose.

He adjusted the Polish P-83 handgun into the dip at the small of his back. It wasn't the best, but he was lucky to have gotten it at all. The cabdriver at the airport directed him to the Marzahn neighborhood, where his journalistic skills paid off in the discovery of an underground network of Turkish document makers and gun dealers. A pile of euros and not a question asked. He had no doubt the serial number had been filed away probably as early as 1984. The piece was a product of the Cold War, and now on the open market, a product of creeping democracy. Still, he was pretty sure it would fire. His knowledge of guns went that far.

Stealth was not in his nature. He had to force himself to think and proceed with caution. He paid in cash for a new iPad and several disposable GoFones for future use. He didn't want to be traced even if he was another continent away. If he had to keep ditching numbers and phones, he would. The one thing that was crystal clear was the fact that whoever was in control of that apartment had the money and organization to find him unless he was careful.

His research during the flight showed the Dresdenhof had been taken over by the Swedish government for its diplomatic corps in the 1920s. That was what was behind the building's long-held notion of foreign jurisdiction. But the public records in 1946 showed the building went to an international security corporation named Tarnhelm. Further research showed Tarnhelm to be a private corporation that seemed a mix of Blackwater meets janitorial services. All their work was under the umbrella of "security services." If this Tarnhelm was the link to Heydrich's SD, it had grown and metastasized over the decades to be something ferocious in its own right. It was a security operation that had subsidiaries all around the world. It boasted its own private military that even the US government used in several Middle East operations. Going against Tarnhelm was insane. But then again, clearly, sanity was no longer his strong point.

He left his room and went downstairs, where the concierge had his new SIM card ready for his phone. Walking by the Victorian grotesque black elephant fountain in the lobby, he made a promise to himself to enjoy a glass of champagne right there if he survived this clusterfuck.

Outside, the Pariserplatz was empty. Nothing blighted the pavement but a stray paper napkin that blew toward the Tiergarten, surreal in its loneliness. In the park in the distance, patches of snow could be seen here and there among the budding linden trees, along with the rare early-morning stroller.

He made his way toward the Brandenburg Tor. Spring was tipping in the warmth of the sun on his forehead, but an icy wind cut through his new jacket. He hardly noticed either. He was driven. By fear and curiosity. Holly's death had been the Big Unanswerable, but Harry's death had a reason. Now adrenaline and caffeine propelled him—and, perhaps, too, if he was truthful, a bit of his own illogical madness.

The Dresdenhof was within walking distance. Near the Memorial of the Murdered Jews of Europe. He wondered bitterly if Harry—though not Jewish—could qualify to be added to them. He himself might eventually need to be too. Truth be known, he was getting in over his head. He was a goddamned writer. The fiercest foe he'd ever encountered was a paper cut. A plan would be better than a hot temper and an old Polish firearm, but it couldn't be helped. This was an *ad hoc* operation. And until he knew what he was up against, the P-83 was staying right where it was.

From a distance, a woman in a vibrant red coat walked toward him from beneath the gate. She was swathed in the scarlet hood like a fairy-tale figure. Beneath it peeked a lock of blond hair. Her hands were encased in pale blue leather gloves.

It was a strangely unsettling combination.

She walked toward him almost with a purpose. The hackles rose on his neck. Perhaps it was the stare. Cool, slate-blue eyes fixed on him, their expression at once dismissive, and yet oddly enticing.

Paranoia slowed his walk. He stared at the woman, stared until she went past him, slightly brushing his sleeve. She murmured an apology, smiled at him, then ducked beneath the canopy of the Hotel Adlon Kempinski.

False alarm. But it served as a warning. He had to stay aware. He didn't know what he was walking into. He knew none of the players in this deadly game. Everyone was suspect. If he was going to get any information, he had to be careful. He was facing a towering opponent. But even if the outcome was dubious, he knew he would spend his last dollar and his last breath to get to the truth. He was the man who'd lost everything. He wasn't going to lose this one without a fight. Because of his mother, because of Holly, because of the fucking Nazis that Harry feared he might have come from, he wasn't going to let this go. His whole life seemed driven to this very mission. And while he was an impotent nobody with no connections and no power, Harry's murder was the last of the fuel to the ice fire that had eaten up his heart. His anger made him incandescent.

He set his jaw. The four-horse chariot, the Quadriga of Victory, built on top of the Tor as a symbol of peace in the 18th century, now looked apocalyptic, galloping above him. He shook off the vision and continued to walk toward the Dresdenhof, the hitch in his gait more pronounced from the long hours traveling. Exhausted and afraid—even wondering if he was a little suicidal—he lied to himself that it was more of a swagger than a limp.

CHAPTER TEN

STAG SCOPED OUT the Dresdenhof as best he could. He stood across the street sipping a hot cup of coffee, his watch cap down in order to obscure his face. As casually as he could, he observed people come and go. Two schoolchildren were loaded into the back of a Maybach, their sleepy mother in her sable coat giving the driver specific instructions from her perch on the sidewalk. Three men separately came down in their uniforms of wool coats and briefcases, and were picked up by their drivers. There was nothing out of the ordinary about the building other than it seemed to cater to the wealthy. And it was certainly older than the adjoining buildings. By decades. That it survived the Allied bombings was a miracle.

Several vans pulled up to the passenger zone. The drivers hopped out and opened up their rear doors. Catering equipment and floral arrangements in hand, they waited for the liveried doorman to open the door for them. Someone was having a party.

Tossing aside the coffee cup, he realized his moment had come. He steeled himself from the jitters that suddenly caused his hands to shake, and crossed the street where the doorman couldn't see him. He didn't expect to be Jason Bourne, still, he had to be smart. He was walking into the fire. Harry had been killed because of one phone call to this building. Inside perhaps was the reason why. They had lured him there with Harry's murder and that business card. He'd come all this way to find out what that reason was, and he sure as hell didn't intend for them to know he was there.

He went to the back of the first truck and grabbed an enormous arrangement of lilies. The flowers obscuring his face, he waited for the doorman to hold the door for him.

He stepped into the ornate green and gilt lobby. To his left was a front desk carved with oak leaves. A dapper man in his early fifties stood behind it, his gaze barely registering him.

Stag pressed the elevator button. Almost immediately the wrought-iron gates clicked open. He stepped in with the huge display of lilies hiding him. He pressed 12, and watched the ornate bronze door close in front of him.

His heart slowed to a less ferocious beat once the lift began moving. He was in and so far, undetected. At the twelfth floor, he stepped out into a black marble hallway. It had only two apartment doors. 12A was to the right. The door was immaculately maintained, painted a glossy black with a transom of black glass. Gold scrolls were painted around the letter A on the glass.

He stashed the lilies in the fire exit, then took out the key that had been slipped into the back of the painting. For a moment, he feared it might not open the door, that he'd come this far on a wild goose chase. In the back of his mind, he thought of the person who had written the note in his pocket. What had happened to him? Nothing good, if Harry was any indication.

A moment of god-awful fear washed over him. He had no idea what waited for him behind the door. Surely bad things could happen just by opening it.

He paused. 12A loomed like the entrance to hell with its unearthly glossy black door and opaque glass. But he'd come this far, he'd risked a lot to find out what was behind it. He was hell-bent to do it.

The key in his hand released a satisfying thump as the tumblers turned in the lock. With a grimace and a look around him, he realized he was about to find out.

Silently, he entered the apartment.

PART TWO

Vernebelt—a Nazi term meaning transformed into mist

CHAPTER ELEVEN

PORTIER TOOK THE hand-delivered note. Since Tarnhelm was a security organization, his important communication was encrypted with the only non-breakable code known: an OTP, a One Time Pad. He worked the code in his armchair. After deciphering it, he tossed it into the fireplace, and watched it burn with the same ferocity that lit up inside him.

Maguire had fled the coop.

He was the only being who possessed secret knowledge of 12A, and now he'd manage to slip away. Like a puff of smoke.

4EVER had always been Luc Portier's go-to man, and now he'd failed. That was why it didn't pay to send an assassin to do an intelligence run. The black man, in his eagerness to make his way onto the board at Tarnhelm, vied for every tough assignment. But he'd choreographed Maguire's exit instead of his debriefing. Unforgivable.

"I need to know what he has," Portier said into a speaker.

The silence at the other end seemed to speak volumes.

"This is going to have to be finessed," he bit out. "When this is under control, we can dispose of him. But until then, I need his information. " He paused. "Every nail does not need a hammer. Make him talk. He can bleed later."

He punched the speaker button. Then sat back in his chair, forcing his anger down to a simmer.

Maguire was not going to escape. And he was not going to take down everything Portier and Tarnhelm had built. But before his end came with blood and silence, Maguire first had to be found and forced to reveal what he knew.

Portier now had the best that Tarnhelm had on him. He would have to be a little more patient and see what they gathered. Later it could be decided how Maguire would die. In a pool of blood. Or, in a more preferred method. In bottomless silence. An eternal darkness.

* * *

The apartment was dim and cool. Stag stood at the entrance for a long moment, his heart thumping with adrenaline while he assessed all threats. But there were none. The place was quiet, devoid of occupants, peopled only with shadows.

Slowly he locked the door behind him and stepped into a time capsule.

The draperies were half-drawn. The robin's egg blue damask at the windows showed a few places where the silk had shattered with age, but other than that, the place was perfectly maintained. The smoky mirrored cornices over the windows gleamed, the French Aubusson rug showed no paths of wear.

All was quiet. It was a tomb. A beautifully preserved sepulcher that hadn't seen human activity in decades by the look of it. And yet, somewhere inside had to be the key to solving the message written on the strip of silk in his pocket.

There was the hauntingly faint scent of perfume in the air, a scent that had so permeated the place, it clung on even decades later. He couldn't identify it. It was heavy and old-fashioned, but compelling. Strangely alive. As if the person who wore it had just turned the corner, out of sight.

Not sure where to start, he figured it was best to explore methodically, bit by bit. He passed through a swinging door to the left of the entrance dais and discovered the kitchen. It was untouched. He went to the refrigerator, something that looked from the 1940s, and opened it. There was nothing in it, and it was not running even though it was plugged in. Clearly the motor had burned out long ago.

Back to the dim living room, he was at a loss as to how to begin. He wanted answers from the place, but he didn't have all the questions yet. All he knew was Harry had been murdered because of the secret inside this apartment. And he was determined to get to the bottom of it.

He stepped to a liquor bar set up on a steel trolley. The bottles were still filled with random measures of alcohol, an impossibility given the years they had been opened. The contents would surely have evaporated. But whoever maintained the apartment kept the bottles in their original state. He even found marks that someone had placed on the bottles with a Sharpie to keep the level intact.

Next to the bottles was a beautiful stag-horn corkscrew. Runic letters of R-H were engraved on the sterling endcap. He picked it up and studied it. It gleamed ominously in the dim light. He wondered how many bottles it had opened. He didn't ruminate for whom.

At the far side of the fireplace, there was a nook of windows. An artist's easel stood abandoned in the center of the space and the palette sat next to it, dried blobs of paint smeared together in a fashion only the artist could decipher. Leaning against it all were canvasses with sketches in burnt umber. The hand that had sketched them was clearly the same as the portrait of Heydrich.

He stepped to a shiny black Telefunken console by the bookcases. The pristinely dust-free 78 shellac on the player was a 1934 hit by Libby Holman called "You and the Night and the Music." He wondered when it had last been played.

There was a desk placed near the entrance to the bedroom. A white saber-leg chair was angled up to it, as if the woman who sat on the pink satin had just momentarily stepped away. On top of the desk, next to the ubiquitous photo of Hitler, lay a creamy piece of stationery in anticipation of a letter. The date had been written on it, now in faded peacock blue ink. May 15th, 1942. The name engraved at the top in dove gray script was Isolda Varrick.

Isolda Varrick. There was finally a name.

He pulled out the white silk strip and compared the peacock blue handwriting there to that on the date of the letter. They were the same.

Glancing above the fireplace, he wondered if the painting that hung there was a portrait of Isolda. It was unusual. The young woman stood backlit on a small hill. The breeze blew a few strands of gold hair across her face. She looked down at the portrait's observer, her eyes clear, steady, and knowing. Her head was turned so her face was in half-shadow and her expression hard to read. It could have been desire as much as disdain on her face. One thing was certain; she was no meek character. She owned that hill, everything she walked toward and left behind. What or who she looked back at would be forever a mystery.

Curiously, on the opposite wall there had once been a large mirror. Now it lay shattered on the floor, each shard no doubt right where it first fell. He walked up to the small hole in the wall where it had hung, his feet crunching over glass. No mistaking a bullet hole.

He went to the bedroom, his steps muffled beneath the lush carpeting. Sheer, frilly curtains peeked out from hyacinth blue taffeta draperies, the kind one expected to see in a madcap heiress' bedroom in a black-and-white movie. He tugged at the satin coverlet on the bed and wasn't surprised to see sheets underneath. The place was eerily maintained. Its occupant seemed to have walked away May 15th, 1942, and never returned.

A very tall Biedermeier chest of drawers stood to the right of the entrance to the bath. He opened the drawers. Luscious silk lingerie in colors like ice blue and shell pink sprang from the interior. There were enough stockings in one drawer for an entire navy on shore leave. The lingerie made it clear she was no wallflower. Sex had to be part of the equation of the apartment. If she were mistress to a very powerful man in Berlin in '42, he would be able to get unheard-of luxuries during wartime with no difficulty.

Buried in the bottom was a large square of white silk. He held it up and saw the raw edges where it had been cut. Hastily, he stuffed it in his pocket. He would see if it matched up when he got back to his room.

He peered into the bathroom beyond. There was a porcelain claw-foot tub, green glass tiles, and sleek deco fixtures. Towels embroidered with the letter I hung strangely refreshed on the towel bar.

Opposite the bathroom door was a vanity table, festooned in silk and crowned with an ornate Venetian mirror. It still held her powder and rouge. He picked up her French perfume. The stopper had a large W on it; the star-sprinkled bottle said *Je Reviens—I come back*. He figured it was the scent that still permeated the apartment, a mixture of jasmine and lemon, and something much darker. Mysterious and troubling. Next to it was some kind of face cream called Tho-Radia. He picked the jar and read the label: *methode scientifique de beauté*. Placing it back on the table, he wiped his palm on his jeans and wondered why anyone thought it was a good idea to put radium in cosmetics.

Back to the living room, he appraised the fat slip-covered sofas that flanked the fireplace and pictured the parties that must have been held there. Men in tuxedos, louchely perched on ottomans, laughing with bejeweled women who drank martinis. The place was created for just such a scenario. But the reality of it was something else entirely. It more likely involved field gray uniforms, two thunderbolt runes, and a death's head cocktail of prussic acid.

He sat at the desk and went through it. There was nothing in the drawer but some calling cards and an extra bottle of ink. He opened the oxblood leather portfolio that held her stationery. Thumbing through it, he saw only more of the same that had been left on the desktop.

But then, between the leaves, a card fell out. The name on it:

SS-Obergruppenführer Reinhard Tristan Eugen Heydrich.

High stakes were involved in the apartment. He pictured Isolda, the artist, obtaining a commission to paint a high-ranking officer of the Third Reich. If the silk that she wrote upon was any indication of her politics, she was on the side of the Allies. Coding on parachute silk was their technology. MI-9 even issued silk escape maps to RAF airmen for their flight jackets. Certainly, her recruitment by the enemies of the Reich would be profitable. A beautiful young portrait painter; a long, erotic sitting. If she played her cards right, she'd begin to be privy to all sorts of information. Heydrich was a notorious sexual profligate. He even started his own SS brothel called *Salon Kitty* in order to spy on his men. He was ripe to keep a mistress.

Heydrich probably didn't know it, but it sure looked to Stag that he was sleeping with the enemy.

Stag perused the bookshelves behind the desk. He knew enough about spy craft to know that codes were sometimes linked to a favorite poem or novel. It would correspond to an edition of a book that only the spy knew. Without it, it would be impossible to crack. If that were the code, which book would correspond? Isolda Varrick's library was deep. There was everything from the requisite volume of *Mein Kampf* to *Children's and Household Tales* by the Brothers Grimm.

He began running through the titles on the shelves. It was impossible. He didn't have days, he had minutes. If someone came, discovered the lilies gone from the truck, he would be in danger. He had to get as much information in the shortest amount of time. There was no time to read every book.

Scarcely making a dent in the volumes, he stepped back, frustrated. He could never check each one in the time he had. And that was only assuming the book Isolda Varrick used was on these shelves. Or even assuming it was a code connected with a book.

His gaze skimmed the titles again, until it fixed again on the notable red spine of *Mein Kampf*. Running his fingers along it, he realized Jake was right. Everyone knew about *Mein Kampf*, but even he—a writer—had never read it. Sure, he'd begun it a few times, but it obsessed and rambled, and he lost interest quickly. Now as he stared at the three oak leaves embossed on Isolda Varrick's copy, he found it noteworthy that her volume looked well read. The spine was cracked and downright worn. If she coded with this book, it would certainly begin to look well read.

Pulling the book off the shelf, he opened the first page. It was the special deluxe edition printed for Hitler's fiftieth birthday. He dug out the silk strip again. On the desk, the book fell open on its loosened spine.

Stunned, he couldn't believe his eyes. Inside were pages and pages, not just of the book's original text, but of peacock blue ink. He found whole paragraphs of code written in the margins. He picked it up. It looked like there was an entire other book written in the margins. Instead of *Mein Kampf* being the key to the message on the silk, it was just the opposite. The silk was the key to the writing in *Mein Kampf*. All hidden in plain sight.

He was in shock at his good fortune. The pages and pages of handwriting were in the same hand as that on the slip of silk. Whatever was in the coded margins was probably the reason Harry had been killed. Holding it like the Maltese Falcon, he quickly unbuttoned his shirt and slid the book between his chest and his arm. With the bulk of his jacket over it, it was undetectable.

He'd use the key written on the silk to figure out what the words meant back at the Adlon. Now, he had to exit the Dresdenhof without alerting anyone that he'd been there.

He looked around the apartment one last time. The place had been made into a shrine—with every remembrance frozen in time. It had been meticulously maintained for decades in honor of the woman who once lived there, yet there was nothing personal in the apartment, nothing ugly or messy. Even the shards of mirror seemed too exact. In suspended animation. It had all been cleansed except for the ugly, messy plea written on silk and slid into the back of a portrait.

He wondered if he would ever know what happened to Isolda Varrick. He looked once more at the portrait and her haunting expression. Had she been caught as a spy and executed? Or had she lived out the rest of her life in East Germany, dully waiting in bread lines?

The apartment left him uneasy. Something about it nagged at him, but from stress and jet lag, he couldn't quite put his finger on what it was. Something was missing.

He unlocked the apartment door and couldn't help but take another look back. There was no telling when he'd be able to enter the apartment again. Once they realized he'd infiltrated their precious perimeter, he had no doubt the nice man downstairs would be on the phone to his evil overlord, plotting his demise as they spoke. But until they managed to stop him, the game was on. For Harry, for everything in Stag's life that had been so ruthlessly taken away, he was now prepared to play to the end. He would get everything he could on them. Hell, if he made it out alive, he'd write the exposé to end all exposés.

That would fuck them *and* the cesspool they'd crawled out of.

CHAPTER TWELVE

THE CONCIERGE WAS busy at the desk when Stag arrived back in the lobby of the Dresdenhof. He exited in nonchalant silence and stepped into the cold. The day was dark with typical Berlin spring weather that couldn't decide whether it wanted to snow or rain. He was expecting to see security goons appear behind him at any minute, but no one followed him.

Back at the elevator to the Adlon, he searched his pockets for his room key card. Deep exhaustion was taking over. He ordered food and checked the news. Buried in the Metro section of the Wuttke online paper was a small mention of Harry's death. Heart failure was the cause. *Wuttke Man Found Dead and Abandoned.* The apartment resident was wanted for questioning. Harry's obit ran in the same paper.

The food came, and he ate while doing more research on Tarnhelm. It was ostensibly a small Swedish janitorial service. But what seemed mundane on the surface was far from it. From their website, he discovered their specialties were high-security clean-up operations and controlled document destruction. The Tarnhelm corporate motto was "We are the Dustbin of the World."

The words raised the hairs on the back of his neck. Heydrich, with his usual ironic humor, referred to the Gestapo as a cross between a general maid and the dustbin of the Reich. Trash removal. Jews, gypsies, homosexuals, no exceptions.

He also discovered what a tarnhelm was. It came from Wagnerian mythology; it was a magical helmet that provided a cloak of invisibility.

*   *   *

Einhar Kronbauer stared grimly at the old Polish maid, for a moment unsure of what she was trying to say in her crappy German. He only knew it was concerning apartment 12A. Something was amiss. And if there was one thing he did not enjoy, it was something going amiss in 12A.

The woman chattered away and urged him to go with her. He had to see what she saw.

He went up with her in the elevator. Katrine, with the fat arms and limp hair, nervously rang her hands. When the elevator door opened, she tugged on his sleeve and urged him quickly to the door.

Kronbauer took out his own key and threw open the door. He wasn't sure what to expect, but the maid led him to the desk. There in the carpet were the impressions left of the saber-legs of the chair, impressions clearly marked by decades of the chair's weight being left there, untouched. Only now, the chair was centimeters off target. Obviously moved. And the maid, who was paid an ungodly premium to keep the apartment in EXACT order, was emphatic in her denials.

Einhar had his ideas who had moved the chair. He'd have to make another phone call, something he looked forward to with the same enthusiasm as a colonoscopy.

He stared at the upset maid, his mind wandering to the dread of having to punch in that awful phone number. He knew only one thing: Someone was going to have a funeral. He just hoped like hell it wasn't going to be his.

* * *

Luc Portier still had his hand on the phone that now lay silent on his desk. He'd had the second phone call from Kronbauer. He swiveled in his leather chair and stared out at the spectacular view of the Alps on the horizon.

He knew who'd been in the apartment. The next steps would be crucial to managing this problem before it spun out of control. Stag Maguire had proven to be a bit more wily than they'd given him credit for. He'd disappeared from his Wuttke apartment, and now had somehow managed to enter the Dresdenhof and get inside that apartment with his own key.

Tarnhelm's men would be in the apartment soon, combing every inch of it for a clue as to what Maguire was looking for. But Portier already knew what would be. The copy of *Mein Kampf.* For decades now, Tarnhelm had studied the coding. Their best human and computerized cryptology had produced zero results. The code was based on an absolutely random key and it couldn't be cracked without it.

Goddammit, he was sick of being a slave to that apartment. The cryptographers insisted nothing could be changed because there could be coding in the placement of the shellac records stored in the Telefunken or in the books on the shelves or the level of liquor in the bottles at the bar. For now, everything had to remain exactly as they'd been handed it. Exactly.

Now it appeared that information about 12A had somehow turned up in Wuttke, Wisconsin, in the hands of Stag Maguire. A dipshit journalist who didn't have a clue what he was doing. How many nations would be at once terrified and thrilled at the possibility, should what Portier feared was inside the book be discovered?

He swiveled back to his desk, stood, and walked to the glass wall that separated his office from his private elevator. He took the lift down and stepped out into the sub-basement where Tarnhelm had its boardroom.

The conference table was empty. Just six seats for the entire board. A board meeting was overdue. There'd been talk that one member was losing his enthusiasm for security service. The man was growing too rich and lazy to bother with secrets any longer. He just wanted to fuck whoever happened to enter his plane with a pussy, and not much else.

Perhaps, with the shock of what Maguire might be able to expose, what was needed was a lesson. A real lesson. One they could all reeducate themselves with. Loyalty and enthusiasm could both be bolstered with a dramatic dose of terror. After all, there were no men on earth more obsessed with self-preservation than a bunch of white male executives sitting around a conference table.

A lesson it was, Portier decided. He would bring them in and pick their brains for a solution to Maguire. Plans would have to be formed and implemented. Security had been breached and that was unacceptable for Tarnhelm, much less Luc Portier. They should be made fully aware of it. Then they would all see how he, Portier, planned on going forward. They would get a nice coppery taste of the stakes at play, once they had blood in their mouths.

He walked past the conference table to a jib door set unobtrusively into the exotic blond wood paneling. He pressed both hands on it and it popped open to show another door that was two-feet-thick steel. It led to the small room beyond that was nothing more than cold stainless walls, a concrete floor. It was hewn into the sub-basement in 1942. The kind of brutalist architecture even

Albert Speer would have admired. An old defunct bomb shelter, with no real use any longer except as a panic room. But he wondered why anyone back in '42 would think to devise such a shelter. For a country not at war. Built for a bomb that didn't exist.

He pressed the two-foot-thick steel door shut.

Yes, it was time for a board meeting. Time to test loyalties. Stag Maguire had managed to place everything at stake. Tarnhelm would not survive a meddling journalist who knew more than they did. Yet they couldn't just go after him with an Uzi. Maguire knew things that they needed to know. They would have to finesse it out of him. Or torture it out of him. Then Maguire could be neutralized.

The board would have to convene right away. They would have to find a solution. If not, they wouldn't need Tarnhelm. It would all be over. Maybe even in a flash.

He thought of the SS motto. *My Honor is called Loyalty.* In the end, when tested, some would have it; some would not.

Now he just had to find out who it was.

CHAPTER THIRTEEN

STAG WAS JUST finished with his room service hamburger when the room phone rang next to him.

For a long moment, he stared at the clanging device, paralyzed by an unnamed dread.

"Yes."

"Einhar Kronbauer, Mr. Maguire. I am from the Dresdenhof."

He sat up, his body tensing. Jesus, they were quick.

"I would like to meet you for a drink, if you would be so kind. Perhaps now downstairs?"

Stag paused. He damned himself, helpless at check-in when they required his passport. He'd hoped there'd be more time. Some rest at least.

Now they knew where he was. The Dresdenhof's security cameras would have his face to compare to his US ID. The only reason he was still alive was because they didn't know what he had. They still wanted to talk to him—which was good—but it was only a matter of when before they'd lose patience and forcibly bring him in.

He had to play for time. There was too much he didn't know. He'd barely begun deciphering the lines of code. He'd stumbled into this deadly mess because of that portrait, but now it was clear he had to make sure he stumbled less.

"I'll meet you in the lobby." He hung up the phone. He was going to have trouble sleeping tonight anyway. Might as well have a couple whiskeys. It wouldn't hurt his nerves either.

He looked down at the book. It was next to the silk he'd taken from the apartment, the silk that perfectly matched its edges with the piece from the back of the portrait. There was no way he was leaving the book behind in the room, and no way he was going to walk around Berlin with a copy of *Mein Kampf* in his hands. He grabbed the sport coat he'd bought at the Walmart back in the US. He ripped open the interior breast pocket wide enough to fit the book, and stuffed it inside.

Once downstairs, he would press Kronbauer for whatever details he could. One thing was certain; he had to make sure Kronbauer brought the news back to the Tarnhelm Corporation that Stag Maguire had just enough information to be a wild card. He'd have to bullshit his way through. Make them too terrified to kill him. Then he might make it. He had to. Because that was the only way to keep them from murdering him for another few days.

*   *   *

Kronbauer sat in a chair along the balustrade that curved over the lobby. Stag noticed that he'd changed from earlier. He was quite the sharp dresser, this German with the fancy neckties.

Stag took a seat at the coffee table. After he'd ordered his whiskey, he took in the view of the lobby below and the stained-glass dome that hung above.

"Thank you for meeting me, Mr. Maguire," Kronbauer began with his thick German accent.

Maguire said nothing. His nerves were on edge from lack of sleep and the soul-eating fear of being consumed by a predator. He was exhausted, but terror would keep him focused and alert.

"As you might guess, many people have been quite surprised at your interest in apartment 12A," Kronbauer said.

"I didn't find it, if that's what you and your employer are wondering. But I will."

Stag was pleased by Kronbauer's troubled and confused expression. He himself didn't know what the "it" was, but that there was an "it" related to that apartment, he had no doubt.

Kronbauer put his hand to his tie in the obsequiousness of all concierges. "The owner of the apartment has long since died, Mr. Maguire. The trust that maintains it is self-funding. There seems no apparent purpose in your interest."

Since he was stabbing in the dark, Stag figured he had no choice but to keep fucking with him. "Diamonds are my interest."

"I can assure you, you are on a fool's errand. There are no diamonds in the apartment. I know every nook and cranny."

"Maybe there's something you missed. These are special diamonds."

"The Blood Eagle? It certainly was a famous diamond, but it is not there, Mr. Maguire. If it were, I would know about it. It disappeared after Heydrich bought it. Just like so much associated with Heydrich, when he was assassinated."

Stag weighed this new information in his head. "I have information you don't. And my visit to 12A only confirmed everything I already knew." Good God, he was doing a stellar job of bullshitting. He didn't know he had it in him.

What the fuck was The Blood Eagle?

"May—may I be blunt with you, Mr. Maguire?" Stag was struck by the waver in Kronbauer's voice. "You may be inquiring into things that people would like to keep undercover. I have no personal knowledge about this, but I fear it may not go well for you should you pursue this."

There seemed a strange little humanity in Kronbauer that Stag hadn't expected.

"Germany lost the war," Stag said. "The Holocaust is no longer a secret. What on earth is there to hide in that apartment?"

Kronbauer drilled him with his stare. "What there is to hide, if I might venture a guess, is the horrific truth, sir."

"The truth? And what would that be?"

Kronbauer paused. He didn't seem to want to speak the words. "That most Germans would do it all again, if the circumstances were the same. In fact, I think you now know a good number of Americans that will act in fear and prejudice, and do cruel and inhuman things they may, in hindsight, deeply regret. It is the truth that we all run from. It is the human condition. We hate and fear and exploit the Other. We do not listen to the better angels of our nature. Not without constant vigilance." He looked away and took a deep sip of his drink. Stag guessed it was scotch. "And I tell you as a postwar German, that vigilance is exhausting."

Stag took a moment to ponder his words. Kronbauer was no idiot, and he had now proved he knew a lot more than he was letting on. "Who is it you work for?"

Kronbauer was back to business in a flash. "I invite you to discover that on your own, Mr. Maguire. Mr. Portier asks you join him in Zug for a brief holiday. He will be happy to send his jet."

"Huh. Beats the hell out of the way I've been used to traveling. But you can tell your employer that I have all the information I need already."

Kronbauer took a distracted sip from his glass.

"Mr. Portier can be very persuasive. He has assured me your trip would be profitable."

"Tarnhelm needs to stay out of my business."

"Of course, of course." Kronbauer met his eye. "Perhaps they are only trying to be of service. "

"Bullshit."

Kronbauer almost imperceptibly raised one eyebrow. "They have a stake in 12A. And they do not take prisoners."

Stag stared at him, anger rising up like a fist in his throat. "What is their stake in 12A? I doubt a big international corporation like Tarnhelm needs to worry about a missing diamond, no matter how rare. So what is it? The janitorial service for one lousy apartment? Or could it be that their specialty in document destruction missed a document or two?"

Kronbauer tensed. "Mr. Portier is quite interested in all you have to say, Mr. Maguire. What can I do to persuade you to take him up on his offer to fly you to him?"

"I'm going to get the Blood Eagle. Tell him that. Then maybe we'll talk." Stag slammed the rest of his whiskey.

He stood. "And just to let you know, if anyone's going anywhere, it's Portier. He'll be coming to me, not the other way around. You tell him that."

"I will, Mr. Maguire. But may I offer some advice?"

Stag listened.

"Decades have passed with my family in the service of apartment 12A. There is something . . . quite dark and unsavory in there. And much bigger than either of us. You cannot do this alone." He paused. "If you contact me again through the Dresdenhof, Tarnhelm will know."

Stag nodded and saw sadness and perhaps a little grudging admiration on Kronbauer's face as he watched him go.

Pressing the elevator button, Stag wondered if he'd played it too hard. He was running the words through his head when the elevator doors opened and the blond woman he'd passed in the

Pariserplatz stepped out. She gave him another smile. Her red coat was gone, which meant she'd probably left it in her room. Now she wore a sexy, frayed, vintage suit and clutched an iPad.

"Hello," she said, no immediately identifiable accent in her voice. He nodded.

She walked past him, the iPad clattering to the floor behind her. He reached for it just as she did.

"Always clumsy, I guess," she offered when she took it from him with what could only be described as a dazzlingly smart girl-next-door smile.

She turned to the lobby. He stepped into the waiting elevator. The exchange was pleasant. A nice antidote to the fear and paranoia that engulfed him. But he didn't trust it. Not for a minute.

The elevator doors closed, and he wondered who she was and what her business was in Berlin. Could she have something to do with him? But there was no point in getting paranoid now. Because they really were out to get him. He need speculate no more.

Suddenly he was bone tired, but he knew he would get little sleep in the Adlon. The fight or flight instinct was raging once again and he knew now to listen to it. He was going to have to battle through the fog of weariness and get the hell out of the Adlon without them knowing where he'd gone.

His consolation was that he doubted the strange Mr. Portier with the private jet was going to rest very well in Zug or wherever the hell he laid his head at night.

CHAPTER FOURTEEN

STAG RODE THE elevator to the roof. He stood outside in the cold evening, staring at the lights of the Memorial to the Murdered Jews of Europe. The field of painfully plain cement oblongs looked like an aboveground cemetery for postmodernists, a cubist *Père-Lachaise*. He gazed at the field of concrete, appalled at the numbers they represented, the incomprehensible mass of humans murdered.

The Nazis called it deportation while they skirted the term extermination. For enemies of the Reich, whoever they were, treasonous officers or three-year-olds who happened to be Jews, Heydrich used the term *NN* next to their names. *Nacht und Nabel*. Enemies of the Reich who disappeared in the night and the fog. Now, by sheer dint of will, the memories of these people were put into slabs of stone, never to be forgotten again.

Hopefully.

He felt acutely small at the top of the Adlon above the field of gray concrete boxes. It was near impossible to believe in platitudes like "God's will" when facing the corporatized extermination of eleven million people. He didn't fool himself. He was no match for even the shadow of the force that had managed to kill all those represented down below. He was a loner, a cripple, a nobody. The *why* of the Nazi mass murder was still being analyzed. It still

danced on the edge of disbelief. How would he add anything to
the answer of it?

He rubbed the exhaustion from his eyes, feeling overwhelmed
and defeated. When he came to his end, there was no child or spouse
to mourn him or remember. There would be no one to care that
there was a stone marker for him. He would be one of the
forgotten.

So what else was there but to take the forgotten as his people?
Like the victims of Heydrich's *Einsatzgruppen*, he, too, had watched
everything he loved in the world destroyed by the dispassionate
muzzle of a gun. But instead of falling into the merciful earth at
Babi Yar, he was left with the cruelty of being alive and alone.
Protecting Holly hadn't been an act of bravery as the newspapers
had said. It had been the meaning and sole purpose of his existence.
And he'd lost. He'd failed. While his leg had healed, he'd spend
months staring at the bottom of bottles of hydrocodone. He'd
counted and recounted the pills, sometimes every hour. *One too
many*. That's what they'd warned him about. One too many, and
he'd no longer have to know what he knew, see what he'd seen, feel
what he felt. He would no longer have to get up out of bed and function. The frustration and fury would melt away to sleep. He could
drift off into the sweet darkness, and never have to picture puddling
shades of bright red ever again.

Cold and alone, he stared down at the monstrous number of
stone oblongs. *Nacht und Nebel* was ultimately about the pain of
stolen good byes. He did know about those. The needle had stolen
his goodbye from his mom, blood-loss had stolen it from Holly.
Whole villages had disappeared once the *Einsatzgruppen* arrived.
Others were rounded up by the Gestapo and crushed into cattle
cars, then sent to a "bathhouse" to the east. It was called "protective
custody." But he was never clear whether the lie was used to

manipulate the Reich or the people they were rounding up. But few good Germans asked such questions back then. Those who watched and knew about Heydrich's operations urged others to remain sane and reasonable. Close your shutters to the roundups—it wouldn't do to disturb the children! Ignore the pleas for water from the cattle car stopped at the siding—would you want your family involved with criminals? You must be deaf to the thousands of gunshots in the woods. They were necessary to protect good folks from the faceless boogeyman who would hurt their precious Reich.

And the smell? Well, the smell was what happened when the Reich was efficiently going about their business. You couldn't avoid the smell, so you didn't answer for it at all. Silence was the route when dealing with the smell. Without silence, the olfactory path would force you to wander into the realm of *why*. To survive, it was logical not to be among those smells. Best to turn away and "let Germany be Germany." Silence was safe. Shut up and be grateful they were fighting for you. It was the only reasonable thing to do in such circumstances.

But Stag was an unreasonable man. Staring at that field of concrete, he knew his only salvation was in grappling with the *why*. The very struggle to answer it was eternal in his soul. The *why* must be brought to light with facts. The *why* must be reckoned with in the mirror. The very struggle was the only thing necessary to the world. Because therein lay hope.

Night and fog was now reason enough for him to chase this demon that killed Harry. Strange as it was, Harry's death was bringing purpose back to him, little by little. He didn't fool himself thinking he was going to be able to destroy Tarnhelm. If bullets and diplomacy were the only things that could make a country behave, then tort lawyers and other countries were the only things to make a corporation behave. He was neither a tort lawyer nor a country. But he sure as hell could try making one or two near-fatal wounds. It only would involve research and planning, and he was excellent at both.

The sting of the cold air atop the Adlon was good in his lungs. And the gun—no matter how shitty it might be—felt comforting tucked into the back waistband of his pants. He didn't know how much time he had until they came for him full-throttle. They were still assessing him. He would have to push himself as far as he physically could, to get as much done as he could.

First, he needed to get some rest. Then get some reading done.

His hand reached for the solid rectangle of the book.

* * * *

Ordering coffee in the lobby of the Hostel-Berlin, Stag tucked himself into a plastic chair by the front door and settled in to read. After an hour's journey, switching subway cars, and finally a long walk in the dark of the Tiergarten, he'd settled on a bunk in the hostel because they were unlikely to ask for his ID with cash at the ready.

In public, he felt a little more safe. It was an illusion; they were smart enough to take him out no matter where he was. His plan to stall for time was to keep them guessing and chasing until he knew what he had and what he needed to do. The best way was to throw them off balance. The only way to do it was to play a hellacious game of whack-a-mole.

Taking the book out from his jacket, he made a point to keep the cover from public view. He lay it open on his lap, took a gulp of coffee, and began to translate from the code.

CHAPTER FIFTEEN

THIS MORNING, *I opened my eyes to find you still asleep next to me. I lay next to you, still as a mouse, and for a brief moment, I had the luxury of honesty. Of my truest emotions. Because you did not see me, I could stare at you with everything buried deep in my soul and not think how placid I must keep my expression, how delight-filled I must keep my eyes.*

I stared at your eyelids with their sparse brush of lashes, your fine slim nose with the impressive commanding profile. Your cheeks were flush with the color that must've glowed like radium in your youth.

I studied your mouth. A strange mouth for a man such as you. The lips were mobile and sensitive. Tender. In my mind, it was really the only feature that made you handsome. I confess with terrible pleasure that I sometimes enjoyed your kisses. And when you rise up above me for your little death, I found sometimes I loved how I made you groan. The power over you at those moments could make me drunk with it. If I had you at my command for those few seconds, might I be able to have you at my command forever? You would be mine. All mine. And it is I who would control those infernal papers you sign by the pile. I would control who knew what. I would have the final say over who lived and who died.

So I lay this morning staring at you, bitter about all I had to do, all still left undone. I no longer think of myself as just another U-boat trying to find shelter in a sea of mines. I am different now entirely. I am with you. I am protected. No one could hurt me. No one would dare.

Except you.

And today this most unusual U-boat stared at you and knew that I cannot hurt you back. For how does one cut off the head of the Hydra without it growing ten more? It would be easy in this moment of vulnerability to seize upon you. But I do not. Instead, when you wake, I must hand the power to hurt me back to you once more. I'll know with every painful second that the breath I take today will only be because you allowed me to have it.

I write this diary as a testament. A testament to you and all that you made this little U-boat do in this tragi-comedy of no hope, only war. Every day I am alone, even with you at my side, so this little diary will be the friend that I will never have in you. In it, I shall confess all my unholy experiences, and I shall do it fully and truthfully. The way I can never do with you. I'll write it down for the small humanity left in me that longs for someone to find this diary and know that I existed at all. What I did in the name and falsity of love. I share with you all the intimacies of the bedroom. I have surrendered to that mouth in my most sacred of places, and its release brought tears to my eyes. But I want you to know that in this world you have created of gray and black, of all night, all the time, I still found my secret little joy. I still defy you with my imaginary colors. There is still release.

A U-boat doesn't have the luxury of honesty. Not when its very essence is to hide. But this morning, I wanted you to know, my lover, my tall blond Aryan beast, the one I surrender to at your every whim and notion, that today I revealed my inner most hidden feelings to you while you slept. I laid bare my self to you. I stared at you with everything in my heart and mind. I stared at you with sheer and utter naked honesty. From the deepest and truest part of my broken and now tarnished soul. For one brief moment I was no longer a U-boat, and you were no longer the Young Evil God of Death. No, at that moment, I was a lioness.

And, I looked at you with all the dispassion of a starving lioness that stares at a pile of bleached bones.

* * *

Stag looked up and gazed at the dingy, institutional lobby of the hostel. It was more and more evident that this remarkable woman was Heydrich's mistress, even referring to him as the Young Evil God of Death, just one of his lovely nicknames. But what was a U-boat? U-boat in this sense was a term for something other than a submarine, but for what?

He grabbed one of his unused GoFones and dialed Jake.

"Jake? It's Stag."

"Jesus, Stag, where are you? Where the hell are you calling from? Harry was found dead of a heart attack in your goddamned apartment, and no one knows where you are."

"I had to go out of town for a while—"

"The authorities have a lot questions—and frankly, so do I!"

"I know that, Jake. I know. And I know about Harry. I've run into some problems."

"You left your apartment open with Harry dead inside it. I'm glad to hear from you. I was worried something had happened to you."

Stag grappled with the need to tell Jake what was going on. He knew he could trust the older man, but he was uneasy about getting him involved if he didn't have to. "I . . . I know."

Jake's voice was thick. Clearly Stag had woken him up. "The funeral's tomorrow."

"Listen, Jake, I'm not going to be there. It can't be helped. And I don't want to tell you where I am."

The silence at the other end of the line was heavy. "That bad?"

"Yes."

"Okay."

By Jake's blind acceptance, Stag was able to continue. "I need help."

"You've got it. Anything."

Stag was relieved to hear it. "I've got a question. This is kind of random but I'm working on a piece right now and—have you ever heard the term U-boat?"

"You mean like a submarine?"

"Yeah, but I don't think they're referring to a sub. They're referring to themselves as a U-boat."

"Ahhh . . ." Jake seemed to understand. "Referring to people, you say? What kind of piece are you doing? Glad you're working, by the way, but this isn't how I pictured you getting back to it."

Stag tasted the bitter words. "Trust me when I tell you it isn't the way I saw it either. But it can't be helped. Now, do you know another term for U-boat?"

"Yes. 'U-boat' refers to a Jew who went to ground in Berlin. It began around the time of the pogrom—you know, Kristallnacht."

"Were there a lot of them?"

"More than we know. Certainly, after November 1938, they left Germany if they could, or went underground if they knew what was good for them."

"I see."

"I can't imagine you missing Harry's funeral. You guys were like brothers."

"As far as I'll ever be concerned, we were brothers." The words cut at Stag.

"I've got to tell you ... ah ... Interpol questioned me about knowing you. Yes, that's right. *Interpol*."

Stag's chest tightened. His situation was as dicey as he thought it was.

"I've got to go, Jake. I'm sorry about Interpol." The words brought new bitterness. "Could you put a wreath on Harry's coffin for me?"

"Let me know what else I can do. I mean it. With Ruthie gone, you know I have nothing but time."

Stag tapped the end call button. He leaned his head back in the chair and thought about the diary. He wasn't quite shocked by the revelation as much as he was impressed by it. Isolda Varrick was a Jew in hiding. And somehow, perhaps through her painting, she'd managed to find herself the object of Heydrich's desire.

Weariness was overtaking him, and he knew he would have to get some rest or collapse. At some point they were going to come for him, but they hadn't shown up yet.

He closed the book and put it back in his jacket. He went to the elevator and punched the floor number of his bunk. He hoped like hell he could sleep. Because, without a doubt, when they got a bead on him again—they were going to run him to ground like a Jew in 1938 Berlin.

That is, if he lived long enough.

CHAPTER SIXTEEN

HENRY SADLER LOOKED nervously around the table. There were six of them. All present. The entire board of Tarnhelm awaiting Portier's pleasure in his private conference room. All had flown to Zürich in their jets on a moment's notice, when Portier had called the meeting.

No distance was too great, no meeting too inconvenient when the puppet master said dance, Sadler thought with a sour taste in his mouth. After all, Portier was as close to being God as any human on earth. He hid behind the Tarnhelm cloak, reaping information as God reaped bodies in war. One click of the mouse and Portier was ahead of the information curve. He got there first, and everyone else jockeyed behind him in order to come in second.

"We mustn't overthink this, gentlemen," Portier said, standing before them in a bespoke winter white suit of the finest vicuña. In spite of his slick apparel, he looked worried and tired, Sadler thought. Like he'd been up all night, fighting off devils.

Or maybe just trying to masturbate that limp dick of his.

Sadler swallowed his glee every time he thought of it: Prostate cancer. Total removal. No more working dick. *No, Dorothy, you can never go home again.* Sadler had been resentful of Portier's power for three decades now, and it was with a good amount of schadenfreude when he'd heard the lovely slut from Slovenia who he liked to be seen with on his arm was going to have to get her rocks off with the pool boy.

"How did this Maguire know of the Blood Eagle?" Sadler, like most executives, could fall into harness quickly. He asked the question with complete authority, with no hint at his real thoughts. Everyone at the table referred to him as *the Ugly American* for his support of the last bid for the White House, but he didn't care. He was in no mood to tap-dance around the subject. He'd had to be called off an Antarctic cruise in order to be there. He was exhausted and nauseous, which is how he usually felt at these meetings with Portier. "I, for one, knew nothing about the Blood Eagle before this meeting," he interjected. "So how the hell did he?"

"We will get to the bottom of it." Portier looked at his wristwatch as if he were already counting down the seconds. The platinum of his Tourbillon Mars gleamed on his wrist like the legend it was. Made from part of a Martian meteorite, the watch was rumored to cost in the millions. It was a signature piece of Portier's, along with his ubiquitous green American alligator briefcase from Hermès.

And now his flaccid member. Sadler's eyes narrowed to hide the pleasure.

"How much is the Blood Eagle worth?" Georges Zellner, the Canadian, interjected. "Sure, red diamonds are rare, but with Tarnhelm operating more than a trillion dollars worldwide, I don't see why we give a sh—"

"It's not about the fucking diamond." Tall blond Erik Rikhardsson gave him a quelling glance. The cold Norseman looked around imperiously. "How is it we control the largest information security service in the world and we don't know what this guy wants?"

"Enough." Portier glanced again at the watch. "We don't know if the Blood Eagle still exists because it disappeared with Heydrich before he left for Paris in '42. He went to Prague after that, and we all know how that ended," he said, referring to Heydrich's assassination by Czech patriots. "If we do not know what happened to the Blood Eagle, neither, I wager, does Maguire."

Portier looked at each face at the table. They were in the infamous boardroom deep in the sub-basement. It was Tarnehlm's SCIF room. Sensitive information only. So secure, the boardroom came with its own bomb shelter. Across from him was Doug Roberts, in from their branch in Australia. Jan Vanderloos was the last one to arrive, from South Africa. Each and every man watched Portier expectantly.

"There are perhaps thirty red diamonds in the entire world, and the Blood Eagle was the most famous of them," Portier announced. "Should it reappear . . . Well, there will be questions. It's known that Heydrich acquired it in '42. We've been meticulous in our disinformation to stay clear of links to Heydrich and the SD. They would be catastrophic to our business model."

"This is more. This is much more," Rikhardsson said. "We're the kind of corporation that gets the job done, not the kind that worries about a sterling reputation. Our clients certainly don't worry about theirs."

Portier contemplated the faces around him. "This is about more. Maguire showing up at that apartment means he's in possession of information we have sought since '42."

"What kind of information?" Vanderloos sputtered.

"Heydrich's SD was involved not only in maintaining the secrecy of the death camps and the Final Solution, but it also kept hidden the most secure operations of the entire war. I needn't remind you, Heydrich was very adept. We didn't officially know about the Holocaust until our military and the Red Army stumbled into the concentration camps."

"Specifics please," Rikhardsson demanded.

A muscle jumped in Portier's jaw. "With the V-1 and V-2 rockets, Hitler was, of course, developing secret weapons, which he believed would win the war. There was one that was even more secret than the rocket program. We have exclusive historical evidence that Heydrich was cloaking an operation through the Škoda Werks plant outside of Prague that was much further along than first thought. Heydrich was assassinated, Germany was bombed to smithereens, and the secret weapon information disappeared. No one could find out what Heydrich had after that. Not even Hitler. *Der Führer* went to his bunker hoping that the 'secret weapon' would somehow be found and win the war for him. But the only things discovered after Heydrich's death were the documents ordering that apartment 12A was to be kept intact in perpetuity. The directions were absolutely clear. And for all these years, we've done exactly that. We've been too afraid not to do it. One thing out of place, one thing destroyed, and we may be out of luck ever finding what Heydrich was hiding."

"What are you saying? That Heydrich may have collected some fissile material? Big deal. The world has a surplus of that, if you haven't heard. Just ask North Korea," Sadler piped in.

Portier snapped back, "We don't know what state of development this weapon was in, we don't know where it is, we don't know who has access to it. We don't fucking know anything. And this is unacceptable. For me. For Tarnhelm."

"Why haven't we forced the information from Maguire?" Vanderloos interjected.

Portier tossed a stack of papers on the table. "This is his dossier. Our analysts say he's the worst sort to respond to torture."

Vanderloos sputtered, "He's a nobody! Surely we can—"

"All we will do is manage to kill him—and there goes his information." Portier nodded to the dossier. "A deranged gunman took out several bystanders in a Starbucks. Maguire's wife was one of them. With a leg shattered by bullets, he still managed to get his dying wife behind a barricade, reach the dead security guard's gun, and take out the gunman. The press called it a pure act of suicide. If he can function under that kind of emotional and physical pain, there's not much more we can do to him that's short of killing."

"We're a security and information company—there are other ways," Roberts said.

"Yes. We need information. As of right now, we don't know what he has, or who he's talked to." Portier gave a meaningful pause. "Nor who he's working with."

Portier's expression took on a nasty new edge to it. "I needn't remind you gentlemen that we supply information to the Sinaloa cartels as well as to the NSA. This man and his questions are unsettling; he will eventually be swatted like a fly. But before that happens, I want everyone in this room to know that every person in our organization is to be put on this. We *must* know what he knows."

He looked at the face of each member of the board. "We sit upon a precipice, gentlemen. We've brought Tarnhelm into the 3rd millennium. The Marianas Web does indeed exist because we created it. Our information infrastructure includes the development of the darkest of web platforms and continues all the way down to receiving the mundane reports of our network of janitors who pick through the trash baskets. Our entire *raison d'être* is built upon security information, which we use and trade like cryptocurrency."

He stared at the board. "When there's chaos in the world, we make money. We like it. But there will be no chaos in *this* organization. *None.*" He shook his head. "Maguire's interest in the apartment in the Dresdenhof could make public a connection to us that has been long suspected. In which case, we are ruined. The Israelis will cease doing business with us, along with the Americans. That will leave us with the Chinese and Russians, and I don't have to tell you, that while technologically proficient, they have all the finesse of a bunch of offal-swilling peasants being seated at *Epicure*. Without connections to information on the West, they would be gone also. Then. We. Are. Finished."

"We must rid ourselves of that apartment! Why do we still keep it?" Sadler demanded.

"There are secrets in there. Heydrich's secrets. He was methodical. Meticulous. Diabolical. We've never known why he placed the apartment in trust. We're afraid there could be messages there: in the pattern of shattered glass, in the level of whiskey in the bottle. We've yet to figure it out and until we do, the apartment stays intact." He released a weary breath. "After all these years, after all our research and study, we have yet to decipher anything. We don't dare get rid of it until we do. If Heydrich had developed a weapon, perhaps the only way to save ourselves from it is the message of that apartment."

"An answer to a question we don't know," Vanderloos interjected.

"Exactly. Besides, at Heydrich's unexpected death, his trust required we keep the apartment *intacta* in perpetuity, and that same trust started Tarnhelm in Stockholm in '46. That trust is what made us, gentlemen, but nonetheless, it marks us like a tattoo." Portier rolled his eyes in frustration. "Whether we like it or not, the Heydrich connection is absolute and irrefutable once made. Whoever traces us to the apartment can trace us all the way back to the RSHA, the Reich Security Main Office. I will not see our corporation compromised by stupid Nazi bullshit."

He took a long, stony look at the faces around him. "And I will not allow a loose cannon to operate in our midst."

"What are you implying?" Vanderloos spit out, incredulously.

Portier answered woodenly. "The words speak for themselves."

"I don't understand," Vanderloos complained. "You sound as if you believe one of us could be working with him."

"I would never be so incautious as to imply that." Portier's gaze still circled the occupants at the table.

"Roberts," Sadler overheard Rikhardsson whisper mischievously, "you've always had an interest in diamonds, have you not? Particularly pink ones from Australia?"

Sadler saw the heat rise in Roberts' cheeks. The man stared back at Rikhardsson with the same chilly stare the Scandinavian gave him.

Under his breath, Sadler heard him retort, "At one time or another, herringfucker, I think everyone at this table has taken an interest in diamonds."

"The longer the man remains active, the more of a threat he becomes," Zellner announced to the table. "I say we bring him in."

"We'll get more information if we manipulate him. We know that from other operations," Sadler said.

"I think it's prudent to send in agents to get to the bottom of this. Find out what he knows, who he's talked with," Roberts added nervously.

"Put him in the Baltic!" For emphasis, Vanderloos beat his fist on the table.

All the men seemed shocked by the sudden pounding.

All except Portier.

"That is an inevitability," Portier said. "But in the meantime, I would like to remind everyone of the seriousness of my intentions." His gaze slid over to the only other door to the conference room.

Everyone knew the room. The old bomb shelter. The nickname among them was The Honor Room after the SS motto. It was Tarnhelm's sick joke, homage to SS Reichsführer Himmler's ridiculous fascination with "Aryan" occult. If you were the focus of questioning, if you were put in time-out in The Honor Room, then either way, like the witches in Salem, innocent or guilty, you were dead.

Sadler had to give the old SS credit where credit was due: they were cartoon villains, but they certainly did not lack style and substance in their villainy. And God knows, they were good at their jobs. Like Tarnhelm was now.

"We deal in information. That is our business. In fact, there is no business if we cannot be relied upon to keep our secrets," Portier said, ambling around the table.

He paused at Roberts' seat, but he didn't look at him. Regardless, Sadler saw the blood violently drain from his face.

Portier turned his attention to Rikhardsson. He stared at the Viking who sat stiffly, defiant and yet trapped. Then, without further contemplation, Portier announced, "No one is going to take Tarnhelm for a ride."

He pressed a button on the table. Four large men arrived, each in bespoke dark gray suits. Each looking like they ate bull sharks for breakfast.

"Mr. Roberts, it has come to my attention that you've been running a side operation in illegal gem trading in Liberia. Would you care to elaborate?" Portier paused and looked him dead in the face.

Roberts choked.

Even Sadler could feel his own insides turned to concrete with sudden fear.

"You can't be serious!" Roberts blurted out.

Rikhardsson stared at Roberts, along with all the others at the table.

"You can't believe this conniving herringfucker any further than you can throw him!" Roberts spat furiously at Rikhardsson. "I've been loyal for more years than this fool has been an adult!"

Rikhardsson turned his eyes to Portier.

"People get weary. They forget those to whom they owe their loyalty," Portier added, his own weariness showing in his voice.

"This is bullshit. *Bullshit*," Roberts blasted.

"Nonetheless, with this Maguire stirring up trouble, now is the time to confirm loyalty to Tarnhelm. I cannot go forward until I have complete assurance that everyone is on the same team." Portier went to the bomb shelter door. He opened it. It was twenty-four inches of solid steel.

"No one has proven his loyalty better than me! No one! You would not have your army of Muscle Men without me! It was my idea. *My idea*!" Roberts screamed in his Aussie twang.

"And as thanks for the Muscle Men, I offer you an out. A gun is provided inside. I suggest you take it," Portier said coldly.

Roberts looked at the others in the room, silently begging for one of them to speak up, to defend him.

"Look, I took a few baubles from the Liberian trade in undocumented gems, but that was only because my wife is the fucking Imelda Marcos of Tarnhelm. I mean she's a vampire! There's no quenching her thirst for sparkle. She's like an old whore who must wear all her rhinestones at once!

"You men know me! I would never betray a trust! It was more like skimming the inventory to please that bitch of a new wife so she would give up some pussy! Surely you can all understand this?"

Desperately, he looked around the table, his very soul begging. "Someone? After all these years of service?"

The board said nothing. The silence was absolute. Vanderloos looked especially uncomfortable but whether that was because he'd done his own skimming or the Dutchman truly felt bad for him, Sadler couldn't tell.

"'My Honor is called Loyalty,'" Portier announced in a tired rumble. "Go and retrieve yours."

The four elegantly suited mammoths surrounded Roberts' chair. One put a hand on his arm and forced him to his feet.

"This is a mistake! I won't go!" Roberts shouted, trying to twist his arm out of the grip holding it.

Portier said nothing. He merely nodded to the gang of four.

They held Roberts on either side and guided him to the room. Sadler watched the rest of the board heroically wash the horror from their faces as Roberts was led to the bomb shelter, a room that amounted to a walk-in safe. Inside, highlighted by a spotlight, was a semi-automatic handgun encased in glass.

Break glass in case of emergency.

Roberts pulled back. He fought and kicked and struggled but to no avail. He was a sixty-year-old man surrounded by more muscle than the US Olympic Weightlifting Team. He was dragged into the vault and deposited there. Everyone knew that once Sadler was inside, there would be nothing for him except perhaps his own merciful self-inflicted death. Either way, to go quickly and violently or to go mad and rot away hour by hour, the only way he would be leaving the vault would be in a dustpan.

Crushing Roberts' screams, two of the goons closed the door. There was an eerie and immediate dead silence. It was like Roberts had never existed at all.

Portier resolutely looked around the table. "Loyalty, gentlemen. Are there any questions?"

Strangely enough, there were none.

CHAPTER SEVENTEEN

STAG WOKE UP in the dorm of the Hostel-Berlin more surprised than rested. The room full of bunks was completely at peace, the only disturbance, the snores of the young hippies that had bailed from their night of partying. *Mein Kampf* was still next to him, open on the page he'd been translating when he finally passed out.

He closed his eyes and wondered about Tarnhelm. Did they know about the writings? He couldn't believe they'd missed them. They were, after all, a security organization. They had to know every inch of that apartment. Only they never had the key to the code.

He'd eluded them, but the translating was going slower than he'd like. And at this point there were no real answers. What in God's name were they so afraid of that they sent someone out to kill Harry just to get his buddy to pick up the phone? It was all darkness right now.

But one thing he did know was that if the SD was still around as some kind of security service, it could be everywhere, and the implications were chilling. Pissing them off was a suicide mission. But he'd never be able to find out what they were up to by making nice and heading into the sunset. His inquiries were going to bring him attention. He would have to deal with it.

He sat up and put his legs over the edge of the bunk. Randomness was the key. It was his only advantage. Tarnhelm probably had people everywhere. He could picture someone tampering with his breakfast in the kitchen.

Nothing like a little paranoia with your morning coffee, he thought to himself with a grimace. He stood and walked a bit, his leg stiffer than usual. The pain brought back memories of Holly. Her room-brightening smile, the comforting way she liked to stroke his chest after they made love, the moment she went to tell him about the pregnancy test and then didn't have to when she brought his hand to her belly.

Find what you love, then let it kill you. He could never figure out if that was Bukowski or Kinky Friedman who said it, but the real truth was that it didn't kill you. Holly had left him behind. All the pain had just left him alive and still kicking. And thoroughly, radiantly pissed off.

With Harry's death, the feeling sure as hell wasn't getting any better.

When his leg loosened, he shrugged on his jacket. In case of rain, he placed *Mein Kampf* and the white silk strip in the Ziploc bag he carried his toiletries in. With both secure inside his tattered inside breast pocket, he left the hostel.

There was a cafe two blocks away. The day was already warming, and in the sun, it was downright pleasant. He set up shop at a table by a budding linden tree that smelled strangely of honeysuckle and bleach. He was careful to sit under the awning. No telling what spy satellites could be aimed at him. He ordered coffee and rolls, then pulled out the book and began reading his latest deciphering.

* * *

This story ends with death.

I am not a fortuneteller, my dearest Reinhardt; all your stories end with death, and it follows that this one shall, too. You have the power to make it so, and so it must be. Every minute of every day, I think of how this may end, and I hate you for it. The very night and fog that you create for others lifts you up onto the pink cloud of power and optimism. You show me the pictures of your beautiful little girl Silke. How is it that you may have pictures of a messy child grinning at you on a blanket in the sunshine, and not me? That you may see your angel-faced children—every evening if you wish it—while I may only imagine the cherub forever denied me? How dare God be that cruel?

Yes, how dare he. And how dare you.

You are the Hangman, and I am nothing in your wake. That is undeniable. So this story will indeed end in death. The only question is whose death shall it be? We shall have to let the play run its course. But what you don't know is how this story began, so allow me to tell you.

My parents were German-born Poles who worked as buyers for Israel's Department Store. I can remember as a girl going to the Schiap Shop at the Place Vendôme, and having very grown-up tea with my mother in the Ritz. There was art school in Paris, summers in Linz and along the Wannsee. When I took my first job at Israel's, as an artist for their ad department, I was a proud young Berliner. By then, of course, you and your kind had boycotted the store. Hardship loomed, but in my youth and naiveté, I believed everyone who said it could not last. "Things will change," Wilfred Israel would tell me, patting my cheek affectionately. "It will get better," he proclaimed. And I believed him. I wanted to believe him like everyone else did. After all, it made no sense why the Nazis would do such a thing. Had not Israel's been a part of Berlin since 1815? Of course, it would continue!

My parents' permit was canceled in October of 1938. Wilfred Israel tried to get my parents out of Germany, but my paperwork lagged, and they would not leave me. The Polenaktion expelled them. Do you remember? Your Gestapo rounded them up. Then they were refused entry because Poland refused German-born Jews. They were held in the rain and the cold, with no food or anything of comfort. My mother wrote that the worst part was having to relieve herself in front of everyone in the courtyard. My gorgeous mother? Sleeping and shitting in a bare-earthen courtyard? There are no words for the horror I felt then. The disbelief. This could not be. My mother was on a first-name basis with Mademoiselle Chanel and Elsa Schiaparelli; my father had two thousand workers beneath him at Israel's! No, this could not happen! I would save them! But I was caught myself. Israel's Department Store was looted and burned in your November pogrom—the Kristallnacht. *Or—if you insist as all of you do— the* Reichskristallnacht—*Even the infamy, you Nazis are so eager to tag all your own!*

And so, this story truly begins with a knock on the door. The Gestapo told me when and where to report for my "treatment" because my parents had been shot trying to escape their inhumane detention. And I was the criminal Jew who had written to them to tell them to escape. So I was to report. And report I did . . .

* * *

Stag put down the book and made some notes on his iPad. For a long moment, he simply sat at the table, contemplating the drip marks on his coffee cup. He needed to research, to concentrate, to really read the "book" Isolda had left behind. She and that apartment were key, but whatever it was, it was not obvious to him nor all the generations that had gone before.

He pulled out the white silk with her writing on it. *The diamonds are in a truck at the bottom of the lake.* Which lake? And what diamonds? De Beers was known for selling both the Allies and the Axis industrial diamonds to make their weapons. An argument could be made that they alone kept the war going longer than necessary by refusing to take sides. So was he chasing something like that? A truckload of crude industrial material? Or Holocaust booty?

He flipped to the Wikipedia page on the Blood Eagle. It was a legendary red diamond from Belgian Congo. Herman Goering had been interested in acquiring it, only to be dismayed that Heydrich had beat him to it. It was another blow the younger Heydrich had dealt to his peers. By the time of Heydrich's death, Goering was high on opiates and mismanaging the Luftwaffe. It was hard not to be dazzled by Heydrich's rising star.

Upon further research, he found that Heydrich's wife had, in one of the world's greatest ironies, been granted a widow's pension after the war. There was no sale of the Blood Eagle to fund her lifestyle. She ran her former summer home as a restaurant and inn. No fabulous jewelry showing up there.

But if Heydrich acquired the Blood Eagle, he must've given it to someone.

He looked down at the diary. His mistress was the place to start. He again wondered what had become of Isolda Varrick. Was it possible she was even alive today? In a home somewhere, ancient and obscure, no longer in touch with her memories? But while she was an intriguing mystery, Tarnhelm's interest wasn't just to acquire a piece of jewelry. There was more to this. Much more.

He perused his bookmarked photo of Luc Portier. The CEO was at a fundraiser sitting next to Bill Gates and a Rothschild heir. He was a well-dressed man in his fifties, a big man, with a full head of graying hair. Even at a dinner, Stag could see his shiny alligator briefcase next to him. He'd read Portier carried it personally, though it was rumored to be lined in lead to keep anyone from scanning the contents. Luc Portier's nuclear football. The legendary Mars Tourbillon watch was ubiquitously strapped to his wrist.

The photo gave Stag pause. Not so much because of Portier's slick appearance but because of Bill Gates's expression. Gates looked at Portier with fear in his eyes.

Tarnhelm was everywhere and nowhere. The cloak of invisibility was far-reaching. It seemed there was nothing they couldn't buy, no information out of their reach. Men like Portier didn't bother with two men from Wuttke, Wisconsin. He was definitely protecting something. Whatever it was, it was bad fucking news. And Stag was going to find out what it was and reveal it to the world.

He looked up the address of the Bundesarchiv in Berlin. It was a repository for SS documents, at least those that survived the bombings and document destruction at the end of the war. It was as good a place to start as any. He stretched his leg and rubbed the ridge of scar tissue that ran down the length of his thigh. He was just about to reach in his pocket for a few bills to leave as a tip when he found himself staring across the boulevard.

There she stood, watching him, in her Red Riding Hood coat and pale blue gloves. The blond.

The notorious blond.

CHAPTER EIGHTEEN

IN A MOMENT of clarity, Stag remembered her brushing against his sleeve in Pariserplatz and her murmured apology. He looked down at his sleeve but could find nothing. No GPS dot, nothing. Again, he recalled her smile as he handed her her iPad at the Adlon elevator. Now here she was again, this time staring at him: Her mark. Her dupe.

When he looked again, she was gone. Like a spirit dissipating in the mist.

Jogging across the busy boulevard, he took a shot at finding her, but there was no sign of her. All around him on the sidewalk were women in athletic shoes and briefcases heading for work and men in Burberry trench coats looking like young George Smileys.

But no blond. No scarlet coat.

He stood there amidst the morning work commuters, unsure of his next move, his mind whirling. Tarnhelm was close. It was all around. The only way to survive long enough to get the information he wanted was to *Nacht und Nabel* himself. Let him disappear into the night and fog for a little while. To get his research done, he needed to exit Berlin, pronto.

He made to disappear into the crowd, but three men in suits suddenly blocked him. They stared, mute and immobile as stone. Then one man, older, with the short stature of a Russian president, stepped forward, his hand up with a badge. It said in large letters, INTERPOL.

"Mr. Maguire." The little man put away his badge. A black Mercedes pulled up and one of the men opened the door.

"May we go for a little ride?" he said as he gestured elegantly toward the car.

Stag gave them all a long, assessing stare. But he was outnumbered and overwhelmed.

"What's this all about?" he demanded, already knowing the answer. They were looking for him. To answer questions; why he ditched Harry's body in his apartment in Wuttke.

"If you would be so kind? We have some things we'd like to ask you." The older man motioned again to the Mercedes.

Resentfully, but without protest, Stag ducked his head and slid into the back seat. Two special agents flanked him on either side and they pulled away.

* * *

"I don't know who she is. She was staying at the Adlon. I kept seeing her." Stag sent a hostile stare at the small man.

He'd been bundled out of the car and into the Berlin office of Interpol. The little man was Chief Aldernay Troost, an American, who had now proven to be very good at asking questions, and very bad at answering them.

Stag again looked at the two bits of video Troost had shown him. The first was an exterior shot of Pariserplatz. It showed in grainy black and white his first little encounter with Red Riding Hood when she obviously intentionally bumped into his naive ass. Vid number two was of them in HD, smiling at each other at the elevators like polite, normal people do.

"Her name is Angelika Aradi. A most unusual woman. She has an uncanny knack of appearing and disappearing, wouldn't you agree?" Troost raised his eyebrow. "I don't mind telling you, we've had a helluva time tracking her. But here you've met with her twice."

"Again, what do you want with me? I don't know her."

Chief Troost perched on the desk between them. They were ensconced in an interrogation room complete with hospital-green walls and dirty baseboards from the fifties. Troost took his time before speaking. He seemed to be weighing the pros and cons of telling him anything. Stag observed his worn cuffs and out-of-date tie. Troost was an old cold warrior if there ever was one, at war in his old Cold War surroundings. He wondered if the fight had been worth it. A lifetime of bureaucratic frustration on a public servant's salary.

"You're wanted for questioning in Wisconsin. I could send you back there on our first plane out of Tegel."

"I take it you're not planning to. I'm wondering why." Stag gnawed the inside of his cheek.

Troost turned his baggy eyes to a framed poster of a beach. It was a generic South Pacific paradise, beaten egg-white sand, irradiated blue water, neo-plastic palm tree. "Sometime, do you ever think, 'Why bother?' Nothing we do in this life is bound to have a lasting effect. Why not just drop out?"

"I'm not much of a philosopher," Stag said.

Troost laughed. "Me either. I'd like to think I was instrumental in bringing that wall down out there. That great big nasty wall." He seemed to laugh to himself. "And I'll be goddamned if it isn't happening all over again."

"Communism?"

The older man snorted. He pulled on the worn-shiny knees of his gray trousers, adjusting them. "No. No. That never worked.

Nobody's going to be conned into that again. No, I'm talking fascism. Dictatorship. Megalomania. And all the lemmings that hurl themselves off the cliff in their name."

"Who would we be talking about here? Germany today is about as anti-fascist—"

"Of course. Yes. But what I'm talking about is corporate fascism. I'm talking about that kind of dictatorship."

"What corporation would you be talking about?" Stag asked warily.

Troost raised one eyebrow and his humor made him seem suddenly younger and more vigorous. "There's a transparency to government—even a bad one. It's not that they don't hide things; it's just in government, there are too many people to control. There's only so far you can go these days. You can't control all the media like you could in the 1930s. You can't round up six million people today without other countries knowing about it.

"But a corporation—well, they don't operate under any real moral or ethical purpose, now do they? They aren't a group of people trying to bring order or reform. No matter how screwed up the Nazis were, they were pretty fucking sincere about their ideals. But a corporation—they exist to make money. That's it. That's their god, their philosophy, their sole endeavor. If governments are bacteria in the wake of penicillin, then corporations are the unkillable viruses of the new millennium."

He face-palmed his aging, hangdog face. "And the worst, the very worst, are ones that control the information. Control the 'facts' and you control the people."

"Who does the woman work for?" Stag tensed. He pretty much knew the answer.

"We don't quite know but we have our theories." Troost frowned. "Of course, we haven't verified them. We must talk to her and soon."

"Why do you want her?"

"There's a little murder we'd like to ask her about."

Stag recalled Harry's grotesque death. He had a little murder he'd like to ask about too.

"We have a high-level NATO official dead in a hotel room. Sir Roger Burnett was an expert in the anti-terrorism arm of NATO. He claimed he'd found a concrete connection between information sold by the Tarnhelm Corporation and the radical Daesh terrorist organization of Almawt Al'Aswad. The Plague. Sir Roger was going to come out with it. But before he did, he ended up dead. And she was around for it all, it seems, perennially in our sights, yet forever elusive."

"You think this Angelika Aradi murdered this man for Tarnhelm?"

"We do. Yes."

Stag kept his expression tight.

"We are interested in getting information from her but we haven't enough to bring her in, and so far, she has managed to elude our undercover people. She will not talk to us. But she seems to have an interest in you. I don't want to frighten you, but that could go very badly for you, from our experience."

Stag consoled himself with the irony that that last statement was not shocking information. "I know nothing about her. She may be following me or it might be coincidence." No matter what cards he was dealt, he was going to continue to play them all close to his chest.

"What is your business in Berlin?"

"I'm thinking of doing a series of articles on modern Berlin. Milwaukee, if you didn't know, has a German ancestry."

Troost perused a file. "That sounds very speculative for a man who was in such a hurry to leave Wuttke, Wisconsin, that he left his buddy dead in his own apartment."

"When you got a deadline, you got a deadline." Stag gave him a level stare.

"You don't have much family, do you, Mr. Maguire?"

Shifting in his seat, Stag grunted.

"Terrible thing that happened to your wife." Troost frowned. "But I guess we all have our sad stories, do we not?"

"My wife's death has no bearing on this matter."

"Of course not. Of course not." The older man seemed to be pondering an idea. He wobbled his jaw and reread a couple of items in the file.

"I don't want to alarm you, Mr. Maguire, but we have reason to believe you may need our protection."

"Why?"

"Simply because all is not as it seems."

"What is Tarnhelm anyway? If they're assassinating people, why don't you guys know about it?" Stag tamped down his anger.

"Tarnhelm is a corporation that was developed in Sweden after the war, but it's not necessarily Swedish. Its funds are directed by a holding company into a Dutch *stichting*, a tax-exempt nonprofit foundation. The head of the company lives in tax exile in Zug, Switzerland."

The man paused and looked down at the shiny knees of his suit. "I don't have to tell you there's virtually no evidence of any charitable giving from the *stichting*. Tarnhelm is flush. Very liquid, with almost no financial oversight. And without that, it is admirably free to do what it will."

"Even assassinate?" Stag could feel his anger rise.

"We have no proof so far . . ." Troost shrugged. He looked at Stag. "We'd like your help, Mr. Maguire."

"My help?" Stag looked around. "I don't know what I could do for you. I'm a spec journalist who hasn't worked in years. I can't see what—"

"Angelika Aradi has an interest in you for some reason. We'd like to find out why."

So the fuck would I, Stag thought. "I don't know who she is, who she works for, or what her interest is. I don't see how I could help."

"Go to the Adlon. Be visible. If you can pull her out in the open, perhaps you might be able to talk to her, find out what her interest is, whom exactly she works for. For that, we can offer protection. You need it." Troost looked back to the poster of paradise. "I'm hoping to retire next year, Mr. Maguire. I don't have a big fat pension like many corporate sellouts of my generation. Tragically, I won't be retiring there." He nodded to the picture. "But this final project will be the jewel in my crown. Will you help me?"

Every instinct told him to refuse. Going back to the Adlon would be suicide. Tarnhelm would put a bead on him, and he'd never escape their snare. It was crucial for him to get out of Berlin and do his research alone and in peace. That was the much more prudent way to get Tarnhelm. Bring it down from without.

But here was a chance to bring it down from within. Much less likely a positive outcome. The odds weren't good. Harry proved what direct contact with Tarnhelm could entail. Meeting up with a strange woman in the Adlon for the police didn't quite sit well.

But his back was against the wall. How could he justify saying no without divulging information?

"If this woman's as dangerous as you say, I'll need some kind of protection, won't I?"

"I'll see that our very best men are in the lobby at all times monitoring any meeting."

God, he didn't want to do it. But the woman was his best contact with Tarnhelm right now. If he could find out what she knew, he 'd be ahead.

"I guess I'll have to," he said.

Troost seemed strangely relieved. "Good man."

CHAPTER NINETEEN

VANDERLOOS SAT IN his plane, talking into his iPhone. The conversation was succinct.

"It must look like an accident. " He paused. "I believe you're qualified to take care of this." Pause. "The money's been wired to your Belize account.

"Take. Him. Out." He tapped the red dot and ended the call. Then he looked out the window. They were just over the Sahara, the orange-red sand melting at the horizon to the blue sky.

He had never gone rogue before now. But Doug Roberts' eradication in The Honor Room shook him. No matter what Tarnhelm might be capable of, he had never been on the ground to see it. It was always a memo slipped innocuously to him at cocktail hour or diagramed on a PowerPoint. Death had always had the cleansing factor of distance. Now it was at his doorstep.

He couldn't stop thinking of Roberts, the shrill, soul-clawing screams, and then the silence, the unbearable silence. Nor could he forget that the gems Roberts had skimmed were part of his own criminal take of the mining concern. Roberts hadn't known their origin, thank God. But Vanderloos didn't need Portier to go digging. Connections were fatal.

He now had to take matters into his own hands. There was no way he was going to pay the price Roberts had. They didn't know the Blood Eagle had been sold to Heydrich decades ago by a family diamond concern in South Africa. The fact that it had been his family's mine was not something he was going to pay for. It had all happened way before his birth; he'd had nothing to do with it. But if that Maguire was even hinting the Blood Eagle might be found and connections were made, he could not take the risk. He sure as hell wasn't going the way of Roberts when someone on the board—no doubt Rikhardsson, the Aryan scum—decided to dig for nefarious deeds.

No. No. Nope. He was not waiting around for that scenario. He was in the business of paranoia. The best way to make yourself secure was to get rid of the security problem and that was Stag Maguire. Vanderloos didn't give a shit about a long-forgotten weapon. South Africa was far enough away from Europe and the arms race for now. And, of course, there was also the very real security of the fact that this weapon had not come to light in all the years since. It very likely did not even exist. But in the meantime, Portier was going to use the entire organization to extract information from Maguire, including anything he might have on the Blood Eagle.

Vanderloos wasn't going to wait around for that. The only solution was to take out Maguire and shut him up for good. Let the pieces fall where they may. He wasn't going to go down like Roberts.

No. No. Nope.

* * *

Stag sat in the Lobby Bar, waiting and drinking. It was after eleven. He'd returned to his room at the Adlon and found everything as he'd left it. Tarnhelm had to have sifted through his room several times while he'd been gone. But the real question that nagged him:

if Red Riding Hood found him, Tarnhelm had to know where he was, so why the hell had they kept their distance?

The answer had to be they were biding their time, studying him, figuring how to best extract his information. He swallowed his fear and paranoia with every sip of whiskey.

He looked around, seeing the usual suspects: business associates having nightcaps and going through their tablets, an older couple enjoying a bottle of the familiar orange label of Veuve Cliquot. Nothing out of the ordinary. But no little Red Riding Hood.

He perused the news on his iPad. The headlines led with a Tarnhelm executive's private plane that was missing over the Baltic. Terrorism was suspect given the sensitivity of Mr. Roberts' work with private contractors in Iraq, the article said. Wreckage of the plane, remnants of a small explosive device, and the pilot's body were all found. Roberts, however, was feeding the fishes. No body. The usual groups were being held accountable. More than one had already claimed responsibility.

Knowing Tarnhelm, there was more to the story than that. But right now, that was not his circus, not his monkey. Instead, he took the diary from the Ziploc bag and flipped to the page he'd last been deciphering.

* * *

I did not plan to be a U-boat. I did not expect to survive at all. The Gestapo told this criminal Jew that she would have to report to the Freibourg Clinic for Racial Hygiene. I was one of the lucky ones, I was told. Because of my blond hair and blue eyes, I was to be allowed to remain and simply receive "treatment." A new experiment was being tried as a cure for my tainted blood. A series of X-ray treatments were prescribed. Painless at first.

But then the bleeding began. The terrible, unending flow. They were most pleased how quickly it started. Then my hair began to fall out. Not entirely. I was blessed with an overabundance of hair, and I was able to pin and pad what I had left after I went to ground.

You never knew that you did this to me, did you? But you were a hair-puller, weren't you, my darling? When you would fall on top of me, I would lay there beneath you, pretending to revel in your caress, all the while seeing my hair, my precious, precious hair, intertwined in your fingers, tickling my breast, mocking every effort of mine to stay upon this earth.

How did I become a U-boat, you ask?

I dutifully went for my treatments until one day the nurse who greeted me decided to take mercy upon me. Or perhaps she was simply resentful of her betters at that moment and decided to rebel. She announced to me in her best Bund Deutscher Mädel voice that the treatments were being discontinued. The powers that be at Tiergartenstrasse 4 had decided the process was taking too long to be effective. New plans were being developed. I was no longer required to return.

Then she did the most astonishing thing.

She whispered as I was leaving, "Don't go home."

Numb, I left the doctor's and took exile on the trolley bus. I traveled for miles, it seemed, unsure of my destiny. Those were the days before rationing. Traveling then in a crowded trolley was still pleasant, before ersatz soap made every soul stink and ersatz butter made every body flatulent. No, to ride the streetcar then was to see happy productive people, to smell perfume and tobacco, and hear laughter. But none of that comforted me then. I was terrified and I rode for hours trying desperately to think of what to do. But where does one go when you are an ersatz human?

I went to make my plea to Wilfred Israel. He could not get me out. But to my relief, he was able to supply me with new papers. I was now a real German again, with papers going back to my great grandparents. With them, I took a job as my new Aryan self as a hatcheck girl at the Scala. And that is where I met you, my lover.

That is where I met you.

* * *

Stag rubbed his eyes and looked around. He was chasing mist, he told himself. First the haunting Isolda, then Red Riding Hood with her pale blue gloves and matching stare.

He threw some bills on the table and packed up. Heading to the elevator, he half-expected to see her standing at the concierge, or ensconced by the elephant fountain in her vintage suit. But she was nowhere.

He barely looked at the two special agents sent to watch him at the Adlon. It was imperative, Troost told him, that nobody know he was being watched. Now one agent sat in the Lobby Bar, studiously nursing a Coke, while the other nonchalantly rode in the elevator with him, making sure to observe him as he headed to his room, cardkey in hand.

He unlocked the door and heard the comforting sound of Sinatra being played on his sound system. Turndown service had prepared his room. He dropped his cardkey in the entrance.

And there she was.

Waiting for him in the beige deco chair, like a spectre greeting the dead at the entrance to a crypt.

For a long moment, he said nothing, simply stared at her. The hair had risen at the back of his neck. The only comfort he had was the fact that she'd had plenty of opportunity to take him out before now. If she hadn't, it meant that she, too, was out for information. But for whom? He was going to find out.

"How did you get in here?" Captain Obvious. Sometimes he truly wondered how a little guy like him was going to survive against Tarnhelm.

She looked to the bed. Draped there was a maid's smock with the Adlon logo. She must've slid by Interpol dressed as the help.

Easy to ignore the powerless, he thought.

He noted how calm she appeared, her legs crossed and slung to the side, one hand resting lightly on a silenced Walther PPK that was casually placed on the table next to her, the other hand cradling the fresh white rose that had been left in a bud vase next to his bed at turndown.

"Who the fuck are you?" He saw no point in vacillating. "And why are you interested in me?"

"You're an interesting man, Mr. Maguire," she answered, her accent cultured, painfully neutral. British, perhaps, with a trace of Eastern Europe. "Truthfully, you interest me, regardless."

"Regardless of Tarnhelm?" he shot back.

"Regardless."

"You've attracted some interest too," he said. "Interpol asked about you."

She didn't look surprised. The intelligence in her eyes was only eclipsed by her cynicism. He took note of the worn vintage suit she wore this time, different than the last, but somehow the same. The deconstruction of it struck him. It jarringly reminded him of the aged clothing you would find on a corpse, but she was hardly corpse-like with her fine symmetrical features, her pink cheeks, and her curves beneath the lines of the suit. No, she was very much alive. Not some cold, dead shell that could harm no one. This woman breathed threat like an intoxicating perfume.

He thought about *Je Reviens*—I come back. Briefly, he believed in spirits.

"They told me you assassinated a NATO official for Tarnhelm." Stag cut to the chase. "Then why the hell haven't you put a bullet in me?"

"Killing you right now goes against their purpose. They want to know what information you have, Mr. Maguire. They will go to great lengths to find out."

He met her eye. "What I have is mine alone."

"You've rattled cages," she said. "They will use all means. Means you can't even guess at."

He thought of Harry's gruesome death. "I'm getting good at guessing."

"Mr. Portier would like you to not have to guess."

"I'll be happy to have a nice long discussion with Portier."

She shook her head. "You won't have a long one."

"He'll see me dead first, I imagine?"

"After he gets his information, you will be a dead man." A brief empathy crossed her face. "Your wife would have probably preferred you retire with your money to some beautiful palazzo in Ibiza, Mr. Maguire, than martyr yourself for a dubious cause. I wonder if this is not the hill to die on."

"Yeah?" He shifted in his seat and wondered briefly if he should introduce the P83 right now. "What's the hill you would die on?"

The wariness lowered for a moment. Then she spoke with matter-of-factness. "There is only one hill. I have a child."

"I don't."

"No."

She knew about Holly's pregnancy, too. He had to give it to Tarnhelm, they were thorough.

"How did they get Harry?"

"Ice needle, I imagine." She stroked the silencer on the PPK with the fresh white rose.

"That's why we couldn't find a wound on him. The needle goes in and melts. Poison?"

She nodded. "Probably Micotil, a bovine antibiotic. Difficult to detect and causes heart failure in humans. It has a two-pronged hit. If the patient makes it to the hospital, the standard dose of epinephrine just speeds it along."

He nodded. He hurt for Harry.

"Mr. Maguire—you're only one man. You cannot fight Tarnhelm. Tell me what you know, and perhaps I can get them to call off the chase."

"Bullshit. They murdered Harry. They're never going to call it off on me."

She conceded the point by pursing her lips. "If you tell me what it is you know—"

"Why don't we start by you telling me what you know, such as what this big bad company is so afraid of?"

She looked at him with a grudging admiration. "You can't threaten Tarnhelm. You're not big enough. I know this very, very well."

"Maybe not, but I can go for all the collateral damage I can."

He swore she almost smiled.

"May I bring Mr. Portier a message? He's anxious to hear from you," she said.

"Tell him I'll be calling him to meet with me as soon as I'm good and ready." He gestured to the PPK. "Are we done?" he asked.

"I doubt it."

She stood.

He instinctively stepped back. "What's your stake in this? Money? Power? Or are you fucking Portier?" He waited for the reply.

"Good evening." She handed him the white rose.

When she left, he swore he'd just seen a ghost.

CHAPTER TWENTY

AFTER SHE'D GONE, Stag assessed what he had in his hotel room. Interpol had done a bang-up job already; he sure as hell wasn't counting on them giving him a good night's rest. But weaponry was hard to come by. All he had was the P-83 and it would do him absolutely no good while he was asleep.

He went to his computer and searched for creative methods of self-protection. After a few minutes of research, he figured out what to do.

In the bathroom, he stared at the cut-crystal glass on the sink for his drinking water. In his pocket, he dug out a pair of nail clippers he'd bought in the airport and assessed them.

Angelika Aradi was perhaps more interrogator and less assassin, but he didn't trust her. Hell, right now, he didn't trust anybody. He made up his mind to take care of his own damned security.

* * *

Duke Farnsworth loved Berlin. It appealed to his every white, male, conservative sensibility. The women were blond, the wine was French, the architecture clean and modern. To do a job there was pleasure upon pleasure.

He checked his weaponry. The bulk of the ice needle gun was more than he liked to carry. It ruined the cut of his suit. But it was everybody's favorite. Clean and quick. The only mess was in the after-effects. You couldn't disable the person right away, so the ice needle was only for certain circumstances. For the rest, he carried a Beretta 8000. The "Cougar" was sleek, swift, and now readily concealed beneath his suit jacket.

Duke Farnsworth had started out with a silver spoon in his mouth and a Yale degree. He was a bright baby investment banker who got his thrills and his insider stock tips from his good friends at Tarnhelm. That there was something inherently evil about a young, good-looking male in a Hugo Boss suit was a given. Farnsworth had no handicaps. The world just unfolded for him.

Of course, a complete lack of conscience could be a handicap. But in the business of assassination, it was a golden asset. There were some who worked very hard to keep theirs under control. Not Duke.

Which is why he didn't bill himself to Tarnhelm as an independent contractor. No point in highlighting the fact that a lack of conscience came with an absolute lack of loyalty. It made him a huge whore, but who wasn't a whore? Even the exalted Portier was a whore. It was obvious he was afraid of that Maguire guy in Wuttke. He wanted Maguire to talk.

But now, after Duke was done with him, there would only be infuriating silence.

He checked his bank account. The Vanderloos wire payment had hit. All set. He looked down at the master key card to the rooms at the Adlon. Bought at great expense but all part of the contract.

He smirked. It was three a.m. The electronic key card would gain him entrance to the elevator and to Maguire's room. The job was about as direct as he'd ever had: Take. Him. Out.

* * *

Stag stepped out into the hallway outside his room and upended a glass of water. It was absorbed and camouflaged by the swirl pattern of the carpeting. For good measure, he splattered two more glasses, and then shut his door.

With the nail clippers, he clipped the cord to a table lamp and stripped the plastic coating off the wires, flushing the telltale plastic down the toilet. Then he wrapped the raw wires around the room's door handle that was in turn wired to the electronic lock that used the key card.

Stepping back, he appraised his handiwork. He was no genius but he was sure good at an internet search and following directions.

Anxious about the setup, he placed a chair in front of the door, not so much to protect him from whomever entered, but to protect himself should he awake in the dark, befuddled, and head for the door. He smirked. That would be just like him to stumble into his own trap.

Now he had nothing to do but get some restless sleep.

* * *

Stag opened his eyes to the sound. Not quite to a scream; it was a kind of violent gurgle. The door rattled like barbarians at the gate, and for a far greater time than it would need to kill.

In the darkened room, he had a good, sickening mental picture of what was happening outside. The current was driving through the arm of the person on the other side of the door. Where the current drove through his body, the ATP—adenosine triphosphate—would be burned off and his muscles would stiffen. A kind of pre-dead rigor mortis. Then the current would blow out one or more wounds on the person's calves where the current exited to reach the ground. Urine would run down his legs as his bladder involuntarily emptied, and when the medics came, they would think the victim had wet the carpet.

Not the perp.

There was a flurry of activity outside, as down the hallway, doors opened to discover the source of the strange sounds. Stag anxiously leapt out of bed and switched on a light. He unplugged the cord to the door and took it off the door handle. Sitting on the edge of the mattress, he twisted together the wires inside the lamp and refastened the sticky felt covering on its base. Then he put it back on the table where it belonged, plugged it in, and turned it on. It worked perfectly. The staff would never notice the slightly truncated cord.

The phone rang in his room. He picked up the receiver.

"Herr Maguire! Emergency!" came the voice at the other end. "Please, please do not touch your door! We've had accident! Z' fire department will open it for you! *Attention! Attention!*"

Maguire gave his calm assurances. Then, his message delivered to Tarnhelm to fuck off, he lay down to wait.

* * *

Of course, the Adlon lawyers wanted to meet with him. He knew too well there was no shortage of them when something bad occurred. Maguire refused the meeting. The last thing he wanted was a bunch of questions. He told the management he was fine and he didn't know what happened. No, he didn't want to sign anything; and he didn't know the dead man outside his door in the security video that they showed him.

And he most certainly had no idea why the black guy stood watching the execution at the end of the hallway. Never coming to the man's aid.

CHAPTER TWENTY-ONE

4EVER GRIMLY EASED himself into the marble tub, drawn and waiting for him in his apartment overlooking the river Spree. As he leaned back against the warm white Carrera, he cursed himself for taking a hit with the fiasco at the Adlon. Sure, it could've been him with his hand stuck on the door handle, frying like a pigeon on a live wire, but that was why he never took side jobs on his own. Death was the ultimate game of bait and switch. Which was why he was still alive. But today had been most unsatisfactory. He never should have subcontracted the hit, but he hadn't expected an out-of-work journalist to come up with anything that elegant. Now it was a black mark on him, not Maguire.

He was 4EVER. He fucking knew better.

Checking the news feed on his device, he tapped in the queries about the accident at the Adlon, wiping the steam off the screen with a pristine white towel. 4EVER draped the towel on the tub wall behind him, taking a pen from the tub-side table, and began his report to Vanderloos.

Tarnhelm didn't believe in inter-office memos when the dirty work had to be performed. One Time Pad, OTP all the way. It was their key to success. No email to trace, no memos left in a file for the authorities to find. Ever. And with it, the absolute secrecy that made them the top of the food chain in security service. Of course, they always required an outline of everything that went wrong or right. Then the recipient would read it, absorb it, and watch the document burn. There was no hacking that system.

4EVER made sure of it now, stating in his memo to Vanderloos that Farnsworth was a clean agent as far as Interpol and the authorities were concerned. That meant: no fingerprints on file, no DNA on file, no mug shots. Anywhere. Farnsworth's body would go to the unidentified remains department at the morgue until they were compelled to give him an anonymous burial as a homeless indigent. For anyone who knew Farnsworth in another capacity, Vanderloos would instruct the PD arm of Tarnhelm to concoct an artful story about his untimely end or disappearance. A swaggering, entitled asshole like Farnsworth was easy to get rid of—his failed attempt at Everest—just like him!—without oxygen!—and he's still lying up there! Or—his heroic—and losing—battle to sail the cross sea at Tierra Del Fuego alone. The PD stood for the Pollution Department. On paper, it specialized in environmental cleanup of wars and other disasters. But on the inside, everyone knew it stood for Plausible Deniability. They cleaned up all right. *We are the Dustbin of the World.* The entire incident would be just that—a curiosity—with all parties silent and blessedly uncurious.

He rubbed his jaw, still tight with anger over the botched assignment. It was unlike him. With every word he wrote, he made clear that Maguire was getting no more chances. Still, it wasn't good for him. The way the current left Farnsworth, it had skittered across the carpet in a haze of static. 4EVER'd been actually paralyzed for a moment, and it took all his strength to get out of there. Now as he wrote in his memo, he mentioned that Maguire had either been the luckiest man in the world to have his lock short out on him, or he was much more wily than they first believed.

A knock came at the door.

"Who is it?" 4EVER snapped, irritated that his housemaid would interrupt him.

"Sir. Monsieur Portier's asked for you."

The voice was familiar. The door opened. 4EVER's eyes narrowed in recognition at who stepped into the bathroom.

"What are *you* doing *here*?" he said, shock on his face.

"We've heard you and Mr. Vanderloos have been driving outside your lane," was all the figure said before a black-clad assassin drove a dagger below 4EVER's left clavicle.

Blood oozed into the bathwater, the smell of iron mixing with the pungent smell of bath salt. 4EVER slumped to the right over the beautifully draped towel. With the table next to him, his writings in one hand, and the pen languishing on the floor by the black man's outstretched fingers, the scene looked strangely familiar.

"Another one for the PD," the assassin said to his companion, matter-of-factly. He stepped to the tub and placed the end of a silencer against 4EVER's temple. But he was stopped from pulling the trigger by his boss.

"Don't ruin the tableau. It's *The Death of Marat*. Don't you see?"

"The death of who?"

"*The Death of Marat*. The painting by Jacques-Louis David. *'N'ayant pu me corrompre ils m'ont assassin*—Unable to corrupt me, they murdered me.'"

"You've got to be shitting me. He was not corrupted?" the second said, gesturing to 4EVER's artfully collapsed body.

Quoting a speech, the first figure said, "'Like Jesus, Marat loved ardently the people, and only them. Like Jesus, Marat hated kings, nobles, priests, rogues, and, like Jesus, he never stopped fighting against these plagues of the people.'"

There was a strange momentary silence while the two of them looked down at 4EVER.

"Where the hell's that from? He's no fucking Jesus."

"It was Marat's eulogy," the first said simply. "Given by the Marquis de Sade."

* * *

Stag couldn't get his mind off of her. She followed him into his dreams that night. A rare occurrence. Usually Stag's nights consisted of nightmares of Holly. Her desperate pleas torturing him as he watched her die in that pool of arterial blood and, lastly, the stench of excrement. But when he woke the next morning, he realized he'd dreamed of Red Riding Hood. And the strangest moment of all was when he realized that he—not Portier—was the Big Bad Wolf.

The edition of *Mein Kampf* was next to him in his bunk in the hostel. He'd gone back there after several subway switches and a long walk through the dark Tiergarten. Another night and he was still breathing. Today was the day to go to the Bundesarchiv. He rose. It was time to *carpe diem*. There was one thing he wanted to look into before he left Berlin.

* * *

"I can get your information," Angelika Aradi said into the LCD screen to Portier. "But you have to give him room. I know the Tarnhelm board has the urge to strong-arm him, but I'm telling you, that won't get you what you need. We'll just end up killing him and lose the opportunity forever." She frowned. "What's the time frame?"

"The corrosion rate of aluminum is eighty years, solder far, far less," he said acidly. "There's your time frame."

"I understand."

Portier looked at her through the screen. "May I inquire about darling Genevieve?"

The question hung in the air for a moment.

"Vieve is very well, thank you," Angelika answered, her voice scrubbed of emotion.

"Did she start school this year?"

"Kindergarten."

"Kindergarten! What a charming age. I suppose there were days you never thought she would make it to kindergarten. The leukemia is undetectable, is it?"

"Yes," she breathed, running her hand through her hair. "I will never be able to thank you enough."

"I've always thought Switzerland had the best doctors. Imagine my surprise when I found that clinic in Norway. Absolutely the best. It was worth any expense."

"It cost you millions. You'll forever have my gratitude." She kept her expression implacable.

"I would like more, my angel. I was never able to have children. And now . . . " His voice wandered off.

"I don't think an angel is what you want."

"Then be my devil. You already are."

"I'm indebted to you. I always will be."

"You're the woman I need. The one to cure me of my afflictions. I'm sick of shallow, stupid beauty. I need mental stimulation . . . as well as physical to heal me. You could give me both."

"You know I will do whatever you ask." Again, her voice was meticulously wiped clean.

"Ah, but always there's work to be done. And you are the very best I have."

"Yes."

"I can't give you very much time."

"I can be quick."

"Then be quick. I have better things I'd like you to be doing."

"I shall do my best."

"I know you will. You always have."

She hit the disconnect. Her screen went blank.

She stood and went to the window. Her room across from the Adlon looked right out over Brandenburg Gate and the Quadriga. In the distance, the horses pounded forward with the conundrum of frozen perpetual motion. "Victory" held her laurel wreath aloft for all to see.

Peace was upon them.

For now.

CHAPTER TWENTY-TWO

"You're in luck. We do have some documents under the name Isolda Varrick." The Bundesarchiv researcher leaned closer to the screen. "Letters . . . aaahhh . . . " She squinted. "It looks like you are the first to ask about them. They've been in a private collection and just arrived. They're being manually documented now." She wrote down some numbers on a Post-It.

"What file will they be placed in?"

"The Red Army liberation of Auschwitz."

"Auschwitz?" Stag felt the punch to his gut, but he wasn't quite surprised. "Was Isolda Varrick taken there?"

"Let me see. We have the Death Books online in our database." The researcher took up her glasses that dangled onto her blouse by a cord. She typed in a few more strokes. "No. Isolda Varrick is not among the names in the Death Books. But, as you know, given what went on at the time and the destruction of documents, our records are far from complete. She certainly could have been there."

"Does it say in whose possession the letters were when they were found?"

She looked at the screen and cross-referenced a few items. "All it says here is that the letters were donated by the family of a Soviet liberator."

Stag ruminated on the idea that Isolda was shipped off to Auschwitz. But where was the logic of her being caught there with letters written by herself to another? No, it was probably someone else who'd somehow had them on themselves in the final hour.

"The copies have been ordered. You may collect them at the desk." The middle-aged woman gave him a smile. "Anything else?"

He shook his head. With a nod, he headed to the main desk.

He did not see the Interpol Special Agent behind him saunter to the desk and pull out his badge on the clerk.

* * *

Stag had the copies of the three Auschwitz letters tucked into Isolda's *Mein Kampf.* They were all three addressed to a man named Eduard Schulte in Berlin. He burned to hole up somewhere and read them, study them, correlate them to the diary, but right now, he didn't have time. He had people to evade and housekeeping to do. And a trip to plan.

He assumed he was being followed. The only way to shake it was to head to Alexanderplatz Station. He spent two hours getting on and off departing trains until he was sure no one could be on him. The next stop was back to Marzahn to get his supplies. He'd collected a large amount of cash at Deutschebank from a wire transfer of his US account. In exchange for a mere 15,000 Euros, he was able to collect all the documents he'd ordered when he'd gotten the P83.

He was now set.

He walked into Citibank with the rest of the cash of the wire transfer, and all the pages he'd translated out of the diary along with the copies of the white silk key. At the International Customer Desk, he whipped out his "British passport" under the ironic name of John Dedman, and said, "I'd like to open an account and safety deposit box."

When the friendly young clerk asked if it would be cash or check, he answered, "Cash." He dumped a stack of 500-euro notes on the desk. The clerk's eyes widened, but she was only too happy to be of service.

PART THREE

The angel would like to stay, awaken the dead, and make whole what has been smashed. But a storm is blowing in from Paradise; it has got caught in his wings with such violence that the angel can no longer close them. This storm irresistibly propels him into the future to which his back is turned, while the pile of debris before him grows skyward. This storm is what we call progress.

WALTER BENJAMIN
In his *Theses on the Philosophy of History*, which he
wrote shortly before he killed himself, in 1940,
while attempting to escape from the Nazis.

CHAPTER TWENTY-THREE

THE FLIGHT TO Zürich was pleasant. First class was certainly the way to travel. Not knowing how much time one had, had its advantages. There was no reason to cut corners now.

"More champagne, Mr. Dedman?" the svelte airline attendant asked.

He waved it away, still ticking down his list. *Nacht und Nebel*. He was now invisible to a cyber search for Stag Maguire. He'd left everything he had in his room at the Adlon in case Tarnhelm had placed a GPS on his belongings. He had a new iPhone, iPad, debit card, and bank account, all untraceable to him. From now on there would be no passport movement, no IP addresses from his old devices, no debits from his accounts, no receipts. He was off the grid. As scrubbed as a felon with new DNA and fingerprints.

He pulled out the Ziploc bag holding his book and letters. He began with the first letter.

* * *

23 February 1942
Dearest Eduard,

I thank you for the beautiful silk! My dream has been answered! I have it packed carefully away until the day comes to send myself to you. I shall arrive as a bride and my dress shall be white with many secret layers. Your gift is a lifesaver in these days of want. I would like you to know I have listened to your every instruction. I will pay attention to every detail. I will make no errors. I will not waste an inch of my precious, precious bridal silk.

I hope you received my first letter, which was sent through our friends. I confessed all in it, all my secret longings. I shall write as often as I can!

Your blushing bride-to-be,
Isolda

* * *

He leaned back and thought about the cryptic writing. Isolda Varrick was no blushing bride. The wedding silk was the spy technology of using it as a code pad for secret messages. What those messages were that she sent, penned onto white silk and tucked behind the lining of a garment, could now only be guessed at. They were long gone, either in a sable coat later purloined by the neighborhood German "citizen" or, perhaps, sorted and shipped with the stories-high piles of garments that left the death camps during the Holocaust.

What remained now were these letters, long held and forgotten in the Byzantine network of the old Soviet Union. She'd been taking a risk to write in her name to this Eduard Schulte. But it must have been she'd had no choice. It had been the only way to get the letters through.

He pulled out the second letter by date. It made less sense than the first.

* * *

7 April 1942
My dearest Eduard,

I urge you to hear my pleas! I cannot be silent any longer, nor should you! I want the world to know (that you are mine, of course!) and I have given you the messages that proclaim ALL. Your family in Geneva will listen to our cries (and see us married, forthwith!)

Today I received my honeymoon suit. It is made of a beautiful shade of Berlin blue. Everything they say about it is true! If you aren't familiar with the color, it will soon be all the RAGE for thousands. Hundreds of thousands perhaps!

To marry, we must, my darling. I cannot bear to go on like this and I demand you tell all now, so that we and those who love like us may plan our salvation from this hell.

Your very loving,
Isolda

* * *

It was an awkward letter, but there seemed nothing to it. Just a dull, little obscure missive of unrequited love. Stag could almost see the Nazi censors falling asleep over the pheromonal pleas of a fiancée to speed along the nuptials. One thing that did stand out, however, was her urging the recipient to look up Berlin blue.

He typed in *Berlin blue*. The definition came up as follows:

> Prussian blue, also known as Berlin blue, is a dark blue color
> that is artificially made. It is one of the first pigments made
> synthetically. It was accidentally found in 1704 by two
> chemists in Berlin. The dark blue uniforms of the Prussian
> army were dyed this color. It is produced by oxidation of
> ferrous ferrocyanide salts.

Ferrocyanide.
Which made Prussic acid.
Known by its more infamous name, Zyklon B.
It didn't take him long to find photographs online of the interior
of a gas chamber. At Madjanek, the walls were stained with the dis-
tinctive intense blue. Beautiful Berlin blue.

He took the research further. He began with the name Eduard
Schulte. The name wasn't unusual, particularly in Germany. He expected there to be thousands, and certainly there were. But the first
search astounded him.

> Eduard Schulte (4 January 1891 in Düsseldorf–6 January
> 1966 in Zürich) was a prominent German industrialist. He
> was one of the first to warn the Allies and tell the world of
> the Holocaust and systematic exterminations of Jews in
> Nazi Germany occupied Europe. In August 1942, the
> Reigner Telegram notified the Allies through the World
> Jewish Congress in Geneva, that 3.5 to 4 million Jews were
> to be exterminated by the planned use of hydrogen cyanide.
> The Allies largely ignored Schulte's information as not
> believable.

He next Googled the Reigner Telegram and read what Reigner
wrote:

August 8, 1942

Received alarming report stating that, in the Führer's Headquarters, a plan has been discussed, and is under consideration, according to which all Jews in countries occupied or controlled by Germany number 3 1/2 to 4 million should, after deportation and concentration in the East, be at one blow exterminated, in order to resolve, once and for all the Jewish question in Europe. Action is reported to be planned for the autumn. Ways of execution are still being discussed including the use of prussic acid. We transmit this information with all the necessary reservation, as exactitude cannot be confirmed by us. Our informant is reported to have close connexions with the highest German authorities, and his reports are generally reliable. Please inform and consult New York.

Stag's blood began to boil. *August 1942.* So much for the excuse of, "*We didn't know till after the war.*" He found it sickening how much could have been done with that knowledge. There were none higher than Heydrich when it came to implementing the Final Solution. Goering, too fat and addicted to run even the Luftwaffe properly, had passed the baton of Hitler's *Mein Kampf* vision to Heydrich, who'd dutifully streamlined it at the Wannsee conference. If Isolde had tried to warn the world of Heydrich's plans, it was beyond credible. It was from the source itself.

Now all he could think of was the waste of Isolda's effort to get the word out. Even if her other missives had reached Schulte—she was writing him in *April 1942*, before the mechanization of death had really gotten under way—these letters had either been waylaid or ignored, like the Reigner Telegram itself.

And the rest, as they say, was history.

Holding down his fury and nausea, Stag reread the second letter. What had seemed mundane at first glance now sent ice through his veins.

* * *

Hear my pleas! Your family in Geneva will listen to our cries! Berlin blue... All the RAGE for thousands. Hundreds of thousands perhaps!

Schulte could have gotten some of his information through Isolda, and she obviously got hers directly from the pillow talk with Heydrich. Now Isolda's early demise seemed more and more likely. She'd been playing a dangerous game, writing Shulte as his fiancée while playing mistress to Heydrich. Had that gotten her killed—not being discovered as a spy, but out of a lover's jealousy? The letters were found in Auschwitz after the liberation, and Schulte didn't die in the Holocaust. It must've been a courier who'd had them. The courier had handed the information down the line, but had been unable to unload the three letters until he or she was deported to Poland. Perhaps Isolda herself had been instrumental in giving the information in the Reigner Telegram, but all he knew for sure was that these three letters had reached a dead end in Auschwitz.

The idea that the world could have been informed of an impending Holocaust as early as April 1942 was hard to swallow. But there it was, in his hands, and on Wikipedia.

Perhaps the idea of mechanized murder had simply been too awful. Perhaps the human mind couldn't fathom it.

No one acted. Millions died.

With deepening dread, he turned to the third letter. It was another to Schulte.

* * *

4 May 1942
My darling betrothed, Eduard,

This is the most pressing plea of all. If you are deaf to me now, I shall be forced to do away with myself, for I tell you this: life without human love is unbearable.

We have what we need to marry in Norway. But my heart is heavy. Water, I think, is the only cure. Our long-planned honeymoon for the Katanga shall bring us home great treasures, and we shall have our glorious union at our address at Vaterhimmelstrasse 235. Because it shall unite us so much more than our time spent at Vaterhimmelstrasse 238, yes? It will be an unstoppable force!

Tell me these plans are first and foremost in your heart? I am surrounded by these cold diamonds, but every minute of every day I long for your warm touch instead. All my diamonds will go in the truck on the last trip to the Königssee. They will not be found without great effort, be assured! But you must do your part. I beg you. I beg you.

Your most despondent lover,
Isolda

* * *

His champagne glass was filled while he typed in Königssee. From the pictures, it was an exquisite lake, south of Berchtesgaden, the alpine retreat infamous for the romps of Eva Braun and Hitler.

He sat back and contemplated it. The outline of the Königssee looked like a long scraggly finger lake between mountains. He dug out the silk message and compared them. He couldn't be sure, of course, the ink had faded and bled but the outline could be the Königssee, certainly. And the string tie at the end of the "finger" could be where the truck was. The truckful of diamonds.

He reread the third letter, unsettled by its opaqueness. Nothing was clear in this one. What the Katanga in the former Belgian Congo, Norway, and a lake in Berchtesgaden had to do with each other, he couldn't begin to guess. The Congo origin of the Blood Eagle diamond seemed tied up in all of it too. Just to confuse matters even more.

He played with Googling the addresses. Nothing came up. There were lots of Himmelstrasses, no Vaterhimmelstrasse.

"Mr. Dedman, may I ask you to check your seat belt?"

Stag looked up. He was mired so deeply in his thoughts, he hadn't realized they were landing. He nodded, then turned off his iPad.

The last letter was going to need some outside help. When he got to the hotel, it was time to get on his new phone and see what Jake had to say.

He checked into the Hotel Baur au Lac, charmed by the immaculately quaint streets of Zürich Old Town. There was also a little James Bond thrill of registering at a luxury hotel under an assumed name. He wasn't sporting a tux, and his limp sure didn't get him noticed as anything more than a pedestrian afterthought. But it didn't matter. He was on a mission.

The bellboy brought him a Swiss SIM card for his new phone number. He scanned the letters to his iPad in the business center, and as soon as he got back to his room, he called Jake.

"I'm sending you something, Jake. Check your email, will you?"

"Christ, Stag. I bought a wreath like you asked. But everyone wants to know where the hell you are."

"I'm in Zürich."

"What?"

Stag smiled bitterly. "Long story. Nothing you want to be involved in. I won't be here long."

"You're coming home when? Julie was worried that you weren't around when Harry died. And she couldn't stop asking questions about where you were when you missed the funeral. I have to say it's mightily strange myself—"

"I really need your help, Jake."

"What is it? I know you're in trouble. I can feel it." The older man's voice grew somber.

"I've kind of stumbled into a story. I can't really talk about it. There isn't time. I'm not sure you'd believe it, even if there was."

"What can I do?" Jake was surely getting the picture. Things were pretty bad.

"I sent you some scanned letters. I want you to read them, and tell me what you think they say."

"Okay." Jake was dead serious. Stag had a moment of relief wash over him. It felt good to not be completely alone, even if he couldn't let on to Jake what was happening.

"Get back to me as soon you read them, huh?" Stag hesitated. "And don't let on to anyone we've talked?"

"Are you in danger? Perhaps you should return?"

"I can't till I'm done. One day we're going to have a long, arm-bending drinking session in Wuttke. Maybe even laugh."

Jake paused. "I hope so," he said, dread in his voice.

CHAPTER TWENTY-FOUR

PORTIER LOOKED UP from his desk and took note of Sadler's hesitant ramble toward him. He sat with Rikhardsson in the Great Room of his office in Zürich. The long walk from the door to his desk was planned by Portier personally. Hitler had Speer use the same technique in his offices in the Reich Chancellery. By the time a visitor got where he was going, he was thoroughly intimidated.

"What have you got?" Portier asked.

Sadler took the proffered seat. "North American cyber surveillance says he's gone—nothing. Vanished. He collected an enormous amount of cash from his accounts and then—poof."

Rikhardsson nodded. "Our satellites are reviewing footage, but he disappeared in the subway in Berlin. This will take some time. His imprint's gone from Europe also. Either he's holed up somewhere not using any technology whatsoever, or he's managed to intentionally evade us."

In silence, Portier went to the Gothic expanse of glass that made up the distinctive top of the Tarnhelm Building. He looked out toward the tip of Lake Zürich as it stabbed into the city.

"Politically, we see he's never been very active, and from his psychiatric history after his wife died, it appears he's almost suicidal." Sadler frowned. "I'm afraid he's rogue."

Rikhardsson stood and went to the window. "We have two choices. We can chase him. Or we can wait until he shows up. Because he will show up. Everybody does. Osama Bin Laden eventually showed up."

Sadler interjected. "He wants something. He would not have gone to that apartment if he didn't."

"We're linked to 12A," Rikhardsson said, "but so far there is no spike in speculation. No electronic chatter, no talk about us on social media. He's played it close to the chest."

"You're asking me for patience, are you?" Portier looked at both men.

Sadler and Rikhardsson both looked wary, unsure how to answer.

"I don't think there's any choice," Rikhardsson said.

"We haven't got infinite time." Portier looked down at the Tourbillon Mars on his tanned wrist. "No matter how fine the timepiece."

"Even if there is a special weapon, we don't know for sure what it is," Rikhardsson said.

"We have a pretty good fucking idea," Sadler grumbled. "If that thing is what we fear it may be—if it unintentionally goes off, then Maguire can possibly link it to us. If that's the case, the world will be watching and damn us to hell. There'll be nowhere for us to hide."

Rikhardsson tossed off his worries with a flick of his fine, Nordic head. "What I'm entranced with is the street value of it. Daesh would pay a fortune to have a ready-made weapon. We could even get Putin's little man to make a very, very good deal for it. That's what he does, doesn't he? Very, very good deals? Fine. Let him. What do we care of their personal squabbles?"

Portier interjected, "You don't seem to grasp the obvious, gentlemen." He paused. "What if the thing is underfoot?"

A strange heavy pause ensued.

"Do we have any reason to believe it is?" Sadler asked.

"Do we have any reason to believe it *isn't*?" Rikhardsson retorted.

Grimly, Portier said, "I would sleep better knowing Heydrich's SD had had the thing safely stored in the underground at Dora-Mittelbau or maybe hauled off to the Hohlgangsanlage tunnels in the Isle of Jersey. But we don't know. And for all we do, it could be rotting in a salt mine between here and Obersaltzberg." He looked off at the breathtakingly beautiful Alps surrounding the Canton of Zürich. The jagged peaks now looked less like a picture postcard, and a lot more ominous. Like a thunderstorm hovering in the distance, ready to blow in their direction.

"I needn't tell you, gentlemen, the corrosion rate of aluminum is around eighty years. Add another factor to that, say, a corrosive like uranium, and we are looking at something quite precarious. Which is one reason I don't want that flea, Maguire, dead yet." Portier knocked on the desk in frustration. "I've got to get that information."

All three men turned quiet. Below, the beautiful sprawl of Zürich lay out around them, framed by the distant snow-covered Alps. It was one of the most beautiful and livable cities in the world, and one of the most important financial districts. It was impossible to imagine it gone.

"Have we any evidence of that?" Sadler suddenly looked quite eager to get back to the relative safety of his US operations, pronto.

"We've been searching for this thing for decades precisely because the information about it was lost in the bombings and in Heydrich's assassination. We don't know where the fuck it is, nor the state it's in."

"Do we even know it exists, for sure? Could we be fearful of nothing?"

"If we had any doubts, Maguire's very appearance has put them to rest. He's not after the Blood Eagle."

"Surely, if there is a weapon, it could be anywhere," Rikhardsson said.

"Anywhere in Europe, that is," Sadler, the American, added, noticeably relieved.

Portier turned to face them. "I want every resource on this. Double it again. And again. I want Maguire to be found and brought in."

Sadler looked at Rikhardsson. Rikhardsson returned the stare. They all agreed on that at least.

*   *   *

Stag jumped at the ring of his cell phone. The number was Jake's.

"Hey," Stag said, stretching his stiffening leg on the bed.

"Sorry that took a while. I had to do some research." Jake cleared his throat.

"What's the verdict?"

"Well, certainly, the first letter is dealing with a shipment of silk. Silk was all but impossible to get during wartime because every last inch was used for parachutes. The white silk referred to is, doubtless, a quantity of parachute silk—sometimes used for a bridal gown during the war years—if it could be obtained in that quantity. I don't believe it was gained in quantity to make a bridal gown. I believe the silk was used as a one-time pad."

"Spies."

"Yes," Jake affirmed what Stag had already surmised. "In cryptography, there is only one encryption technique that cannot be cracked. A spy would receive his message in a Vernam cipher or an OTP, a one-time pad. After the message was deciphered, the pad was discarded. He had to be delivered a key to read further messages. It was brilliant."

Stag rubbed his jaw. "She needed the silk to send and receive messages."

"I believe so. But obviously these letters are sending encoded messages also. The first is acknowledging the receipt of the silk and perhaps her training in the use of it; the second—well, I guess you've researched Eduard Schulte and the Reigner Telegram."

"She was clearly sending Schulte messages in these letters."

"Schulte was an industrialist and secretly anti-Nazi. He was in the unique position of traveling through the Reich, through Poland, and to Switzerland whereby he came into contact with the Allies. She seems to be alluding quite clearly to *Aktion Reinhard*. After Heydrich's death, they used his first name to refer to the death camps' gassing of Jews."

"She took a great risk."

"Yes. Indeed, a brave woman. Who was she? I could find nothing on her."

"She's been lost to history. For now," Stag added.

"Well, she was certainly in the thick of things. That last letter—" Jake abruptly stopped. Stag could hear him take a deep breath.

"Yes?" Stag said.

"I wasn't sure about it. Something niggled at the back of my brain so I asked an expert." He paused again. "I hope you're sitting down, Stag. I think I have some very unsettling information."

CHAPTER TWENTY-FIVE

ANGELIKA ARADI WALKED through the passenger terminal of Zürich Airport, heading toward the cabstand. There was a private plane available to her at all hours through the corporation, but when she went deep, she sometimes found it more useful to travel commercial. That way it was harder for Tarnhelm to track her. Not impossible, of course, but they had no reason to keep an eye on her when they thought she was still in Berlin, studiously pursuing her quarry from there.

She grabbed her wheelie and stepped to the front of the cabstand.

"Hotel Baur au Lac," she said to the cab driver as she got into the back seat. They drove to Old Town, and in her mind's eye, she pictured all the maneuvers Maguire had used to evade the Tarnhelm men rather artfully in the subway. Of course, he was an amateur. But he was one helluva amateur. And now he was nowhere they could find.

Except for her.

They pulled up to the columned front of the old hotel. She paid the driver and immediately a distinctive Baur au Lac white cap-and-coat bellman lifted her luggage to the curb.

"Welcome," he said politely.

She got out of the cab and looked up at the old hotel, its striped awnings giving it a bandbox freshness one didn't see except in Switzerland.

"Will you be staying long with us?"

She smiled at the bellman. "We'll see."

*   *   *

Chief Aldernay Troost logged notes onto his computer. Maguire still hadn't called, nor had he returned to the Adlon. It seemed he may have disappeared, and on Troost's watch. He didn't like it. He could feel the frustration mount as he typed in the details.

The American had no idea how much trouble he was in. Not just with Interpol and its potential to issue a Red Notice, but with the little spook. The blond. She was full of bad tidings, indeed. For Maguire. For him. Perhaps everybody.

He slammed the laptop closed and stared across his desk to Special Agent Jones who stared back.

"I want to know the minute he calls."

Jones nodded.

"Has anybody got an explanation for these letters our men got from the Bundesarchiv? What's Maguire's interest there?"

"We don't know yet. The letters seem pretty clear cut, but no one knows where Vaterhimmelstrasse is. That's what's taking so long."

Troost stood and rubbed the stubble on his jaw. "The minute they know anything, I want a report. *Anything,* okay?"

"You think they've got him?" Jones asked.

"No."

"Which worries you more?"

Aldernay Troost gave him the truth. "I don't know."

CHAPTER TWENTY-SIX

"THREE THINGS CONCERNED me in this letter," Jake said over the phone to Stag. "The first was the street address of 235 and 238. Then the name of the street: Father Sky Street. I could find no Vaterhimmelstrasse. It doesn't exist as a street anywhere that I could find. Of course, with the war, street names in Germany have changed many, many times. But Father Sky Street bothered me."

Jake took another deep breath. "But the real worry were these two sentences: *My heart is heavy. Water, I think, is the only cure.*"

There was a thick pause before Jake asked, "Do you know the term 'heavy water'?"

Maguire felt his muscles seize. "I'm not sure. Wasn't there a plant up in Norway somewhere..." He frowned, trying to remember what he knew.

"Yes, the Nordsk Hydro plant. It was sabotaged by the Norwegians during the war to deprive Germany of its heavy water."

"And heavy water used for..."

"I'm no rocket scientist," Jake said, modestly, "but I have to tell you, Stag, I'm quite disturbed by this letter. Especially by the date of it."

"What do you mean?"

Jake's voice seemed to get older with every word. "Well, to be sure, I asked a colleague for the etymology of the word Vaterhimmelstrasse.

It's Father Sky Street. Father Sky is an old term for the planet Uranus. And Uranus is ... well, it's the reference used when we named uranium."

Stag said nothing. The hair was beginning to prickle at the back of his neck.

Jake continued. "This is certainly not my expertise, but I've done a bit of further research and found that uranium comes in two natural forms: U-238 and the much rarer form of U-235. It's U-235 that is necessary to cause chain reactions. To get it, we take the abundant U-238—or what we would call naturally forming uranium—and then it must be centrifuged in a quite complicated process using heavy water to create U-235. It's a very costly and difficult procedure." He added as an aside, "Which is lucky for us, because that means not just anyone or any country can come up with enough U-235 to build a bomb. Turns out we have more control over the proliferation of nuclear bombs than we thought. They just don't happen. They are difficult to create. Things must be precise."

"Are you telling me Isolda Varrick wrote to Schulte about the ingredients of a nuclear bomb?" The implications were just beginning to sink in. "In 1942?"

"All the materials are there. She mentions Norway and heavy water. And early in the war, Germany had huge resources of uranium under their control in the Belgian Congo—the sources of U-238 and the much rarer U-235. In fact, the bombs of Hiroshima and Nagasaki got their uranium from the Belgian Congo after the Germans lost it. But it's a stone-cold fact the Germans most definitely got to the Congo's uranium first."

"Jesus. This can't be—" Stag was numb.

"Before you panic, let me tell you the part that really concerns me. *'Our long-planned honeymoon for the Katanga shall bring us home great treasures, and we shall have our glorious union at our address at Vaterhimmelstrasse 235. Because it shall unite us so much more than our time spent at Vaterhimmelstrasse 238.'"*

Jake's breathing became erratic as if he were continually catching his breath. "U-235 was needed during the development of nuclear weapons but it was difficult and expensive to process. It occurs naturally but in minute amounts. The Katanga deposit in the Belgian Congo was supposed to be the world's richest naturally occurring deposit of U-235, but we've only known it to be rumor. When we took control of the Congo and mined it for the uranium for the Trinity Bomb, we never found the fabled Katanga deposit, and in the end, we believed it never existed. That it remained strictly rumor. Well, I fear . . . I fear it may be true after all. If the Katanga treasure Isolda Varrick mentions was there, and was indeed U-235, then that would mean the Germans got it. Which would have put them leaps and bounds ahead of us in developing the bomb. In 1942."

"But they didn't have the bomb. *We* had the bomb," Stag pointed out almost defensively.

"We were the first to use the bomb, but we weren't the first to think of it. The Germans had the *Uranverein,* the Uranium Club, in 1939. In fact, it was in its second incarnation the day WWII began—September 1, 1939. After that, they had the Virus House— the name of the plutonium lab next to the Kaiser Wilhelm Institute of Physics. They named it that to discourage unwelcome visitors. I have to tell you, Stag, the Germans were extremely good with secrecy. Look at how much information they kept in the dark just on the Holocaust. They were master obfuscators."

"It doesn't follow they were able to develop a bomb and not use it."

Jake was silent. He spoke his words slowly. "It follows, if it fell to a security organization expert in managing secret information to keep it under wraps till they planned to use it. And then, it follows

that the information became lost when the head of this organization was unexpectedly and violently struck down. There was no
more insidious organization anywhere than Heydrich's SD. They
managed to kill millions without us believing it. *For years.*"

Stag felt like he'd been knocked back on his heels. When he came
to his senses, he said, "Look, this is getting a little crazy. I'm here
looking for the diamonds she mentions in this letter. Not a bomb."

"If there'd been a bomb, it does seem we'd have known about it
by now," Jake interjected.

"We'd have found it and decommissioned it after we took over
Germany," Stag said with a little more certainty than he felt.

"Except—" Jake left the word hanging in midair.

Except.

"Except Heydrich was assassinated in '42. In the chaos of that,
perhaps documents went missing. Perhaps crucial information was
lost when he died." Stag finished the thought. "But I can't believe
there could be some kind of nuclear device just hanging around—"

"Perhaps not hanging around. The Alpine Redoubt."

Stag knew what Jake was referring to. The Germans in their hy-
pothetical last stand had talked of storing ordinance high in the
Alps in order to wage the final war against the Allies. Nothing came
of it. The theory was the Alps would be easy for a decimated army to
defend, and the Germans could use their cache of weapons to hold
out until the mythical, much-talked-about "super weapon" promised by their Führer could be launched to save them.

"The Alpine Redoubt has been proven to be nothing but a fairy
tale," Stag said.

"Yes," Jake agreed. "But what's not a myth is that the Germans
brought weapons and valuables to the Alps because of the many salt
mines there that could preserve them. Salzburg, Austria, is *salt for-
tress* in English, if I may remind you. The Alps are littered with these

mines, and they go back at least to the medieval period. We do not, by a long shot, know where they all are . . . or what may have been tucked into them."

"Look," Stag interjected, "I think no matter how well connected Isolda Varrick was, she could not be talking about a bomb. The materials to make a bomb, perhaps, but a *bomb,* no, it's too unbelievable."

"'. . . *it shall unite us so much more* . . .' A troubling sentence." Jake grew quiet. "Unite what is essentially a hollow bullet of U-235 into a separate mass of U-235 and you get . . . well, you get a chain reaction. Fission. *An unstoppable force.*"

Stag lowered himself to a chair. Without even knowing it, he'd been pacing the room while he and Jake spoke.

"What are you in the middle of, Stag? You sure picked a time and place to revive your journalism career."

He could almost hear Jake shaking his head. Stag released a deep breath he hadn't known he was holding. "Right now, I have more immediate worries than a bomb that may or may not exist—and, nonetheless, hasn't gone off—in decades now." His gaze went to the copy of *Mein Kampf* in its raggedy Ziploc bag. There was still more to decipher there. He should get to it. "Are you going to be available should I have more questions?" he asked, rather ironically. After all, Jake was going nowhere. Stag was the one who might be rubbed out at any moment.

"Of course. Anything. Do you want me to come there?"

Stag was moved by the man's concern. "Wherever I am these days, there is no here, here," he answered. "But thanks. Look for my calls."

"I'm concerned about you, Stag. This is dangerous. There may be a significant population at risk should this thing be real."

Stag nodded to no one. "I'm doing everything I can. But I don't know enough. I don't know who to trust."

"You can trust me."

"Don't talk to anyone. Don't tell anyone you've talked to me."

"I won't. But let me hear from you, okay?"

Stag grunted. He looked at *Mein Kampf*, then disconnected the phone.

CHAPTER TWENTY-SEVEN

THIS EVENING WE went to a private party at Horcher's Restaurant. We dined on Viennese fried chicken—because even you agreed that a corpulent man like Goering couldn't be wrong when it came to his favorite fare. The night was rare. You don't like to take me anywhere. Instead we nest and idle in my apartment. But this was a secret party, your favorite kind, the room full of high-ranking SD and their Salon Kitty girlfriends awash in jewels and peroxide. So you arrived at my door and said we must attend to escape the boredom of the apartment.

Imagine Goebbels' chagrin when he saw you there? The good doctor had his hand stroking the exiled actress Lida Baarová's thigh, and when he saw you, the fear and distaste made his little troll face crumble like rubble. At one point, Joseph and his "pet" went to the wine room, an auspicious place for a man who loves not wine, but I don't think he took Lida there to browse the vintages. And when they disappeared, you looked at me, the derisive tug on your lips for me alone. You tolerate Goebbels much better than Himmler, with his silly fascination for the occult and spurious Aryan folklore. While Goebbels has no interest in food, his face usually carries the sheen of Lida on it. You, in your inimitable way, always remarked it was too bad Lida's juice couldn't cure his bad skin.

Through all these antics, you drunkenly put your usual quell on the atmosphere. The band attempted to revive the crowd, and during a sweet little tune, you stroked your fingers against my palm, and then played with my hand, as if a tender mood had caught you up in the music, and you couldn't help yourself.

The whole time you held my hand I couldn't help but think how intimate the simple gesture was. How much is communicated through the clasping of hands. The warmth comes through, the respect. Even more than a kiss, it seems. Perhaps it is the furtiveness of it, the lack of possession. It asks permission, it doesn't demand. We sat together, holding hands, and the entire time I longed for the comfort of it, while you longed for the intimacy I shall never give.

But then I had my first laugh. Gigli, your favorite blond from the SS orchestra, turned to you, and in her solo, almost mockingly began to sing the old Johnny Mercer favorite from the Garrick Gaeties of 1930. She ended pointedly with the famous line:

All you had to do is say, "Boo."
Out of breath (and scared to death of you)

Her song ended and a terrible silence filled the room. Everyone was frozen, waiting to see if our Hangman would get the joke.

It was then I began to laugh.

I laughed and laughed, unable to control myself, until tears streamed down my cheeks. My God but it felt good! To release all the black absurdities I'd been living with. To lose myself in a primal surge of rueful hilarity. I wanted more and more of the opiate until I finally came back to my senses and found the room had begun to laugh with me. And you even laughed, in a moment of self-knowledge that I rarely see in those cold, wretched eyes of yours. Then you took me home, and you made love, and I thought of clasped hands. Clasped hands and bleached bones.

* * *

Stag turned the page and continued reading. His leg throbbed. He stuffed a couple of pillows underneath it and kept going. It was difficult keeping his mind on the diary. He was exhausted, overwhelmed by Jake's information and its implications. Tomorrow he was going to scope out Tarnhelm. After that, he would have to take it one limp at a time.

Against his will, he thought of Red Riding Hood. He couldn't stop picturing her as she sat in his room holding that white rose, dressed in that degraded, beautiful suit, the suit that matched the degraded, worn look in her eyes. Eyes that had seen too much.

He wondered if his eyes looked the same. Perhaps they did to others. How could they not hold the reflections of all the sorrow he'd been through—and now held all the sorrow he knew was surely to come?

His thoughts went back to the idea of the bomb. He'd yet found no direct reference to heavy water or Vaterhimmelstrasse in the coded diary. It left him with an ill-defined nausea to imagine a bomb out there, decaying and unstable, but the nausea was constantly being overridden with frustration. After all, he couldn't find those fucking diamonds and he had real clues to them; how the hell was he going to find a bomb that may or may not exist with no clues?

He had to keep plugging away to decode the diary. It seemed Isolda had written it for catharsis, and, perhaps, a grasp at immortality. She'd had to know her situation was as precarious as anyone's could be. But so far, the diary mostly seemed to be a cry of, "I was here, damn it! I existed, and this is what happened to me!" Her secret war information, on the other hand, was imparted in these letters, and perhaps in silk messages she tucked into the back of the paintings.

He went through the apartment in his head—that strange, closed place that reeked of decades past. Something bothered him about it more than just the freak nature of a time capsule. The place was really more like a tomb. But what was buried there that he did not find?

He closed the diary and flipped off the light. He lay in the dark for a while, trying to figure things out in a rare moment of peace and solitude.

They wouldn't come for him tonight. Not only had he secured his door, but he'd registered at the Swiss Star under the name of Maguire. At the Baur au Lac, he traveled under the name of Dedman. He figured this way he could unnerve them. Spring up, place to place, like that mole-and-mallet game, with hopefully enough lead-time to stay ahead of them. Under this system, it would take them a minute to realize he was even in town.

It was risky, taunting Goliath. But there was no other way to kick the chair out from under a man like Portier except to take the offensive. He was going to have to be bold and aggressive when he finally met Portier.

Then, he would disappear again. *Nacht und nebel.*

Tonight, he would sleep. He was damned tired. He needed to dream good, restful things, but his mind went back to the ominous picture of Red Riding Hood in his room at the Adlon, with her coat off and her legs gathered to the side of the chair. He wondered what her eyes would look like full of something more like joy rather than dread. She was at that woman's age where her face had a kind of wasting to it. The bones had become more delicate and defined, the hollows more vulnerable. It now seemed much sexier than the plump, unworldly face of a younger woman.

But he knew he wouldn't dream of her.

He would dream of Holly. And wake, alone and shrouded with grief.

CHAPTER TWENTY-EIGHT

STAG WOKE AS he thought he would, bathed in sweat, clutching the twisted sheets like a life rope. He lay there for a long time, the shadow of his dreams still suffocating him. Skeletal men groped their way through the haze of a nuclear winter. Mushroom clouds dotted the Dali landscape like obscene trees. In the distance, a woman and her newborn stood stock still, staring at him. Only him. Then in an instant roll of hellfire, they were gone. Transformed into the mist.

He ordered coffee. When he was dressed and out, he bought a disposable GoFone to call Interpol.

He didn't want to talk to Troost. Law enforcement was never going to provide him any information, but he'd promised he would report back every now and then. Besides, it didn't hurt to have a few friends in high places.

"You left the Adlon, Mr. Maguire." Troost didn't bother hiding the frustration in his voice. "We'd like to protect you, but if you insist on—"

"Look, I appreciate the sentiments, but I have things to do."

"Such as?" Troost asked.

"Business."

"You're going to need help. It's foolish for you to be poking into Tarnhelm's affairs without some kind of safety net. These people are very dangerous."

"Yeah."

"Stay where you are and we'll send—"

"I have one question—Why would Tarnhelm have anything to do with NATO?"

There was a long pause at the end of the line. "Tarnhelm deals in secrets, Mr. Maguire. Regular people don't understand the cost of secrets."

"They rubbed out this Sir Roger so they could continue keeping whose secrets? NATO's or Tarnhelm's? Who is their client?"

"We don't know." Troost breathed into the phone. "That's why we'd like to talk to Angelika Aradi. If we find that connection between client and Tarnhelm, we'll be able to do something about it. But what we need is for you to stay alive. Stay alive so you can give us information."

"The two are mutually exclusive."

Stag hung up.

* * *

Stag stepped into the lobby of the Baur au Lac and again made the mental note to get some better clothes. The hotel, like the Adlon, was another relentlessly chic place, but between the probable recurring need to exit quickly and the fact that he was getting attached to his jacket that held *Mein Kampf,* he knew he wouldn't bother. Shabby and limping was no way to impress the elite, but being a writer, telling folks to fuck off was.

He left the Baur au Lac in the rental car Dedman had ordered. He parked it on a random street, then walked to the Zurich Cantonal Bank. After he'd opened up a Maguire account there, he took a cab to Tarnhelm headquarters. At the huge oak door, he felt like he was infiltrating a very exclusive club. The building was eighteenth century. The stairway, marble. The secretaries looked like they'd been handpicked by Fox News—all of them capable, fat-free, and willing to work their way to the top by their knees and botox.

Yep. It was all just as he imagined. He looked as out of place in his cheap sagging jacket as a cockroach in a Junior League Show house.

"May I help you?" The sheath-clad receptionist barely contained her distaste at his appearance.

He looked at her. He swore there was a factory somewhere in Scandinavia that made women like her just to be wallpaper for men like Portier.

"Luc Portier."

She looked doubtful. "Mr. Portier? I'm afraid I must ask if you have an appointment?" It didn't take long to scratch down to the bitch in her.

"Oh, I don't need an appointment." He went to a bank of seating upholstered in thick silk damask. He sat and stared back at her. "Just tell him Stag Maguire wants to see him."

He smiled. It wasn't often that a scraggly cripple made demands on Luc Portier. But these were no longer normal times. No, these were extraordinary times, and it was best they all get up to speed. No time like the present.

* * *

Angelika watched Maguire enter the Tarnhelm building. Maguire didn't know who or what he was dealing with or he'd never have been so bold. But she couldn't help but be a little impressed by his steadfast, awkward gait. He walked into the dragon's den without hesitation, and the sheer audacity of it left her wanting to hold her hand over her mouth, breathless.

CHAPTER TWENTY-NINE

STAG SAT ACROSS from Portier's spectacular glass desk in an office that looked more like a futuristic hall of mirrors. From his seat, Portier stared at him. He returned the favor. Finally, once the secretary had shut the double doors behind her, Portier spoke.

"What can I do for you, Mr. Maguire?"

The hostility gave Stag pause. He'd found Portier to be like his pictures, an older gentleman, handsome, well dressed, the ultimate flashy watch on his wrist, the Hermès alligator briefcase next to him as if it held the launch codes for the US arsenal. According to the picture with Bill Gates, Portier rattled people more than people rattled him.

"I have some information," Stag said, never taking his eyes from Portier. "About *Mein Kampf.*"

"How did you get it?" Portier was clearly a man who had his questions answered.

"My friend you murdered found it. I want to know what you'd be willing to pay."

"Yes. I've expected you. We've read about your interest in settlements."

A rage volcanoed up in Stag for a moment. But then with Herculean willpower, he tamped it down. "Unless you can bring Harry back, what else is there?"

Portier assessed him. "What suits a man like yourself? An island in the South Pacific? A town house in Mayfair? Nothing is out of reach, of course."

"How about I want to be Prime Minister of the UK? Or perhaps I want the House of Saud to work for me for a change?"

Caution seeped into Portier's cold stare. "Those things would surely take time, but, certainly, they are not impossible."

"I can give you what you want."

The words hung between them.

Portier nodded. "Can you prove this?"

"Yes." Stag stared full bore. He took the sheet of silk out from his pocket and flashed it at Portier, not long enough for him to see anything but the fact that there was a lot of writing on it. "Just call me a close acquaintance of Heydrich's."

The hatred on Portier's face sparked, but it was quickly replaced by the facade of reason. He was, after all, the consummate businessman.

"I see," he said.

"I plan on doing a trade. A lucrative trade. With you," Stag said. "However, I insist you treat me fairly. This"—he gestured to the silk stuffed in his pocket—"has been copied and is with various persons. I think this is what they call the Dead Man Switch. Should anything happen to me, it will trigger several emails to Interpol that will reveal the rest of our complicated relationship, along with your connection to 12A and the need to autopsy Harry for traces of Micotil."

Portier nodded slowly. "We are open to negotiation. What are your terms?"

"I want to meet with the full board of Tarnhelm. The negotiations will be with them and you, not you alone."

The older man was clearly not used to meeting demands. It obviously galled him. "That, of course, can be arranged, but perhaps it would be more efficient to deal with me. Here and now."

"No. I demand witnesses."

"It's an unnecessary precaution. I can do anything you might need."

"I want the entire board."

Portier seemed to mull this in his head. "You really don't need—"

"And I want full third-party participation in my safety, or there will be no meeting."

"If you'd like the board to meet with you, that can be arranged."

"I'm the 'little guy'," Stag said. "I want it my way."

"Of course. When would you like to schedule this meeting?" Portier made no attempt to hide his impatience. He clearly didn't like anything Stag was saying.

"Wait for my phone call. I'll set the terms."

Portier's mouth turned down. His stare remained unbroken. "We will meet your terms, Mr. Maguire. Simply let me know when you can return and meet the board."

"The board will meet with me, not the other way around."

Grudgingly, Portier said, "However you like."

"I'll arrange the flight."

"Flight?"

Stag nodded. "Yes. You and the board will meet using my choice of security force, not yours."

"You hardly look like a man who has his own security force."

"Oh, but I do. We're going to have a board meeting aboard a commercial Airbus A380. My security system will be TSA approved."

"What?"

"Singapore Airlines, first class, from Frankfurt to Singapore. That's the kind it will be. A secure one. And that is not negotiable. Our next meeting will take place aboard the commercial flight of my choosing with you and the rest of the board in tow, or it will not take place at all. And if it does not take place, then you can watch this beautiful little dream"—Stag gestured around the enormous office with the Picassos on the wall and the Modigliani sculptures on pedestals—"become nothing but a forlorn memory of days past."

Portier finally boomed out in anger. "Who are you to dictate these absurd terms to me?"

Stag stood and began his stilted journey to the double doors, his back to Portier's shouting. Then he paused but he did not turn around. "To rich and privileged people like you, I'm your worst nightmare. I am an unreasonable man."

Portier stared knives into Stag's back until he disappeared through the glossy double doors.

Alone in his office, Portier knew he should take a moment of reflection and ponder his options. But when he looked down at his newly arrived blood tests, now neatly stacked on his desk, the rage was impossible to bite back.

He was not going to have terms dictated to him by some cripple from Wisconsin. And Tarnhelm was not the corporation it was, to take orders from a snickering little journalist.

No, this was not going to happen.

Vengeance is mine, sayeth the Lord.

And he was the fucking Lord—of Tarnhelm, of the entire world.

It didn't matter how many blood tests they took. He was still here, and he would be till his last breath.

He reveled in the lowbrow, peasant satisfaction of being able to annihilate his enemies, the ones who mocked him, underestimated him, weighed upon him. But as much as Stag Maguire affronted him, Portier knew it was prudent to get as much information as he could before Maguire was snuffed. He hadn't become head of Tarnhelm by being a hothead, or by behaving like a renegade. He was known for his patience, his astuteness. It was the bedrock upon which Tarnhelm had thrived.

No, it would not do to pick up the phone and order Maguire to be crushed. There was the Dead Man Switch to think of. And the information they still needed. Besides, if Luc Portier was honest with himself, as the white count on his blood tests insisted he be, the man he most wanted gone was Sadler. The American blueblood. His Washington connections went so far back that his family farm had made up the land for Congressional Country Club. It didn't pass Portier's notice that Sadler seemed mighty relieved his home was in America. Away from whatever beast Heydrich still could unleash on Europe.

His anger intensified. Sadler was always snickering behind his back. The man's amusement at his prostate problems was legend. Payback from years of competition was still not settled, though Portier had been at the top of Tarnhelm for years.

Oh, but the sweet foolish notion of getting rid of all of them was delicious. Until then he would need to wring out the very last drop of his patience.

CHAPTER THIRTY

It was now a calculated risk. Taking down Tarnhelm was not going to be easy. Not when he was the consummate nobody, left behind by everyone he'd ever loved, to limp through life with a bullet-scarred leg. Stag didn't know if that made him weak or nihilistic or both, but deep inside, it seemed to have created a strong place for him to reside. He was going forward. No matter what.

Logic told him that the only way to take out Portier and Tarnhelm would be with something bigger. The Settlement was a drop in the bucket of Tarnhelm's worth. He could not compete with money. The only thing he could do well was research and write. He was a journalist.

He would have to take that skill and strangle them with it.

Back in his room at the Baur au Lac, he propped his leg up with pillows and took out the diary.

* * *

A miserable January.

You've come back from your "very important" meeting at the house on the lake, and now you're quite pleased with yourself. You've got everyone's cooperation for your grand plans, including mine, it would seem.

It is cold and snowy in Prague as well. Instead of rushing back there, you landed your plane in Templehof and came to me. The world and I blossom for you, as is your right as the übermenschen. If only those damned Russians were not entrenched at the front! But that is not your worry. No, your cares all end at the tip of your nose, and I make sure to keep it that way for you.

But behind your back, I take my slips of silk to the art shop in the guise of buying more paint. "Cerulean, please, and some tubes of flake white!" I say cheerfully to the clerk, while taking the silk from beneath my sleeve lining. I pass it along, then tote my oils home to paint your portrait, content in the knowledge that today I told them about your meeting at Wannsee. And gave them news of the new bomb being developed in secret.

You've been instructed to guard this new weapon more fiercely than the heaped-up bodies of all your Jews.

* * *

Stag leaned back on the pillows and closed his eyes, running a timeline. The Wannsee conference was where Heydrich organized the necessary factions of the Third Reich in order to implement the Final Solution. The date of the conference was January 20, 1942. A few months later, Heydrich died June 4th in Prague. Everything in the diary going forth would be relevant to the letters he'd discovered in the Bundesarchiv.

The diamonds are in a truck at the bottom of the lake.

There was much more than diamonds at stake here. He couldn't quite figure it out. The diamonds might have been financing for arms. They could have been industrial diamonds needed for Heydrich's Skoda Werks in Prague. To fashion a bomb casing perhaps?

His thoughts began drifting. He wondered if there were more letters tucked into the National Archives in DC or perhaps in Moscow. But even if there were, Tarnhelm had to already know about them. Also, it was highly unlikely they hadn't already investigated the newly available letters at the Bundesarchiv by now. They were, after all, in the security and information business. The only thing they didn't know was what was on the slip of silk in his possession. They didn't know how to translate the diary. That was the key.

The next logical step was to head to the Königssee and look for that truck at the bottom of the lake. If it still existed.

He probably had enough money in the Settlement to run a salvage operation if he found it. Diamonds would sure come in handy in going against Tarnhelm, he thought blackly. He was taking on a behemoth that fed on shadows. Tarnhelm lurked in every dark corner. He didn't know how to break their nefarious hold, but, in the end, if the SD had been defanged, Tarnhelm could be too. If the creature was afraid of the dark, then light must be cast upon it, to see it for what it really was, cowering in the corner and shivering in the spotlight. Tarnhelm had to be revealed in words, just as Isolda Varrick forcefully cried out her very existence in words written in her copy of *Mein Kampf*.

Tomorrow he would buy a laptop and begin his first article. He already knew what he wanted to research and how he would like it all to end. That was his last coherent thought before he fell asleep.

CHAPTER THIRTY-ONE

STAG WALKED THE few blocks to where he'd parked his rental car, making sure he was not followed in the darkness of pre-dawn.

Then he climbed into the buttery leather seat of the Porsche. It was a five-hour drive to Königssee through the beautiful Alps, and he saw no reason not to enjoy every bit of it.

The sun just lightened the mountains as he drove east into the Alps. The ice and snow had been scrupulously removed from the roadways—*nothing like that German engineering*, he thought to himself ironically, putting the roadster on cruise control.

* * *

The lowering sun cast deep teal shadows across the waters of the Königssee. Above, the mountains were tipped in red-gold. Buds had begun to explode on the beech trees. Evergreens deepened the blue shadows into black. A boating party was out on the lake. The electric motor was drowned by the tinkle of music. It went past, finally hushed by the creeping darkness.

One thing struck Stag as he stood on the shore. Sometimes a writer has to put all his research aside and just experience what he's writing about. Just go there. Smell the smells, see the sights. This was the perfect example. The Königssee, indescribably beautiful, was also the clearest body of water he'd ever seen. It wasn't just clear, it was fucking crystal clear all the way down to its cold, clear, magnified bottom.

There was no way a truck had fallen into this lake that everybody didn't already know about. And if they knew about it, it had certainly been explored thoroughly. There was no secret Nazi treasure in the bottom of the Königssee. It was a dead end. There was nothing else to do but get ready to fly to Singapore.

* * *

Troost got on the phone to Interpol's Operations and Command Center in Washington, DC.

"I'll need the Wisconsin authorities to issue a warrant for Hyortur Maguire." He paused and listened. "The reason?" Troost looked at the poster of the beach mocking him. He sighed. It certainly wasn't getting any closer. "Fugitive wanted for questioning in the death of Harold Gerde." He looked down at his notes.

He ended the call with a nod. Looking up, he saw Special Agent Jones.

"We've lost him again."

Troost couldn't hide his annoyance. "The man has so many people following him, we're bumping up against the crowd at his elbow. How the hell can we lose him?"

"He has another set of IDs. Has to have."

"Obviously," Troost said, his voice enough to freeze-dry. "Why don't we know who they are?"

"We're on it. But without being able to question Aradi—"

"Fuck Aradi and her little spook operation. I want you to do your job, not depend on others."

Jones nodded. "Of course. But you can imagine it's hard to toss his room without a warrant."

"We are Interpol. We do not search rooms without a warrant. That would be illegal."

"I understand."

Troost stared. "I wonder if you do."

* * *

I went for a walk today. The Nazi banners flying along the Ku'damm snapped, their color in sharp contrast to the pale blue sky overhead. I could do nothing but marvel at them. The Nazi red is a most beautiful red. It is not at all the blood red one would think, but an optimistic carmine with the slightest hint of orange. One can't help but be impressed to walk down a street alive with these glowing red banners. And you cannot flee the swastika. A little boy ran in front of me on the sidewalk, bouncing his rubber ball; again, the hakenkreuz printed on it. The clerk at the KaDeWe jangled as she wrapped my package. I admired her charm bracelet, full of little Nazi flags from all her Strength Through Joy travels. She proudly showed me all the lovely swastikas on her bracelet from Frankfurt A.M. to Dortmund. How mighty the Thousand-Year-Reich will seem to be from all the swastika-laden debris that will be left behind.

And left behind it shall be, for I went to the art store today with my little slip of silk. I told my contacts how they are baling the hair shorn from the victims in the east. You, of course, laughed when you told me about these bales. You then bragged about your German efficiency. The hair will provide superior soundproofing for our submarines, you told me—your U-boat. The hair would be appropriately used to bring about the end to the enemies of the Reich.

I reply like the smart Aryan I am.

At last, the Jews shall merit some worth! I say, laughing.

CHAPTER THIRTY-TWO

THE ALPINERS CRAWLED down the face of the cliff via ropes and carabineers. Up top, Macintosh "Mac" Killburn looked down at them with all the burly pride of Reinhold Messner reaching Everest for the first time. "That's it. Belay! Belay!" he bellowed down to his students. The acne-bloomed fifteen-year-old faces looked up at him, encouraged and terrified all at once.

The Berchtesgaden Alps were the picture-perfect place for mountain climbing. It was Mac's penance in life that, in order to live there, he was forced to teach the brats of the wealthy how to maneuver a lame twenty-five-foot cliff. He'd much rather have taken his expertise to K2, but climbing the Himalayas was expensive. And there was no need for a children's instructor there. Broke children didn't take climbing lessons, and if they did, the Sherpas already had their future jobs covered. Hell, the Sherpas put him to shame. They put them all to shame.

"Mac! Mac!" A young voice below him cried out. He looked down past the snow bank and saw the problem immediately. The rope was caught on a rock and little Dallas Ann Vetrova was dangling over the cliff trying to swing it free.

"Hold on there!" He swooped down on his line. Dallas, all red hair and freckles, smiled her relief. Mac gave her line a confident yank. "You've got this!" he told her, pleased by the renewed look of confidence and determination on her face. She gripped the rope and continued her descent. Little Dallas was as hell-bent to rappel the cliff as her mother had been to escape the strip club. Certainly no one could accuse Dallas's daddy of cowardice. He'd been the first to encroach upon Soviet oil. His buddy Putin, strangely, never put up a grumble.

Mac's sudden laughter boomed all the way down to the Königssee, the sublime crystal-clear lake below the ice-covered peaks. He sure as hell would rather be in the Himalayas, earning renown, breaking records on K2. But due to a case of adulthood mumps and the news of his dashed dreams of a big family full of children, he'd come to realize that the wholesome smiles of some of these fucked-up kids was, in the end, perhaps enough.

Clinging to the side like Spider-Man, he watched as the other two kids, one, the scion of a tech genius, and the other, a mass-tort attorney who was now two wives removed from this kid's mom, got to the ledge. The cliff was Mac's go-to favorite climb, easy for beginners, not too far to fall in case disaster happened.

Plus, it had the benefits of a history lesson. He followed the group to the ledge below, stood, and released his carabineers. Walking to the hump of rusted metal, he placed his hand on the truck door handle, pulling it open in a flurry of green-gray flakes. The truck had been here since the war. It had crashed off the roadside above, probably because of ice, and fell down the mountainside to finally lodge in the crevice between the ledge and the rock face. Other than climbers, most didn't even know it was there. It was impossible to see from the road, and because of the crevices in the rock face, it was hidden from below. The cleanup after the war had probably left it because it wasn't really visible, and from the mountain, it would have been cost prohibitive to retrieve.

The three teens released their carabineers and grinned with accomplishment. Chet Logan, the skinny youth with the name of a cowboy and the heart of a bean-counter, was the first to identify it. "It's a German Eiheits Diesel!" he exclaimed. "Look! You can still see the mount where the Breda gun was on top of the truck bed!"

"How long has this been here?" Dallas Ann asked, perusing it suspiciously.

"A long time. Just look at the rust," Chet said, watching the orangey red dust sprinkle to the ground where his hand touched the truck.

"Yep, it's been here since the war." Mac was happy to give the kids a lesson. "The Nazis planned the *Alpenfestung,* the Alpine Redoubt, as they called it, where they might make a last stand. It was rumored to mostly just be an invention by their propaganda minister, Goebbels, but it's a fact they used these mountains to stash arms, valuables, documents, from the beginning."

He watched Wentford Holmes III climb into the driver's seat of the truck and pretend to take the wheel, long since pillaged.

Chet cautiously climbed into the back of the truck. Wentford followed, ploughing him aside. "Where's the gun?" Wentford demanded, kicking the mount as if the huge gun might just appear.

There was always an asshole in the group, Mac thought, and they were usually the children of tort attorneys or evangelicals. Go figure.

"Long gone. The Allies were pretty thorough removing ordnance after the surrender." He helped Dallas Ann scramble to the truck bed. The sun had melted all the snow, revealing wet rusty metal. "Just don't fall through. I think it's solid but it's been through seventy or more winters."

Wentford leapt to the top of the mount and pretended to play battle with an imaginary gun, evaporating Dallas Ann and Chet who stood politely by. He leapt and pounded away foolishly, as teens do when they become the perfect storm of Adderall and narcissism.

Dallas laughed. Chet looked resentful. Wentford made particular effort to annihilate him, pounding his feet for emphasis.

Suddenly the truck shuddered. The sound of metal ripping was followed by a heavy boom.

"Whoa!" Dallas Ann exclaimed, lunging for the metal bars along the edge of the truck bed.

They all watched as a huge barrel-like structure was birthed below the crumbling truck. The tank rolled to the edge of the cliff and fell, bouncing once, then twice along the rock face before becoming lodged in a crevice about fifty feet below. Mac squatted and looked down, where the tank clung to the precious space on the ledge.

"That must've been the gas tank."

"Why is it not rusted like the truck?" Dallas Ann asked, squatting next him.

"Not made of steel, that's for sure. Pretty high-grade aluminum for a gas tank." Mac shrugged. "Sorry to have to tell you this, guys." He looked up the face of the cliff. "The fun part's over. Now we have to go back. Up there." He jabbed his thumb upward.

The four of them looked up the mountainside, like angels to heaven.

Behind them, the grotesque form of the rusted truck appeared crouched as if it were ready for a meal. A beast out of Dante's *Inferno*.

PART FOUR

Upon Heydrich's death, Hitler had his safe blown open and acquired the documents therein. With incredible anger and agitation, Hitler read Heydrich's big file named Adolf Hitler. When he was finished, he shouted like a madman and told Bormann, "Heydrich was more dangerous that we thought! He had us all within the grasp of his hands!!! What would have happened to us had he lived!?"

Testimony of the SS Officer who was present

CHAPTER THIRTY-THREE

THE FRANKFURT GATE for Singapore Airlines was an odd mix of manufactured German rathskeller stuck in a cold corridor of terrazzo marble and uninspired mall from 1974. There was access to a first-class lounge, but Stag decided to pass. No point in meeting up with the crowd early, he reckoned, ironically. Things were going to get awkward soon enough.

In the meantime, he was on the internet with a new device in Maguire's name. Dedman's documents and devices were safe in his carry-on. He had just started to read about Jan Vanderloos, President of Tarnhelm South Africa, who had been struck by a debilitating stroke, when Suites Class seating was announced. The Airbus 380 was the largest aircraft commercially available. It had twelve single suites that could convert to six doubles, and he was pretty confident Tarnhelm had booked all of them. They sure as fuck didn't want an audience.

He was the first to board. The suites were like individual cubicles that each had an adjoining wall to another. The wall could come down and create a double bed when it was time for sleeping. Individual privacy was maximum, which he was happy to have. He didn't relish spending the next few hours staring at a bunch of men who wanted to kill him. No, he was going to take the meeting, outline his plan to them, then try to relax in that viper's nest, in his double bed in the sky.

Make that a double bed in the sky with Givenchy pajamas.

The attendant was quick to bring him a Blue Mountain coffee. He'd read it went for about $120.00 a pound, and he longed to taste it. But he didn't dare. Not when Tarnhelm had a target on his forehead. So he stirred it with a spoon and ruefully thought about the life that awaited him when his money was gone and he was back to flying economy. If he lived that long. He was watching the coffee cool when the first of the board members arrived in the suite forward to his.

He figured the tall Norseman was Rikhardsson. The guy looked at him like the bloodthirsty pagan he was, all ice-blue stare and heartless beheading. His attendant took his carry-on and swished by in her Balmain-designed batik uniform. Stag had read that the Singapore Girl was required to have a certain waist-to-hip ratio. It was, of course, completely sexist and unacceptable, until you were watching them bend and stretch, their ass in your face. Then, for a man, it was heaven.

"Mr. Maguire? Henry Sadler. President of North American Operations." A nondescript American shoved his hand in and pumped his. "Mr. Portier will be here shortly."

Stag said nothing. From the shuffling and obsequious murmurs behind him, he figured the other board members were getting settled.

Portier arrived looking like Marie Antoinette being forced to tour the slums near the Paris sewers. He handed his alligator briefcase to his personal airline attendant—Stag thought her name was Nor—who took it and placed it elegantly under the bench in front of his seat. For one second, Portier met his eye across the aisle. It said, "I am going to eat your face off," then he took a glass of Krug and settled back for takeoff.

The Airbus rose from the tarmac like a floating tanker, with hardly a bump. Once the captain lifted the seat belt sign, Stag figured he would get started. It wouldn't take long.

He went to the first-class lounge at the front of the plane, nodding to Portier to follow. The rest of the board stood and sauntered in. Once the five of them settled in the hip, boxy, white leather lounge seats, Stag whipped out a manila folder and handed it to Portier. Portier opened it and examined the key, which, for the occasion, Stag had slipped in a new Ziploc bag.

"I can't afford fancy Hermès briefcases . . . yet," Stag added with drummed-up humility.

The men each took a long look at the folded silk strip through the Ziploc. The last one to examine it, Rikhardsson, placed it in the manila folder and handed it back to Stag.

Stag sat back. "I just read about Mr. Vanderloos. He seemed young for a stroke. I understand he's in a permanent vegetative state. Very unfortunate. I would have liked for him to be here." It was all he could do not to roll his eyes. He handed Portier an envelope that held his request. It was simple. Fifty million in the numbered account in the Zurich Cantonal Bank, half when they landed, the other half when they received the key. Swiss-numbered accounts weren't what they used to be now that the Holocaust lawyers and US Homeland Security was onto them, but that didn't bother Stag. Especially since there would be no one to complain.

Portier read his demands in stony silence. He motioned for Rikhardsson to take the contents around to the other board members.

Then he said to Stag, "Mr. Maguire, what makes you think you'll be able to get away with this?"

"Well, I figure at the rate your board is going, all I have to do is wait, and you'll cannibalize yourselves." Stag looked at the glass of sparkling spring water that Rikhardsson had just sipped from. It was clearly a nice safe glass of water. He took it from the cocktail table and chugged it down himself, much to Rikhardsson's shock. "Besides, you're here, aren't you?"

He didn't bother to wait around for an answer. Instead, he rose and gimped to his suite. Now all there was left to do was refuse all meals, get tucked into his double bed, and lie awake till they landed at Changi Airport. Without fearing for his life, it was just an endurance test. Like flying economy.

* * *

You've become quite secretive about the new weapon. You talk of the future, that one day there shall be a great bomb affixed to a rocket that will destroy an entire city in one blast. I don't really believe it. Especially when you claim it will be but the size of a pineapple, but I listen with intent even as I look dreamy and distracted at my easel. You murmured the bomb is not yet launchable, but you boast it may be dropped from a plane. You drink as you speak to me of these things. Sometimes, I am not certain what your slurred words are saying. But I write it down as best I can on my white silk. I go to the paint store, and hand it over.

It is my little hammer, you see, knocking away at the bricks of the Thousand-Year-Reich.

* * *

Changi Airport was the most beautiful airport Stag had ever seen, from its celestial architecture to its ridiculous number of high-end shops. But walking through it to catch his flight to Bali, he noted the strange inefficiency of the Singaporeans. Everything was beautiful to the eye, but once you went to your gate, you couldn't get a pedestrian bottle of water without walking a mile back to where the shops had been hubbed. And the internet, forget about it. To get the code, you had to go back through security. But, fuck, you could buy some Ferragamos in a heartbeat.

He passed briefly through the Singapore Airlines SilverKris lounge to send out an email. For the second meeting with Tarnhelm, he decided he needed a more appropriate accoutrement instead of a Ziploc bag. He emailed several photos and specifications to Wuhan, China, where he'd sourced a high-end fake leather goods operation. They were rushing through a "fine" alligator briefcase, just exactly like the one Portier owned. Only he wasn't going to pay Hermès to make it.

He smiled, thinking how pissed off Portier was going to be seeing another Hermès briefcase like his own. For a moment, he even considered getting a fake Tourbillon Mars made in China and wearing it at their next meeting, just to get the guy's goat.

Nah.

His work done, he thought about staying in the first-class lounge, but after his last flight, he was getting tired of staring at douchebags. And sometimes he just wanted to blend with the crowd. Now was such a time. Portier was sure to let him live a few more minutes till they made a deal.

Or not.

He settled into the plane that would take him to Denpasar. He was booked at the St. Regis under his name, but Dedman was at a small upscale hotel called Bali Orchid. He had a nice over-the-water palm-woven villa waiting for him there. He hoped he had enough time to enjoy it and get some research done

* * *

Portier took his own private plane back to Zurich. The rest of the board flew with him.

"Fifty million." Zellner shook his head. "Tell me again why we don't just shoot him out of the air—collateral damage aside?"

"He's fucking with us," Rikhardsson bit out from a blond leather couch.

"Yes," Portier agreed. "But until we have that code, we cannot see him dead." He was determined not to be driven by the rage of his white count. There was too much he still wanted to get done. It was time for ice in his veins as Rikhardsson had handsomely mastered.

The phone rang and he answered it.

The three other men, Sadler, Rikhardsson, and Zellner, all waited, stilled in anticipation.

"Are you sure? The photographs were clear?" Portier listened. Quietly he put down the phone.

"Well?" Sadler asked.

"Our photos sent back from our body cams were crystal clear. The key which Maguire presented us is real." Portier again swallowed an unaccustomed rage. "The first line only, however. The rest is gibberish."

"Jesus Christ," Zellner burst out.

Portier wasted no time. "Maguire most definitely has the key to the diary. But what he showed us on the airplane was not THE key. It was a dupe meant to fool us into the action we've just taken. To see if he has it. To confirm it, then to pay him for the real one."

Zellner ran his hand down his face.

"Let's just get him to talk. Waterboard him. What are we wasting time for?" Rikhardsson demanded.

"No," Sadler interjected. "We bring him in with force and the letters go out. Then the game is lost."

"I have others on this." Portier ended it there. "Let's see what they can find."

"Of course." Rikhardsson fell into silence, unusual for him to be mute and impotent.

Sadler checked his phone. His private plane was waiting in Zurich. Until that bomb was found, he planned on spending as much time safely in the US as possible.

"We can always pay him," Zellner muttered.

"Yes. Perhaps we will have to retrieve it that way. Nothing must be ruled out," Portier said.

"Nothing?" Sadler asked, more derision in his voice than he meant to reveal.

Portier stared at him, and thought of those blood tests waiting for him back on his desk, and Sadler's long trip back to his compound in Potomac, Maryland. "No. Nothing," he added, realizing for the first time what a virtue patience really was.

CHAPTER THIRTY-FOUR

THE MESSAGE HAD come via a numbers station off Wrangel Island between the Chukchi and East Siberian Seas. Numbers stations were uber old school, but still useful. It was hard to pin an espionage charge on someone who possessed nothing more sophisticated than an AM radio. iPhones and computers could be hacked, their IP addresses known. But numbers stations broadcasted a series of codes only one person in the world could decipher. In the black world of spying, there was technology that could get you killed, and then some that couldn't. Numbers stations were like an old friend. A lonesome broadcasting tower sending random messages out into the ether. They were inefficient, but absolutely foolproof, and it was still the go-to practice when someone was in deep and needed to be in the loop. They carried ironclad deniability.

James Duffy, head of Nuclear Terrorism of NATO, looked down at the message that had just come in from his best agent.

Likely gun-type. Likely unstable. P has own plans.

A gun-type nuclear bomb was what was used in Hiroshima. It was inefficient and had long since been phased out for any military use in favor of implosion technology. The gun-type was counterintuitive to the layman because, instead of shooting a "bullet" of uranium into a uranium mass to cause the chain reaction, its explosives shot a larger hollow mass of uranium onto a smaller spike to create the effect. But it was simple, which was why it was most feared. A gun-type was the one kind of nuclear bomb that could be crudely fabricated by Daesh organizations like the Black Plague.

Thank God those organizations were fractured and unprofessional in the extreme, he thought. Their random attacks were horrific, but nothing like the numbers of casualties possible in a nuclear attack. Even a dirty bomb, though psychologically damaging, would leave behind cities to clean up and survive.

But an actual chain-reaction nuclear bomb? Unthinkable.

P has own plans.

That sentence made his breath catch. P stood for Luc Portier of Tarnhelm. Figuring there could be a portable nuclear device out there that Tarnhelm could market made Duffy's stomach drop. Tarnhelm had self-preservation, but no conscience. If they had a bomb, they'd sell it anywhere they were not. Which left a lot of territory for ISIL or the Black Plague or whoever had the funds to set one off.

Duffy sent out his own message. It would be relayed to the numbers station and would require his agent to listen to it at the mutually known time.

Neutralize situation all costs.

He rose from his desk and grabbed his raincoat. It was always raining in Brussels, he thought, hating the weather that blew in from the North Atlantic. The arm of NATO he headed had been stationed ironically right next to the airport in Zaventem, where the 2016 bombing occurred.

Now there was worse to come.

He shrugged into the Burberry and thought about putting more TWR agents in Zurich. TWR was the unofficial anti-terrorism arm of NATO, buried deep and unknown to even the participating countries that were not the top three. Among other things, the initials stood for *There Was Resistance*. The name was to honor those gone before. It also signified ongoing struggles, of which there were many in this world. TWR existed because of the undisputed fact that soon the world's terrorist organizations were going to be in possession of a nuclear device. Whether it was a dirty bomb that spewed radioactive material with the blast, or a true nuclear device that created a chain reaction explosion, no one yet knew. But it was coming as surely as there would be resistance. And TWR would be there to provide resistance, if no one else could.

Duffy snatched his umbrella and cursed the foul weather again. The world was already at war with money, arms, and aggression. Did they have to fight the weather, too? From the cold rain pelting his window's view of the cars on the E40, he figured the answer was yes.

* * *

Stag lay in a teak lounge chair beneath the thatch roof of his over-water villa. The sky was cloudless, the water a perfectly clear turquoise. It was jarring reading about wartime Berlin with such a vista. Still, he forged on. He'd spent all morning and most of the afternoon in Kuta, walking through alleys of addicts who were on *shabu-shabu* or pills of meth and caffeine called *ya ba*. Even the street children were high. Glue was cheaper than food. And the manufacturers refused to add the negligible expense of oil of mustard because it "reduced sales."

It was as depressing as it could be. The tourism industry was booming, but the economic effects didn't translate to the population.

Bali was the second poorest part of Indonesia after Jakarta, and it twisted his heart to see kids blindly hugging trees after huffing a plastic bag, but he knew he couldn't really do anything for them now. He had errands to run. Focus was the only skill he had and he had to get to the bottom of this strange, terrifying organization called Tarnhelm.

His first item in Bali had been to purchase a gun. Now the Glock sat next to him on the table, ready to protect him should he need it. He then procured a large safety deposit box at the Bank Commonwealth to stash his valuables, and took out a mailbox to have his new Wuhan-made briefcase delivered. Afterwards he'd taken a sweet little swim in the Indian Ocean. He was now ready to sit back and do some serious deciphering.

The twenty-five million hadn't arrived in his numbered account in Zurich yet, but he'd be patient.

* * *

Hans is no longer at the art store! He was "removed" by the Gestapo, said the old man, and he won't say where Hans has gone. Very bad tidings. Now I have no one to give my slips of silk to, and yet there is now much terrifying news to deliver. Your little meeting in Wannsee has brought information about Prussic acid and train schedules. And there in your pocket one night I found a diagram of the bomb you say could be made the size of a pineapple. In desperation, I've taken to write to Eduard Schulte, pretending to be his fiancé. I sent the letter to Frau Keils in the hope that she may forward it from Switzerland when she goes. I shall write her again, but I fear for her also. She has been known to hide Jews. Much to her peril.

But if I don't write Schulte, how else to get the information through at this very late hour?

The only answer is to persist. Because the world has gifted you more than your fair share, my darling. So I shall persist because, whether it matters not, I will never gift to you my silence.

* * *

He now realized the letters, unable to be forwarded to Schulte for some reason, must have been with this Frau Keils when she got rounded up and sent to Auschwitz. He checked the Auschwitz Death Books at the United States Holocaust Memorial Museum. And found a woman from Berlin named Anna Keils who died in early 1942.

Well, there was one small mystery solved.

Stag ran his fingers over the handwriting. At times, he felt Isolda was speaking solely to him. He was her companion in her terror. He was the broken man who fit her broken pieces with his own. The unsilent cripple. The first to be mocked. The first to be shunned. The first to be shoved into a shower. She wrote to rebel against Heydrich's secrets the only way she could; he worked to rebel against Tarnhelm's secrets the only way he could. It was a quiet war fought with research and planning, though it was a war he knew how to fight.

But what good would it do? If he were killed and forgotten, it would come to nothing. But if he persisted, with half as much bravery Isolda had shown, and if his plans and research worked, he could leave Tarnhelm limping like he limped. Then he had to somehow pay tribute to Isolda. He would see that her silence was broken. Her words would be published and placed in the timeline of history.

He flipped the page and continued.

* * *

I lay awake all night worrying about what information Hans may give your Gestapo. I've written several letters to My Dear Eduard, and now Frau Keils is no longer reachable. I have no one to help me, except the old man at the paint store, and I cannot tell if there was glee on his face when the Gestapo took Hans away or despair. He sits on his stool and never is there an expression in his dead, watery eyes.

* * *

Stag wondered whether her plea on that last piece of silk was stashed in the painting in a desperate attempt to reach the old man. Perhaps she had sent the painting with the silk to him under the guise of his matching a color she used. If that were the case, the old man had never seen it.

The gnawing feeling that something was amiss in that apartment came back to him. He went through the place in his mind again. Everything was there, right down to the ubiquitous photo of Der Führer. What was bugging him? The missing thing. What the hell was it? He needed to return to Berlin and that apartment, but there was too much to do in the meantime. The best he could do now was keep up with Tarnhelm. He made a note to call Jake on his Dedman phone and ask him to research a list of questions he had. If Jake was good enough to do that for him, he could then finish deciphering the diary.

CHAPTER THIRTY-FIVE

STAG MAGUIRE'S ACTIONS were suicidal, Angelika mused as she ended the session with Portier. Maguire was taking on way too much. While his audacity was impressive, there was no doubt in her mind they would kill him. Tarnhelm was now on the hook for twenty-five million. Portier told her they were paying it to buy time.

Now it was up to her.

She didn't relish going forward. It was a tangle, for Maguire, for her. Her first assessment of Maguire as he walked past her in the Pariserplatz was that he was singularly unimpressive. His only distinction was he had a strange gait, stiff, like a propping horse. Maguire was a bit taller than average perhaps, his face clean-shaven, but his eyes possessed a certain wildness. When they looked around, they were a little too open, showing a sliver too much white. She remembered the last time she'd seen eyes like that. They belonged to a terrified Syrian mother trying to protect her child. They were the eyes of the hunted.

Inexplicably, Maguire had checked into the St. Regis in Bali. Luc had made some disparaging comment about Maguire already attempting to live like the nouveau-riche. Angelika wasn't buying it. Maguire was no self-indulgent fool. It took more than a nice hotel to impress him. He was in Bali for another reason. He wasn't taking a vacation now.

It was doubtful, however, that the weapon was in Indonesia. But his trip to the Königssee bothered her. It was a likely place for a Nazi secret. If Heydrich had a weapon that he wanted to keep to himself for strategic purposes, a nice salt mine was the place for it. It was logical that it had been moved there, secretly.

A car downstairs waited to take her to the plane that would take her to Bali. She didn't know what her next move would be, but she did know Maguire was not staying at the Regis.

But for her, he would not be hard to find.

* * *

I wore your most spectacular diamond ring today. Everyone thought it was a ruby and a tiny one at that! But those who knew spoke of us in whispers, recounting the terrific fight you had with Goering over winning this ugly red stone. It looks like a small sparkling drop of blood on my finger. I didn't know diamonds came in every color. You even told me of green ones tainted by uranium. You said when you win this war you will buy me two green diamonds, one for each ear, in order to look at them when we make love.

How like you to associate the beautiful things in life, Shubert and violin, your love for the rare and the beautiful, with that which is pure, and never see how they in themselves don't translate goodness.

There is only Death and the Maiden in your world.

No meaningful grey. Only black and white. And red.

* * *

Sadler's limo took the George Washington Memorial Parkway out of Reagan National Airport. He was almost home. All they had to do was cross the Potomac at the Beltway, and once in Maryland, head to River Road.

He opened the window of the limo and smelled the air. The Good Old USA never smelled so clean. To the left, was the spring green scent of the golf course at Avenel, and to the right, once they put Potomac Village behind them, he could just catch a whiff of horse manure. His thousand-acre farm and a good old-fashioned gallop through the sod fields would erase Zurich and uranium and that fucking Frenchman from his mind.

His phone rang. He wanted to throw it out the window and make the driver run over it again and again.

"What have you got?"

"There's a blackout on his information. No one knows."

Sadler angered. "Someone knows. His doctor knows."

"There's nothing. He has us locked out."

"Good."

"Good?" came the voice on the other end.

"Yes. If he doesn't want us to know, it means it's bad. Portier's days as head of Tarnhelm are numbered."

"Perhaps. Or he's just fucking with us. That's been known to happen in this organization."

Sadler grunted and ended the call. The fieldstone gates of the compound were coming up to the left. He suddenly realized he'd never been happier to be home in the good ol' USA.

* * *

I want to tell you about my first kiss.

His name was Miki Bloch. Ah, that name! I still feel dreamy thinking it. He was tall and handsome. He was, perhaps, fourteen. We shared realshule in Berlin. My whole school day was devoted to getting a glimpse of him. He, of course, did not know I existed.

I was eleven. A nothing. A child.

But he, he was my lord and savior! I would daydream about holding hands with him and walking through the Tiergarten *on blustery days when he would take off his coat and wrap me in it because I was littler than he, and a lady. How I ached to be noticed! But I was invisible. I met his mother once while waiting in line for my father to pick me up. She was short and fat and, to think of it now, homely, but a truly beautiful woman, if the truth were told! She was always laughing, always happy to know you, always kind. I was grateful she spoke to me. I was Nobody, and here was Miki Bloch's mother telling me how she had just baked some* berlinerkranser, *and if she'd known she'd be waiting with such a nice young girl, she'd have brought some for me!*

I was beside myself with joy. Every day when she should see me in line after that, she would wave and call out my name. How delightful she was . . . Then one day, I was in the schoolyard, bouncing my rubber ball, and Miki Bloch walked by. I was so shocked by his sudden appearance, all I could do was grip my ball and back away, into a flower bed where I fell right on my bottom. Utter ruin! He laughed at me, but then came over to ask if I could use some help getting up. I nodded, and he bent down.

The most amazing thing happened then. He bent close to take my hand and I acted as if I was no longer myself, but a fiery princess overcome by a magic spell. I pressed my mouth on his and closed my eyes.

Then the worst. No magic kiss, no fairy tale. He drew back as if I'd just slapped him. Horror came over his expression. He pulled me up and walked away in embarrassment.

I died of mortification. It was the defining moment of my first walk into womanhood, and I was crushed.

I wish I could meet him again. I wish we could drink martinis at Harry's and laugh about our innocence, perhaps even hold hands now as friends. If he was still the boy I remember, perhaps I could daydream of being his wife, of seeing to his dinner and his socks, with great domesticity and tenderness.

I bought a smock today in the market. I use old men's shirts from the rag merchant since I go through so many. Painting is messy. I brought the shirt home, and as I handed it to my maid to wash, I noticed the black threads on the left shirtfront. They were still there, sewn into the white cotton. The shape of a Star of David. Another Jew who does not need his shirt.

You said to me today in your oddly high-pitched voice that you were sending a diamond over to the apartment until things settled down in Berlin. I dared not question what is unsettled in Berlin. But you told me I am to stay home, for my own sake.

The Gestapo has such talents for torture. So I think of Hans, and Miki Bloch, and the man who does not need his shirt.

I wonder when I shall become the woman who does not need her dress.

CHAPTER THIRTY-SIX

ALDERNAY TROOST LANDED in Bali and went straight to the Regis. He flashed his badge and inquired about Maguire. No one had seen him. No, his bed had not been touched, no, he had had no room service since checking in.

No surprise. Dead end.

He called Berlin to see if anything had happened on their end. Nothing.

He wondered how it was that anyone could remain unfound in this day and age. If Tarnhelm couldn't keep tabs on Maguire, what chance did Interpol have, with their government budgets and legal constraints?

"Do you want me to check other hotels?" Special Agent Jones offered.

"He'd be under another name."

"Any idea where he's going next?"

Troost let out a long, weary release of air. "Yeah. He's going straight into the ground. We just don't know exactly when."

Jones just shrugged.

* * *

Rikhardsson had his own compound in Bygdoy outside of Oslo. Snow was still on the fields, ice on the walkways, but it had been all cleaned up by the time the caravan of black SUVs and limos arrived.

The door was held and the leader of the Daesh offshoot, the Black Plague, entered. In his Saville suit and keffiyeh, the caliph was the perfect mix of west and east. The custom suit, because white men rule; the keffiyeh, because God was the platform to rail from when one was grasping for power.

The men settled in Rikhardsson's study. After libations were offered—tea for the most holy Caliph al-Samarrai—Rikhardsson got down to business.

"Our analysts believe it's a Little Boy gun-type nuclear fission device of uranium 235 with a nitrocellulose propellant." Rikhardsson lowered the note in his hand. "Sorry to get technical, but you went to Oxford, so I assume you understand what all this means."

The caliph sipped his tea with proper English manners. "I understand it. Have they dimensions?" His accent was perfectly English as well.

"No dimensions. But it's projected to be about the size of two 55-gallon steel drums. This is a non-governmental weapon that is currently unknown to any state power, ready for use, and untraceable."

"Have you a price?"

"We estimate in the 5 billion range, but that could go up with competition."

Caliph al-Samarrai took the news in stride. "The usual means of transfer?"

Rikhardsson nodded. "In your case, first to Bank Melli, then we will determine where we park it."

"Lichtenstein?"

"Ah, who knows? We change with the weather and the current state of the Feds. Yesterday it was Panama, tomorrow it's Vanuatu."

Both men laughed.

"How quickly can we take possession?" The caliph cut to the chase.

"You won't take possession at all. We will make a controlled drop, using our people and our security, on your chosen target. All part of the price."

The caliph looked most displeased. "If we purchase it, we must have the authority—"

"You will not have it under any circumstances."

"But, certainly, we would get your approval on the target, of course."

Rikhardsson said nothing.

The caliph understood. "No deal?"

"Mr. Portier makes all the arrangements himself."

"I think four billion is more in order then. If we cannot have control—"

"Four billion will get you in seventeenth place."

"That many?"

"That many." Rikhardsson raised his teacup and smiled.

* * *

I think this must be the end. I keep a placid face, but inside, I screech with terror. In one last attempt to save myself, I wrote a note on silk and put it in back of your portrait. Then I sent your portrait to the old man with the excuse of tightening the loose stretchers. If I am lucky, he will find the note and know who to contact. If not . . .

My God, death has been long in coming. It doesn't seem possible to continue any longer. You have three diamonds here. A very bad sign for me. A delay has kept you from appearing, and so I wait and order coffee from my maid, and worry.

In another life, I think I could have loved you in some small way. I feel certain you would have loved me. Especially that night you talked of your boyhood. "Moses Handel" the children called you because you were musical, and, in their cruelty, they thought to place a curse on you from your rumored Jewish ancestry. Süss was by marriage only in your family but they tainted you with the Semite blood and you never forgave them. You nurse many petty grudges. You should have been Irish, not German!

In strange and little ways, we are very much alike. We both love Shubert. Wagner. Paintings by Bocklin and Monet— though Monet be most degenerate. You asked me to paint myself just like Woman with a Parasol, *and even I had to smile inwardly. It was exactly the way I saw it myself. It haunts me even now. You saw things in me and I saw things in you that go beyond words and description.*

Art and music are our bond.

When you order me gone, I will still take the time to explain to you how many times I wanted to kill you. How much I wanted to see your jaw slacken in death and see what little light in those lifeless eyes of yours drain away. I could have killed you while you slept, but what would serve as a satisfying momentary impulse would, in the grand scheme, go unnoticed by history. The juggernaut of the Reich is set to go forward, and it will move without you or me. The Jews will be murdered, the war will continue until Germany is nothing but rubble, men will starve and bleed, women will cry and wander the streets looking for loved ones lost forever.

And I will live to see none of it. For this one small mercy, I will be grateful.

* * *

Stag couldn't figure out why the number of diamonds Heydrich was placing in her apartment caused her to feel such doom. Was it that she would be killed because she knew he was stealing them? Was he stashing jewels for his escape should Germany not win the war? And first and foremost, what about the weapon? Where in God's name was it and what was in that apartment that Tarnhelm was desperate to understand?

He took out the original silk key. The map of the Königssee seemed to be clearer and clearer now that he thought he'd identified it. But there was more to this hellacious chase than diamonds. It had to be the weapon, and the answer had to be in that apartment. It lay with Heydrich and the SD and with Isolda Varrick.

He had little hope she was still alive. Obituary notices in Germany had held nothing of an Isolda Varrick. But if she disappeared before 1945, there was a good chance she simply vanished into the cloud of war, never to be found.

He looked out at the ocean, now blooming in pink and gold. There was one last entry to the diary. It would tell all. Or he would be left as stumped as Tarnhelm.

CHAPTER THIRTY-SEVEN

THERE WAS NO pomp and circumstance for the meeting in Potomac. No black SUVs and limos, no mic-wearing men in suits. Just a
lone figure in a chauffeur-driven Ford, pulling into the circular
drive with all the status of an Uber arrival.

But Sadler made sure he waited for this man at the door. While
he did not look as if he was due the status of diplomacy, the man was
the Surrogate himself. In fact, if you saw him on the street, with his
handsome, youthful face and crisp blue blazer, you'd dismiss him as
a baby lawyer—just another Damien all grown up from *The Omen*
and now working for an investment bank. But, like Hitler's crippled
dwarf of propaganda, what you might dismiss could be fatal.

When the two men settled in his office, Sadler waited for him to
be the first to speak.

"As we discussed, he invested heavily in a billionaire's suburb outside of Moscow. Every oligarch has a place in his Sputnik Luxe in
Barvikha. Every. Oligarch," he said with meaning.

"How heavily?" Sadler asked.

"Fifty."

Sadler knew this meant billion. *Fifty billion.*

"They're calling in his loans. He's terrified. He won't eat; he won't
drink. He's convinced they're going to sneak polonium in his Diet

Coke, and you know how he feels about his hair. Fuck. If he loses that..."

This, Sadler thought, from the man who once pointed at his head and told the world, "I have a very, very good brain. The best brain." Like he wanted to be rewarded with a cookie.

"He's going to need diapers soon, he's so freaked out," the Surrogate said.

"The man just has to put his name on everything, doesn't he?" Sadler commented acidly.

"No US banks would do business with him. He had no choice but to chum up with the Russians. Then, after he orchestrated the deal with Rosneft, he flooded the oil market, and Tesla sealed his doom with their new battery. Now this over-the-top suburb is being abandoned like rats off a sinking ship. The default rate is breathtaking."

"Therefore in order to pay the loans..."

"He wants total destruction of the community. It's the only way to get the insurer Allianz to pay him—and more importantly, to pay off his loans."

"We can guarantee total destruction. Certainly."

"It needs to look like Daesh. Act of God. All that stuff. Or Allianz won't pay."

"Of course."

The Surrogate paused. "You know we're not looking for a lot of casualties here. Just property destruction."

"Complete property destruction is impossible without collateral casualties. Certainly, we could destroy a compound or two safely, but an entire suburb? With plausible deniability? No."

"What do you suggest?"

"We have a unique opportunity on the horizon. May I get you a drink and explain it to you? I think this is just what your man is looking for." Sadler rose and went to the bar to make the drinks.

* * *

Angelika Aradi took a seat at the bar. Below her sandaled feet, a beautiful spotted cat shark slid by beneath the glass floor. The Bali Orchid was a spectacular tiny resort with private over-the-water bungalows and the best chefs from four continents. Maguire picked well. She would have to remember the place. She ordered a gin and tonic.

She bet that he would stay in the hotel instead of taking a tuk-tuk into Kuta. He was nothing but problems for her. First and foremost, he was not a dupe. Lonely men subject to flattery were easy prey, particularly for a woman, but Maguire was a different species. To get to him, you had to get to his mind first. All of which was proving far more difficult than anyone imagined.

She thought of Portier's expression when they'd last Skyped. She'd never seen him as angry and frustrated as he was then. Maguire was getting the best of everyone.

A Chinese man walked by her and said in Mandarin, "Pillow lace," referring to her blond hair. She took a deep sip of her drink, and pondered the world's fascination for hair. It was nothing but a mass of dead strands, and yet men went mad for it, the blond kind especially, and Asian men in particular.

But there was only one color of hair that she cared about. Nothing made her think of her duty more than seeing hair—or rather the stark lack of it—on her four-year-old's head. When Genevieve had been desperately sick, she'd read to her over and over again, *The Velveteen Rabbit*. Until you were used and worn and loved, you cannot be Real. Angelika looked down at the fraying of the white cuff of her linen suit. It was why she was drawn to vintage. The clothes had become Real after all this time. Each moth hole, each deconstructed lapel, told a story. And now, after the ordeal of

Genevieve's sickness, she and her daughter had their story. They had become Real.

Angelika was wild about the thick dark brown locks that now covered her child's head. No fraying or deconstruction there any longer.

But there was a limit to it. Like the world itself, you could not pull the stuffing from the Velveteen Rabbit, leave it like an abandoned cicada shell, and expect it to revive.

Her only choice in this life was to stay focused on hair. She would calm her nerves with gin and her daughter's fine health, and she would tread this tightrope for now, letting Tarnhelm know she would do her duty.

* * *

You have sent your bomb into hiding. What schemes are you working on? Are you hiding it from the Führer or the Wehrmacht? Or both? You give me no clues, so I wait here, hoping my messages get through. But with all your diamonds surrounding me, I fear I will be unable to do anything until the end.

As much as I want to live, I no longer dream it's possible. The Jews are not long for this earth, and as one of them, I think it is my fate to join them. I suspect I have been seen by a Jew catcher and identified. Many U-boats when they get rounded up by the Gestapo turn Jew catcher. One can never predict who will stick by his fellow man and who will be traitor. Or did you intercept one of my letters to Shulte? I don't know and no longer have the luxury to care. I have no delusions about your sudden coolness.

I want you and the world to know one thing at the end: Even though there was no hope or dignity to my situation, I created those things anyway. It was my intention to pick this horrible book and write upon it. I pray my words break the words printed inside, and that my words may live and tower above the madness that is rich upon every printed page.

People will wonder in the future why we Jews did not fight more when we were staring down the barrel of a gun or standing in the shadow of the gas chamber. It is because we have looked into the eyes of man whose soul is so dark and deep, we no longer wish to remain within his vision. It tells us things about our own humanity we did not wish to know. And when one is naked and broken, there is no longer any ability to deny it. It is a disease of the human heart. It has nothing to do with Germans and Jews. Until we as humans stand up and say, "I will not do this," then it will happen again. And again.

In the end, I tell you, my evil Hangman, my Butcher of Prague, my Blond Beast, the joke is on you. For it is purest salvation to remove one's clothes and stand peacefully in line that we may escape that stare. Death is preferable. A mercy like none other.

I will go peacefully too. For I understand the horror of that stare well by now. In my dying moment, I shall cling to the memory of my parents. And to that shadow figure of hope, my unrequited love, the man who never arrived; the man who does not need his shirt. Perhaps in the end I will finally have a clear vision of the children that were never to be. I don't know if what I have done has helped the survival of the Jews, but in the end, this fight is not about the Jews anyway. It is for the survival of the human soul. There is still good inside me, in spite of all that I've been through. It is smaller now, but brilliant and less fragile. Truly and sincerely earned. My last words will be, "I will NOT do this." And while this warrior will go meekly toward her demise, the good inside her proves she did not concede defeat. And that will be enough.

CHAPTER THIRTY-EIGHT

STAG WAS UP early the next morning. He didn't sleep well, thinking of Isolda Varrick. She had been right. There was a tipping point inside every man: when one could go on, and when one had finally had too much. His tipping point had been Harry. He'd been stuck in the misery of his anger and grief over Holly, but Harry's death had transformed him. First, he wanted to know why they'd killed him. Now, he wanted to take them down or die trying. Not just for Harry, but for everyone Heydrich had murdered. Including, with all probability, Isolda.

And ye shall know the truth, and the truth shall make you free. The line from John 8:32 rang through his head, supplanted with the louder line that said: *And ye shall know the truth, and the truth shall piss you off.*

Back to work, he sat down to breakfast overlooking the radium blue of the Indian Ocean. He checked his bank account on his phone app, and a knot of satisfaction tightened his belly.

He was richer by twenty-five million dollars.

It was amazing what you could accomplish when you had not one fucking thing to lose.

He went back into Kuta to make another trip to the safety deposit box. There was no longer any point in carrying the diary around, so he scanned the pages onto his tablet and placed it in his box. After he left the bank, he opened a mailbox at TIKI, a private postal service. There he deposited his letter ceding ownership of the Zurich Cantonal Bank account to Save the Children. After all, what was he going to do with twenty-five million dollars? He wasn't the millionaire type. Besides, someone had to get these Indonesian kids off the *ngelem*.

I will not *do this.*

Isolda's words clung to his thoughts like the gossamer of a spider's web that you couldn't see, only feel brush against your skin with maddening endurance. He burned to find out what had happened to her. As soon as he could, he was determined to make it back to Berlin and reenter the Dresdenhof. Apartment 12A.

He ate in a small cafe in one of Kuta's most notorious little back alley drug bazaars. He ordered *mie goreng*, the local fried noodles, with shrimp, and a Bintang beer, then sat back to watch the local sights of mopeds and street deals.

"Bintang or Anker, mate?" A man in a Hawaiian shirt of neon orange hibiscus sat down at the table next to him.

"Bintang," Stag offered. "Is Anker better?"

"Dunno. I'm a goddamned Kiwi. Malcolm's the name."

Stag nodded. "First time in Bali?"

"Yeah. You?"

"Yup." He wondered if Malcolm was in Bali for the beach or the drugs. Probably both.

"What brings you 'ere?" the man asked, settling on a Bintang.

"Journalist."

"Ah, writing about Bali?"

"I might. What about you?"

"Honeymoon. The wife's out shopping. Dunno what there is to buy. Everything's shyte as far as I can see."

Stag smiled. He remembered his honeymoon with Holly on St. Kitts. The beach was black sand, the tourist items only some local batik and rum. It had been devoid of cheesy tourist traps and rip-offs. Besides, there'd only been room for the two of them on that big, beautiful island. If there were others, he couldn't remember seeing any of them.

"What're you really writing about? The Bali Nine?" Like the Aussies, the Kiwis were outraged by the current Indonesian president's hard stance on drugs. The Bali Nine were Aussies who'd been jailed or executed for drug smuggling in spite of Australia's protest and diplomatic sanctions. True to his word, Widodo had given zero clemency.

"Should I write about it?"

"You should, mate. It's bullshit! Who does that bloke think he is?"

"Well, he was definitely sincere."

This brought the Kiwi up short. He seemed surprised, and then released a loud boisterous laugh. "You got me there, mate!"

Stag ordered another Bintang. His food arrived, and he and the Kiwi had a lively discussion of the American use of the word football.

When he was full, he stood and put all the rupiahs in his pocket onto the table.

"You looking for a party later, I can hook you up with some good *arak*," Malcolm said, referring to the Balinese liquor made from toddy palm leaves.

Stag told him he'd think about it, suddenly wondering if the guy was on his honeymoon at all and not an illicit *arak* dealer who specialized in selling tourists illegal alcohol laced with methanol.

For being inexpressibly beautiful, he thought, Bali could be a total shithole.

* * *

Stag took his time walking through the tourist section of Kuta. It
was like a cheesier version of Cancun but with more Aussies and
vomit. He stopped to observe a couple of Kiwi women—teenagers
pretty much—drunkenly wobble through a tee shirt shop that had
gems like *Back Door! No Baby!* and *What Part of Deep Throat Don't
You Understand?* He had to squelch the fatherly urge to put them in
a taxi and get them home.

He cut through a small quiet street, hoping it would be a shortcut
to the beach. There he would get a tuk-tuk and take a leisurely ride
back to his resort. But when he got halfway, he had the distinct
feeling he was being followed.

From a plate-glass reflection, he recognized the flash of neon orange in the Hawaiian shirt that the man Malcolm had worn.

It could be coincidence.

But he doubted it.

Ducking into a dead-end alley, abandoned save for the copious
amounts of trash picked through and discarded even by the street
children, he waited, Glock in hand.

"Who the fuck are you working for?" he demanded, cheered by
the surprise on the Kiwi's face as he stood in the street facing him.

"Ease up, mate!"

"How did you find me? GPS? Or is the word out to look for a
white guy with a limp?" Stag readjusted his finger on the trigger.

"Whoa! I dunno what you're talking about!" Malcolm took several steps toward him. "Just thought you might want a little something better than *arak*. Let me show you." Malcolm pulled
something out of the back of his cut-offs.

Stag barely registered the glint of metal before a shot rang out.
The Kiwi slammed into the wall of the alley, then dropped, stone

cold dead in a pile of polychrome plastic. A bullet went clean though his head. His Kel-Tec handgun had skittered over to his left and now lay atop a pile of blown-out flip-flops and Snickers wrappers.

The only problem was Stag hadn't shot him. Someone else had.

His hackles up, Stag stood motionless, unable to find a hiding place in the alley. He waited, expecting. But seconds passed.

Nothing came.

He could hear crowds gathering outside of various shops along the street, everyone curious about the gunshot. He shoved the Glock into his waistband and slowly made his way out of the alley. With his nerves on fire, he casually made his way down the street. He was long gone before the first siren.

CHAPTER THIRTY-NINE

BACK AT HIS hotel, Stag tried to figure out what had happened. But nothing made sense. Had he somehow, someway acquired a guardian angel? It was hard to believe Portier could fit that role, but if Portier wanted him dead, he'd be dead. Since Portier wanted him alive for now, he was going to be protected.

So who the hell was the Kiwi working for? NATO? He doubted it. They weren't in the business of assassination, nor would they want him dead with that bomb out there for anyone to find. No, the only conclusion he could come to was there were players in this game he didn't know yet, but he had no doubt he would meet again. The notion didn't set well. He had enough to worry about.

Shrugging off the stress, he decided to keep working. After he booked a flight back to Berlin, he messaged Jake to see if he was finally set up on WhatsApp.

When Jake called, Stag was sitting beneath the palm-thatched over-water lanai, still enjoying the sunset.

"Stag?" Jake's voice came through. The fuzzy video grew crisp. "Wow! Look at that!" the older man exclaimed.

"How are you, Jake? See what technology can do for you?"

"There's three feet of snow here and there you are, being a beach bum. That water behind you—is that the South China Sea?"

"Indian Ocean."

"Beautiful. Just beautiful." Jake took a moment to appreciate the picture, then he looked down at something. "I've got that research for you."

Stag could hear the trepidation in Jake's voice. But right now, he couldn't comfort him.

"Okay. There were three WWII-era atomic bombs: Trinity, Little Boy, and Fat Man. They all used uranium 235, but if the Germans had a nuclear device, it most likely involved a gun-type bomb like the one that took out Hiroshima."

"Why is that?"

"Because, unlike the other two, Little Boy didn't require plutonium. Plutonium is man-made. It needs a cyclotron and a good bit of work to make it. And that's a lot of people who might know about what they're up to. If Heydrich had the Katanga deposit of U-235, that's all that would be needed to make a Hiroshima-type device."

"Then he really could have kept the lid on it."

"Yes," Jake answered. "With his unexpected death, information got lost perhaps and buried or bombed, and now we don't know what the hell he had or where it might be."

"How big would this thing be? What would it look like?"

"I would venture to say it would be smaller than Little Boy, but not much. Less than ten feet long. A bit less than 9000 lbs. Aluminum casing."

It was horrifyingly small. Stag could hardly get his head around the fact that it could take out a city. The world's nuclear arsenal was thousands of times stronger than Little Boy, but its use was deterrent only. A rogue bomb could change all that forever.

"There's one very unsettling aspect about this type of bomb, Stag. Being a gun-type, Little Boy used one firing mechanism, while Trinity and the Nagasaki bomb used implosion from several coordinated blasts surrounding the atomic core—much more complicated."

Stag gnawed on the inside of his cheek. "I'm not following you. Sorry. This whole nuclear stuff is Greek to me."

"Let me explain the whole thing in a nutshell. Nuclear material in and of itself isn't explosive. The blast of an atom bomb is set off by traditional explosives. They, in turn, force the nuclear material into a collision with itself. That, in turn, creates the chain reaction that causes the immense scale of an atomic detonation."

"Okay. I get it."

"The trouble with this gun-type lying around decaying somewhere isn't in the nuclear material. A leak of nuclear material isn't great for the environment but it's not Hiroshima. No, the problem is that a gun-type bomb takes much less sophistication and luck to detonate it. It doesn't require a coordination of several explosives as in the Nagasaki bomb. That was an implosion device. No, a gun-type, only requires one. There's a very high level of chance that it could detonate on its own. A fall could do it. Static electricity from lightning could do it."

Stag's stomach knotted. "Jesus."

Jake continued. "I took a lot of comfort in the fact that the early bombs the USA had were very high maintenance. The trigger mechanism used a battery that only lasted about a month before the entire device had to be disassembled and the battery recharged." He paused. "I was thinking this gave it a good chance of being a dud, with the battery dead."

"Yes, that is good news."

"Uh, well, not really. My research definitely points to Heydrich having the intelligence network to make a 'wooden bomb'."

"A wooden bomb? Why the fuck would they make a nuke out of wood?"

"It's not made of wood. It's a term they started using in the fifties when the US desired less high-maintenance atomic bombs. The military wanted bombs that could sit on a shelf for years; decades even, like a plank of wood, inert and ready to go. Sandia Laboratory couldn't figure how to make bombs with a shelf life of more than thirty days because their batteries died." Jake frowned. "So Sandia began to study the war interrogations of the German scientists that made the V-2 rockets for the Nazis."

"What'd they find?" Stag hated to even ask. He sure as fuck knew he wouldn't like the answer.

"Georg Otto Erb. During his interrogation, he revealed how the molten salt battery works. It can't be recharged or reused, but you don't really need that on an atomic device. You only need to use it once."

"How long's the shelf life of this battery?"

"Conceivably, centuries. Until the salts completely evaporate, which, as you know, takes a damn long time."

Stag was speechless. Heydrich might not have gotten his hands on this kind of technology early enough to make use of it. But then again, he might have. His fingers were in every pie in the Reich. Walter Schellenberg, Head of Foreign Intelligence of the Third Reich, described Heydrich as "the hidden pivot around which the Nazi régime revolved." Himmler wrote Heydrich about Heisenberg, the lead scientist of the German nuclear weapon project, telling him not to lose or silence Heisenberg. There was no doubt Heydrich knew everything.

In which case, there was a bomb out there, armed and ready to go. "Wooden."

"I know you don't want to hear this, Stag, but I think you're going to have to go to the authorities with this information. This thing needs to be in the hands of those who can disarm it."

"I still don't know where it is." He didn't mention the fact that he still didn't know who to trust. Especially after the Kiwi.

"What do you think happened to it?"

"I think Heydrich was having it moved somewhere. For his own personal leverage, frankly. The guy wasn't selfless, and he wasn't stupid. If he thought this weapon could be brought under his sole control, he would do everything he could to make sure that happened."

"But where could he hide it? Salt mine?"

"I have a map. At least, I think that's what it is. The references are to diamonds, though. Not a bomb. Frankly, I don't know if it pertains to this at all."

"Industrial diamonds, perhaps? Used for making the bomb fittings?"

"Maybe. I've thought of that. I've got to get back to Germany."

"I'll meet you there."

Stag let out a long breath of air. "I have to tell you, Jake, I'm not making any friends with this. It's dangerous."

"You need some help. And I'm the only one old enough to keep his mouth shut."

Stag snorted. "You're not making this easy."

"I'll beat you to Berlin."

"You probably will." Stag paused. "Thanks, Jake."

"If this really is what we fear it is, we're going to need a lot of help. God save us."

CHAPTER FORTY

STAG WAS ON the plane back to Singapore when she took the seat next to him. He couldn't actually say he was surprised. No matter how much he covered his tracks, he was, after all, an amateur.

"How does it feel, Mr. Maguire, to be the most sought-after man on the planet?"

He looked at her, her thin vintage suit, this time in white cotton, set off the faint suntan. Angelika Aradi had followed him to Bali.

"You're the only one who can find me. Why is that?" Stag now realized how odd it was for a flight from Bali to Singapore to be almost empty. He wondered if Ms. Aradi had managed to buy most of the tickets so they could speak.

"My father was a pickpocket in Hungary, my mother was Bosnian." She smiled darkly. "They both gave me skills not necessarily found in those assigned to my job."

"And what job would that be? Spy? Assassin? NATO-destroying subcontractor? What do you do, Ms. Aradi? In fact, what the fuck does Tarnhelm even do?" His guard was up. She was a singular woman. He feared her and was fascinated by her in equal measure.

She raised one eyebrow. "You don't know?"

"No. Enlighten me."

"Tarnhelm starts wars. There's money in that, don't you see?"

He rubbed his jaw. "Yeah, I got that."

"What Tarnhelm does is deal in secrets. The enemy is the truth. Truth makes people very hard to control."

"Then count me as the enemy."

"They already have."

"How much do they pay you to start wars?"

"I'd rather they pay me to stop them. But right now, my fee is my daughter's life. She's in a study. Cancer-free." She paused. "She's not yet five years old."

Stag had nothing against a little kid, particularly one with cancer, but it didn't settle well that Tarnhelm had sicced this woman on him only to find out she was a mama grizzly in disguise. How did you ever win a round with a mother protecting her cub?

"I guess there's no point in offering you a bribe then," he bit out.

"Mr. Maguire—Stag—they think you know where the bomb is. Once they get your information and find the bomb, Tarnhelm will sell it and kill you."

"I'll be happy to take the information to my grave then."

"That's their worst fear."

"I know. So go tell them." Stag's anger was rising. "And fuck off."

She stared at him. "You need to trust someone."

"And I'm going to trust you?"

"No. But I know someone you can trust at NATO—"

"What? Are you telling me you're some kind of 'double agent'? Tarnhelm by day, NATO by night? Bullshit."

"What I'm telling you is that Tarnhelm is very powerful, more than most of the world knows. Its tentacles are everywhere. But you can trust my contact—"

"How do I know the person you refer to is not reporting back to Tarnhelm for a nice set-aside?"

She didn't toss back a smug answer.

Finally, she said what sounded a little too much like the truth. "Because I don't want my daughter in Tarnhelm's world, that's why." Her words were calm. "She's fought too hard. She's too pure. I may be filthy from what I've had to do, but I'm telling you the truth. I work for Portier. He is the one who paid for the study that cured my daughter. I have an allegiance to him. But I don't want my daughter in a world where nuclear arms are bought and sold to the highest bidder."

He stared at her. His back was up. She was good. Damn good. He almost believed her.

"Do you really understand what you're dealing with?" she said. "A rogue nuclear device with the force of a Hiroshima, to the highest bidder? Untraceable to any nation, group, or corporation? I can't think of anything more coveted on this earth except immortality."

He still said nothing.

"You're in deep. You're going to need allies. And you don't know who to trust."

"I sure as fuck don't trust you. According to Interpol, you're wanted for questioning concerning the death of a NATO official."

It was her turn for silence. But she didn't look surprised by his accusation. If anything, she just looked more weary. Like she'd heard it all and seen it all.

"Here's the contact." She handed him a business card. "He's expecting you at any time."

"How do you keep finding me when all the rest can't?"

"Tarnhelm has face-recognition spy satellites, but you can't use it in subways or buildings. Sure, they've hacked into most Visa and MasterCard networks, but they can't trace cash. Sometimes, like the military, they find themselves in love with the technology and fail to get the man on the ground to do the old-fashioned legwork." Her hand slid to the part in his jacket. He looked down. There was the micro GPS he'd suspected she'd put in his sleeve. Her brushing against him on the Pariserplatz was just a diversion for the other hand to slip the GPS between his buttons.

"If I have to kill you in order to save my daughter, I will kill you." She rose from her seat when the captain put on the seat belt sign for their approach into Singapore. "Do everything you can to prevent that."

The plane's lighting lit the wasting beauty on her face, and she turned and walked to the rear of the plane.

* * *

"Stag!" Jake called out from the lobby.

Stag had never been so happy to see someone in his life. He went to him as fast as he could through the expanse of the Berlin Sony Center.

"The apartment's upstairs. Let me take your bag." Stag gripped the older man's shoulder in camaraderie. They walked through the enormous complex just south of the Tiergarten. Stag had found the place on Airbnb.

When they had settled into the stark, modern two-bedroom, Jake was the first to speak. "I've got the Königssee information. There's a historian there—a Herr Professor Hoening—I've already spoken to him. He says there have been rumors of Nazi stash around Königssee since late '42. But he was adamant that there was nothing in the lake. It's too clear and too easy to explore. It's a dead end."

"Maybe it's not the Königssee. Maybe I'm off-base on that one." Stag frowned.

"Perhaps, but there's a lot of abandoned military equipment that was there at the end of the war. He said most of it has been picked off, but there are a few places in the mountains inaccessible. They've been left virtually intact."

"I need to go there. But first, I have to figure out if I have all the pieces in Berlin. There's an apartment here . . . " Stag's voice wandered off. He still couldn't figure out what bothered him about it. "I think the first thing to do is have you get over your jet lag. Then dinner tonight. With an acquaintance."

"Acquaintance?"

"Yes. I don't really trust him, but I think he just may tell us the truth. Besides, I'm kind of running out of friends in Berlin."

Jake nodded, then headed to his bedroom to rest.

* * *

"I am interested in an apartment, " Stag said into the new GoFone he'd bought. The number would be unrecognizable to Kronbauer and whoever might be tracing calls at the Dresdenhof, but he hoped Kronbauer would recognize his American accent and voice even though he spoke German.

There was a long pause at the other end of the line.

"I am sorry. We have nothing available," Kronbauer said slowly.

"I would like to meet with someone anyway. If in the future—"

"I will pass your number on to the appropriate person. Thank you very much."

Stag heard the click at the end of the line. He wasn't sure if the message got through. The only thing he could do now was wait.

CHAPTER FORTY-ONE

"Nuclear weapons can be detonated using two different methods: ground burst and air burst. Hiroshima and Nagasaki were both air burst detonations. Their energy was more evenly distributed over a wider plot of ground. To kill the most people beneath it. However . . ." The retired US Army Lieutenant General "Red" Doyle paused, frowned, and continued. "Ground bursts are recommended when contamination by nuclear fallout is warranted. They are much more deadly. They can suck up enormous amounts of dust in their cloud and disperse it contaminated with alpha particles over many times the area of an air burst ignition."

Portier sat at his desk with the Alps on the horizon in the window behind him. It was a beautiful day, blue-skied and sunny, the first real spring weather they'd had. It didn't show on his expression, since he was in a foul mood. Urinating had become his Armageddon.

"Give me an example of the most destructive scenario of a single detonation, and then the least," he said wearily.

"Most destructive?" Doyle took a moment. "FEMA believes the most destructive would be a single ground burst to Nebraska."

"To take out missiles?"

"God no. A megaton ground burst to the most fertile part of the Great Plains would be a holocaust. Minimum effort, maximum effect. It would destroy America."

"Why?" Portier asked.

"The radioactivity from the dust cloud would disperse and contaminate the US's most vital food source—the Great Plains—not to mention Canada's."

"But surely that would dissipate. Look at Fukushima—"

"It wouldn't be in the ocean to dissipate. It would be in the air. Alpha particles everywhere."

"But what if Washington was hit—"

"It is a quaint notion to worry about military bases and cities being nuked. If they really want to destroy the US, take out the farms in a ground burst and pfffst! America being a superpower is gone. Not only would the famine adversely affect the US, but grain imports to Russia, China, and India would cease. Best estimates are that a billion people would starve worldwide." He shook his head. "No. Cities, missiles, a government, can all be refashioned and cobbled together. Surprisingly in a hurry. But the ability to feed ourselves? Americans can't eat iPhones. No matter how much the USA prides itself on technology and its economy, food is the linchpin. Otherwise the US just becomes Singapore, an island nation beholden to everybody and anybody to send them rice."

"I still don't understand. Nagasaki and Hiroshima have been occupied for decades with no radioactivity—"

"Yes. But again, air burst. Little Boy was detonated two thousand feet *above* Hiroshima. Therefore, limited alpha particle ingestion. No, what you don't understand is there are lots of different kinds of radiation. You can play with plutonium pellets with your bare hands if you like, not that risky. Alpha radiation is so weak it cannot penetrate a sheet of paper, let alone your skin. But ingest it? Just look up the pictures of the radium girls. They painted radial-luminescent paint on watch faces in the 1920s, and were instructed to point their brushes with their mouths. You do not want to die of radium eating out your bones. The alpha particles from a ground-burst detonation would be scattered across almost every food source. The food supply would be either tainted and have to be destroyed, or worse, it would be suspect, perhaps forever. No, that is what would destroy the US."

"Mmmm." Portier took the news with an inscrutable expression. "What is the least damaging scenario?"

"Air burst over a relatively arid, non-populated area. The Gobi Desert, Siberia, some place like that."

"Air burst or ground burst—are the bombs different?"

"Not at all. In fact, they are the same. The only difference is in the timer. Does it detonate early, while still in the air? Or do they allow the bomb explosives to detonate on impact, then triggering the nuclear reaction, kicking up the dust?"

"So, if I had a bomb, any bomb, I would be the one to choose how it is used?" Portier looked interested now.

"Exactly," said Red Doyle.

Portier contemplated this for a moment before saying, "I meant to congratulate you on your appointment. The President is getting a true patriot in his new cabinet."

Doyle nodded. "But we aren't going to tell him about this consult, are we? With all the problems on the staff with the Foreign Agents Registration Act, the last thing I need is for them to think I'm working outside the office."

"Our relationship predates your appointment," said Portier.

"Yes, but the libtards would have a field day if they got a whiff of impropriety."

"Yes, the . . . libtards." Portier smiled. Like he gave a shit.

"The bastards whine very loudly. Then hand over all their rights. I swear it's a mental disease," Doyle said with disgust.

"We want good relationships, General. With you and the rest of the incoming cabinet."

The general smiled. "You have quite an operation here, sir. When I was at Blackwater, we had the luxury of openly admiring you."

"I understand the constraints now. We will keep our secrets. After all, it's what we do," Portier offered.

"Yes. It's what we do," Doyle repeated, toasting him with his snifter of Henri IV cognac.

* * *

Kronbauer looked up expectantly. He sat in the Arema Cafe on the Birkenstrasse in Moabit, a nice little island of old-school refuge in the bustle of modern Berlin. The cafe was a butcher shop from the 1800s and now was a jewel of original art nouveau tile.

Stag sat down at the table.

"I don't have much time," Kronbauer said, looking at his watch.

Stag looked around. Kronbauer was too dressed up and fussy for the casual cafe, but it was the perfect place to meet. It was unlikely any of his rich cronies would happen in on them. It was this or stand on the street eating Döner Kebab.

"I was surprised you called me back. I don't take you for a spy," Stag said.

"By default, everyone who works with Tarnhelm is a spy," Kronbauer answered.

"Yeah. I got that." Which was why Dedman had the apartment in Sony Center and why he refrained from inviting Jake to their meeting. Tarnhelm didn't need to know about him. He'd been

pretty scrupulous in making sure there was no connection between them for Tarnhelm to sniff out. He didn't want Jake to go
the way of Harry. Ice and Micotil made a hellacious cocktail.

"Mr. Maguire, I am taking a chance meeting with you. Not only
do I value my job, but my neck as well."

"I think they've got a bomb. A really bad bomb."

Kronbauer looked unsurprised. "Certainly, they protect that
apartment as if it held the Holy Grail."

"They will sell it to the highest bidder. Unlikely anyone will
bother detonating it in Berlin—"

"My son is a lobbyist for Krupp in Washington, DC."

Stag suddenly knew where Kronbauer's disjointed loyalties came
from.

"We're all kind of spread out these days, aren't we? Hard to decide
what place to protect and what to let go."

"I don't get involved in the workings of Tarnhelm. But that apartment . . . Well, it has me worried."

"I need to get back inside of it. There's something I'm missing
there. If I could figure out what, I think I could solve this whole
problem." Stag silenced as the waitress came with their drinks.
When she left, he said, "I'd like to know the history of the place."

Kronbauer frowned. "There actually isn't much to tell. My family's been maintaining it with the Dresdenhof since before the war.
The only one who had any real experience with the occupants was
my grandfather. He'd met the woman in the portrait."

"Isolda Varrick?"

"Yes. But as I'm sure you know, the apartment didn't actually be-
long to her. It was Heydrich's. He kept her, you see."

"Yes."

"There are only two things I know about the last days of the occupants. My grandfather spoke of these stories in hushed tones with

the promise they were not to be repeated. He was very loyal, you see. SD himself. Quite patriotic."

Stag nodded.

"My grandfather had a bit of a crush on Isolda, I believe. As a child, I can remember accompanying him on his inspections of the apartment. He would stand very still, for long moments, and stare at her portrait. Sometimes, I think there were tears in his eyes.

"The only thing I ever heard about her at all was that, one day, she went up to the apartment after greeting my grandfather at the concierge with *mausebär*, her little endearment for him—he loved the silly name because he was so smitten with her."

Kronbauer paused for effect. "*She never came back down.*"

Stag wasn't exactly shocked by the revelation. It could mean anything really. Where the SD was involved, people just disappeared. *Nacht und nabel.*

"The other story he told me concerned the mirror. When Heydrich had placed the empty apartment in his trust, he walked through it with my grandfather, pointing out how everything must be exactly maintained. Then he did the most unsettling thing. Heydrich caught the reflection of the portrait in the mirror that hung opposite. He stared into the mirror for a very long time. Then, in a rage, he drew his pistol, and fired the shot that shattered it."

The waitress returned to ask if they needed anything. Kronbauer politely waved her away. When she was gone, he leaned in and said, "The thing that got to my grandfather, you see, wasn't that he had to maintain the apartment, nor was it that he could never figure out what had happened to its occupant. I think deep down he half-dreamed Isolda Varrick would show up again, and be pleased her apartment was well cared for, and call him *mausebär*.

"No, the thing that ultimately placed a wedge between my grand-father and his patriotism to the SD was Heydrich's behavior. He was never sure if Heydrich was unhinged by the image of Isolda—or the image of himself."

CHAPTER FORTY-TWO

STAG WOKE WITH a start. This time, the trauma of Holly was fractured with shards of mirror, her last words echoing though his dreams, scratchy and far away. As if recorded on an old shellac 78.

He sat on the edge of the bed, his head in his hands, trying to wake up and pull himself out of the loop of his nightmare. He and Jake had stayed up late while Stag brought him up to speed on the diary, Tarnhelm, and all the strange happenings since they'd last seen each other. Now the comforting smell of freshly brewed coffee was wafting in. When he looked up, Jake appeared at his door with a steamy cup, in the same old wrinkled clothes he'd arrived in.

The one thing Jake could do was pack light.

"I thought I heard you. Rough night?" the older man said.

Stag grunted and gratefully accepted the mug.

"While you explore that strange apartment, I'll do a bit of research." Jake raised an eyebrow. "You never know what a little academic digging can turn up."

"Where the fuck do you start?" Stag asked, rhetorically.

"I think I should start at the German Resistance Memorial Center. We've got a rebel on our hands in Isolda Varrick. Maybe there's something there that can be useful."

"She probably deserves her own damned memorial. But I don't know that we'll ever even know her real name."

Jake said nothing. There was nothing to say.

* * *

Jake stood in the hall of the new exhibit at the German Resistance Memorial Center, in front of the glass display case of uniforms on the mannequins. There they were, the tailored uniforms of the rogues' gallery: the Gestapo, the SS, the SD. Letters in code, along with their translations, were posted along the narrow walls. To make for an eerie effect, the museum piped in the sound of people whispering in order to create the dread and paranoia one must have felt as a lone resister against the Third Reich.

Reading one letter, he went back and forth several times to the display case where the uniforms were. Something clearly bothered him. He stopped in front of the SD uniform, his gaze riveted to the left sleeve. He took as good a picture as he could with his GoFone, then he returned to the wall of letters, one in particular holding his attention. When the photo of it was taken, he hastily placed the phone back in his wrinkled khakis, zipped up his overcoat, and departed, not even noticing it had begun to rain until he was back in the apartment and it pelted against the large plate-glass windows.

* * *

Stag waited in the rear of the Dresdenhof for the service entrance to click. Dressed in workman's overalls and a toolbox he'd snagged from under the sink at the Airbnb, he couldn't shove down the trepidation tightening his throat. Kronbauer was cooperating, and for some strange reason, Stag had trusted him. Perhaps it was the recognition of a fellow conflicted soul, or perhaps it was just that he really was running out of options. But when the service door lock released, Stag knew he'd made the right choice. Kronbauer had done his part and gotten him back in. Now it was Stag's turn.

He stepped inside.

He held the key to 12A in one hand and the P-83 in the other. He met no one as he rode the service elevator. Inside the hallway, he found he didn't even need the key. Kronbauer had kindly left the door to 12A unlocked.

PART FIVE

Most of you know what it means when a hundred corpses are lying side by side, or five hundred, or a thousand. To have stuck it out, and at the same time—apart from exceptions caused by human weakness—to have remained decent fellows, that is what has made us hard. This is a page of glory in our history, which has never been written and is never to be written . . .

SS Reichsfuhrer Heinrich Himmler
in a secret speech about the extermination of
Jews in death camps to his men at Posen,
German-occupied Poland

CHAPTER FORTY-THREE

IT HAUNTED HIM. There was something wrong with the apartment, but every walk through was just like the last. There was the kitchen, the painter's nook, the portrait. Isolda's sensual bedroom of satin and lace, and her large bathroom, full of luxuries to pamper the body. Her clothes were still in the drawers of her bureau. The perfume bottle of *Je Reviens* still sat on her dressing table.

In the living room, the glass shards of the mirror twinkled on the rug, giving the room a surreal star shine in the morning light. In the bookcase, he perused the titles again, making note of the empty space where *Mein Kampf* had been.

If Isolda had come up to the apartment and been taken by the SD, they could have gotten her out of the apartment many ways without being seen. Kronbauer's grandfather could have just missed her exit, somehow. Perhaps he'd been distracted by the agents. Perhaps he'd just stepped away as they escorted her through the lobby on their way to the Gestapo or the train station.

And yet, there was the niggling problem of what was missing. It was there at the edges of his conscious, ebbing and flowing like a tide, never quite still enough to be captured.

He went to the portrait and took it down. Between the stretcher bars and canvas, he checked for any silk messages stuck in there that others might have missed. There was nothing.

Slowly he sat down on the sofa that faced the wide-open double doors of the bedroom. Logically, he reviewed everything he knew. If she had come up to the apartment and was never seen to leave, then it was reasonable to wonder if she was still there. But where? The apartment was sumptuous but small. The spaces were all accounted for . . .

Except.

He stood, the realization running though him like a bolt of electricity. The bedroom, the bath, the bureau. All as they should be. But there was no wardrobe, and no closet. A woman of her means would have gowns and dresses. And goddamnit. A woman would have realized right away the closet was missing.

Stepping into the bedroom, he drew out the apartment's floor plan in his head. The bathroom door was off to the right, with the huge Biedermeier bureau on the wall to the right of it.

The bathroom didn't abut the living room wall. There was a space between them. Unless that space was taken up by the apartment next door, that was exactly where he figured a closet would be if the apartment had one.

He shoved the tall bureau aside, straining with its weight. Beyond, the plaster wall looked undisturbed. Not sure what there might be behind it, he got the toolbox he'd brought with him. He took out the large hammer and chisel, and went to the smooth plaster wall.

If there had been a closet there, perhaps he would find the outline. Perhaps there was even a hallway to an entirely new set of rooms. He wouldn't know until the plaster came off.

Working diligently, he cracked away at the plaster where he supposed a door might have been. The more he chipped away, the more damning the evidence. Finally, when all the plaster had been removed, he stepped back amongst the dust, and stood in awe at his finding. There was the outline of a doorway, its door missing. And in its place was a wall of red brick.

* * *

"The SD had its own salt mines, like much of the Reich's bureaucracy. They were acquired for document storage." Rikhardsson referred to the dossier in his hand. "After the war, everyone was looking for valuables. They still look for Nazi gold and such. But the real gold for the SD was its files. Heydrich kept these little cards on everyone. And he protected them fiercely."

"We have all the files, don't we?" Sadler asked, irritated and weary that he'd been summoned to Zurich again. He was getting damn tired of being a lapdog.

"Not even close," Portier said. "Between Heydrich's nefarious little file cards and then Ernst Kaltenbrunner, who took over after Heydrich's assassination, there's a lot we don't have."

"We have the Berghof Memo in which Heydrich tells the Führer about a shipment of documents to be stored somewhere in the area, but it's unclear where it is referring to. No other records survive that we know of."

"Do you know how big an area that is? Berchtesgaden is a national park, not to mention all the surrounding mountains." Portier was becoming annoyed as he so often did these days.

"And the fact that a lot of the entrances to these mines were dynamited in order to seal them when they knew the war was being lost. The chances of finding anything Heydrich might have hidden there is extremely slim." Rikhardsson, with his cold logic, irritated Portier further.

"If Maguire is in Berlin, it's because he knows something. We will find it. We have him covered," Sadler said.

"Unless we have another incident." Portier looked at Sadler.

Sadler didn't miss the reference. "We've recalled every agent that Vanderloos sent out."

"Every agent that you know of," Portier shot back.

Sadler looked extremely uncomfortable. Rikhardsson, too.

"This is chaos," Portier sighed. Wearily, he picked up his briefcase and buzzed for his car. "Until we have that bomb, I don't want anyone leaving Zurich."

"But I have several deals—" Sadler began.

"No one is leaving. If this thing's around, I want everyone to have the full incentive of it being found."

Sadler looked vaguely ill, as he usually looked.

Portier's assistant arrived at the door to walk him to his limo. After he was gone, Rikhardsson said, "Let's hope to God the thing is closer to Berchtesgaden than here."

"If it exists," Sadler snapped.

"Oh, it exists. Heydrich was power-hungry and no fool."

"Then let's hope it is nearer the North Sea."

"Portier won't bet on it."

"And why not?" Sadler clenched his jaw in frustration. "Why does he insist on staying here if there's a danger?"

"Because he doesn't care."

"Oh, he doesn't? The man with the million-dollar watch, every luxury, every comfort, doesn't care that he might one day be desperately licking the black rain off his briefcase in a search for water?"

"No, he does not."

"And why would that be?" Sadler couldn't control his anger any longer.

"Because he is dying," Rikhardsson said.

CHAPTER FORTY-FOUR

DREAD WEIGHED DOWN on him. Stag gripped the chisel and began removing the bricks. He vaguely wondered if others in the apartments around him could hear him banging, but he didn't stop. He was driven to see the other side.

The bricks piled up on the Aubusson rug, the dust swirled in the morning light. Slowly the hole became large enough for him to reach through.

He shoved his hand into the darkness beyond, and touched a strange, unexpected barrier. In the time it took him to draw back, horror slowly seeped into his blood. He knew what he'd found. Clawing, clinging hair; coarse black ropes of it; red, fuzzy piles of it; here and there, sprinkled with the barest wisps of caramel and blond. When he looked down at his hand, several baby curls clung to his fingers, the color of a fawn.

He found himself on his knees.

The strands of nameless victims were saved and matted into a felt, thick enough to form batting insulation for a German submarine. This was Heydrich's fitting end for his own U-boat. Not a sound would escape.

It took a long time for him to find the courage to stand, and pick up the hammer and chisel again. His heart hammered rebelliously in his chest.

God, he didn't want to know.

She was there in the corner of the closet. She'd mummified, and there were piles of hair around her where she must've clawed at the felt in moments of despair and terror. His heart seized up. He couldn't figure out which was worse at the moment: finding Isolda's body slumped down in the corner of a sealed tomb, or the fact that the very substance that had sealed her inside was the hair of a thousand murdered people.

He knelt down gently to look at her.

She wore the Blood Eagle on the ring finger of her right hand, as many Germans did when signifying a wedding ring. In her other hand, as if tossed in as an afterthought by her tormentor, was a note, perhaps the last she'd ever written, perhaps the thing that Heydrich had caught her with and sealed her fate, the silk hanging limply from her skeletal fingers. To him, it was as if she held out her death warrant.

He gently took the note from her and decoded it then and there. It was another attempt to reach the old man at the paint store. Perhaps he'd been her traitor all along; lost to history now. But she implored him to give the warning.

* * *

The diamonds did not go in the lake. I beg you to reach Shulte and tell him the information is wrong! They ran off the road and went down the mountain to land on a ledge. I've no location yet. Do not search the lake. It is not there. It is on the mountain!

* * *

She gave no more pleas for help in this one. She knew.

* * *

"I'm sure of it," Jake said, sitting at the apartment table. "The museum's evidence was slight, but compelling. In our case, I think there can be no other conclusion."

Stag sat facing him, still stunned by his own discovery. The coffee in front of him had gone cold.

"Diamonds, don't you see? It always struck me as frivolous to be worried about some diamonds instead of a nuke." Jake, as if in nervous reflex, emptied his cold cup in the sink and poured him another. "But this answered it. I saw it in the underground letters. I'd never heard it before."

Jake went to his phone and brought up a picture.

"This is what they were talking about. It was slang used to refer to the SD, the Sicherheitsdienst. Heydrich's security service. The SD's uniform patch was the initials SD framed in a diamond."

Stag looked down at the photo. There it was, a distinct black diamond as the background with the embroidered letters SD in white. A patch identifying the wearer as one of Heydrich's goons. Worn on the left sleeve of the uniform. So obvious that, even in the portrait they had of Heydrich, the SD lozenge patch was up front and center.

"The diamonds in the lake was an oblique reference to the SD men tapped to secure the transport of this bomb. It was her code way of saying they were taken out by the crash," Jake said. "All the diamonds she referred to in the diary are SD men. She was surrounded by them. Watching them, reporting on them. The goddamned bomb and Heydrich were surrounded by them!"

Stag took another long moment to absorb what Jake had told him.

"We've got to reassess that diary now," Jake continued. "I suspect the bomb went into a cliff somewhere. It's probably still there. The transporting was probably so secret that when the truck had an accident, no one knew about it but perhaps Heydrich. Then he was assassinated before he could do anything. The diamonds have all been a red herring." Jake sat down, facing him. Ready for his conclusions.

"Not all of them," Stag said. He stuck his fingers in his coat pocket and gingerly placed the Blood Eagle on the table like it was radioactive.

CHAPTER FORTY-FIVE

STAG FOUND HIMSELF driving another rented Porsche to Königs-see in the afternoon. Jake had acquired it to keep the trail off of Stag, just in case. To be completely sure they weren't leaving a trail, they bought new clothes, luggage, and phones. Now they sped south, a seven-hour drive that would put them in around nine.

He couldn't get his mind off what he'd found in 12A. He'd washed his hands a thousand times, yet the sensation of the clinging hairs was still there.

Heydrich had proven to be strangely sentimental. When he'd found out he was harboring his own U-boat, he'd buried her like one. He'd had her encased in soundproofing, never to be found at the bottom of his own private sea. Then he'd demanded everything be kept intact, perhaps, because he'd had plans to visit with her there. Sit beside her grave, as it were, to work out whatever grief actually could touch that ice-cold heart. Perhaps he'd even morbidly thought to relive his times with her in the exactitude of the surroundings. Stag had no doubt that Heydrich vengefully would have had the entire apartment building removed had he lived long enough. But instead, he'd sunk his little U-boat, encased her in secrecy, and made the rest of the world go insane chasing his red herring. His wishes had posthumously developed into the trust that Tarnhelm received after the war. That had become their mandate: the apartment was never to be changed. Nothing was to be moved. Walls were not knocked on because they were looking for his secret weapon and convinced that the clues lay in the positioning of things. Because why else leave everything so precisely the same? The SD dealt in secrets. They were good at keeping quiet. Tarnhelm was driven to find the secret in the apartment to the point of madness. To the point of even fooling themselves. What they didn't know was that the bomb was the incidental enigma wrapped in the riddle of the apartment.

"Have you given thought to Herr Professor Hoening? What we should ask him?" Jake broke into his thoughts, referring to the historian he'd spoken to earlier who lived in the area.

His voice kicked Stag back into the here and now. "What's your idea?" he asked, shifting gears on an incline. "Is it even in the mountains around the Königssee? It might be somewhere else entirely."

"I think showing the drawing of the lake to Herr Hoening will prove useful. Asking around for Nazi diamonds is very different from asking around for a military truck that crashed down a mountainside."

"We've got to find someone who knows those mountains." Stag shifted up.

"Hoening's the place to start. We can see him first thing in the morning." Jake smiled. "He's just like me, an old guy with plenty of time for questions, not to mention for nutjobs that crawl out of the woodwork."

Stag chewed on the inside of his mouth. "I'm glad you have had time for it. I don't want to do this all alone. Diamonds were one thing, this is completely another now."

Jake grew solemn. "Yes. This is quite another. Quite another."

* * *

"I think it's the Königssee," Hoening said, looking down at the photocopy of the silk key. "What does this say? Some is in German, and some in Martian."

Herr Professor Hoening was a big, smiley bear of a man with a white beard like Santa Claus. He was a retired professor like Jake from the University of Munich, one of Germany's oldest. Behind the man's impressive girth was a gothic bookcase overflowing with tomes on European history of the 20th century. They couldn't have found a better man to ask.

"Are you on the hunt for Nazi treasure, *ja?*" he asked, a twinkle in his eye.

"We're really more interested in finding the truck, if you really want to know. The truck might have museum value."

Stag was impressed with Jake's save. He was beginning to lie as well as Stag.

"I know the US military cleared this area very thoroughly. Looking for the *Alpenfestung*—the Alpine Redoubt—you see?" Hoening went to the bookcase and searched for a moment. He found what he was looking for: a US military manual of Nazi areas around Berchtesgaden that were either cleaned out or destroyed.

"Here it is." Hoening placed the book on his desk and pointed to a section. "*The US policy of ordnance reduction requires all military personnel to take possession of any and all enemy weapons and hardware, where feasible.*"

"What if it wasn't feasible—what if the truck had gone in the lake or was found on some inaccessible site like a cliff face or something?" Stag asked.

"Then it may have been abandoned. After the war, when things were very difficult, if it had been left behind by the US as not salvage-worthy, the locals would have taken it for scrap."

"Even if it was inaccessible?"

"Very little here is inaccessible to our climbers. They're the best in the world." He smiled. "But, of course, an entire truck might be difficult, if not impossible, to get completely off the mountain."

"Do you know any good climbers? One that really knows the area?" Jake asked.

"Ah, there's a fine fellow just down the street quite expert in the mountains here. He's an American, but his grandfather was a climber from here and he decided to come back."

"Would it be too much to ask for his name?"

"Certainly, I shall give it to you." The Herr Professor got out an elaborately old-fashioned fountain pen and wrote it down.

CHAPTER FORTY-SIX

THE MESSAGES CAME in tandem. Updates. Portier unfolded them, studied them, and burned them. His patience was strung as taut as piano wire. He had his two best agents on it: one whom he trusted, one whom he did not.

Wincing, he endured the needle-stick of morphine as his nurse injected him. He'd fought the use of it as long as he could, but some days it was too much. Between the pain and the exhausting, eternal urge to urinate, he was in hell, and the only antidote, this.

Now he embraced the surge in his veins. The sweet relief. Elusive no more.

"Mr. Sadler, sir," his secretary said as she watched the nurse depart. "On line four."

Portier picked up the phone. They spoke in abstracts, but the meaning was clear.

"The client is getting anxious. I'd like to give them encouraging news," Sadler said.

Portier's normal annoyance was now chilled by the blessings of the poppy. "Tell them to be patient. They, of all people, know we must do this right."

"Of course. But they are concerned by the lack of information."

"Information? They dare ask for information?" Portier smiled, the first time in a while. "Tell them I've got information for them:

Russia has 1600 missiles capable of reaching DC. Shall we please the client? Or shall we fuck this up and topple empires?"

"I understand. I'll do what I can to appease them."

"You do that," said Portier, slamming down the phone.

With his heart rate up, the morphine blossomed. And it was pleasant, really, these thoughts of his: One colossally stupid, paying client; one target; one domino; one Armageddon. And it was all under his control. Once the bomb was found, he could do as he wished. And let the world be as damned as he was.

* * *

"See? It's there. Can you see now?" Mac Killburn stabbed his stone-battered finger in the direction below them.

Stag, Jake, and Mac were parked at an overlook, where the mountain seemed to fall away just beyond the car rail straight into the clear waters of the Königssee.

Mac continued, "Right there on the ledge with the scrawny evergreen in front of it—"

Stag took a sharp intake of breath. He suddenly made out the shape of the truck that blended into the stone face. It was unnaturally hunkered down, like a bird settled in a nest, an outline of rust and flaking paint. It had suffered a terrific fall from the road. Anyone inside would have been killed on impact.

"You sure you want to go down there?" Mac asked, eyeing the harnesses and ropes still slung around his shoulders. "I mean, with your leg and all . . ."

"I want to go." Stag turned to Jake. "You fine up here?"

Jake looked a bit unsure. "You know, maybe I'm not so old, after all. Perhaps, you should let me give it a try instead. I could—"

"I'm going," Stag said, not letting him finish.

Mac encouraged. "I'll belay. It's really not a bad climb, just looks—"

"Bad," Stag finished, slinging his metal-scarred leg over the car rail and fastening himself into the harness.

"Just take it slow. You've got time. I do this with kids all the time." Mac gave him a smile.

Stag looked down at the cliff, then back at Jake's grim face. Then he planted his ass in the harness and began the descent.

* * *

Interpol was quiet when Troost arrived. The few agents still there on a late Sunday evening were absorbed in work in their cubicles, eager to get their paperwork filed and be gone.

He closed the door to his office and settled down at his desk, the flashing screen on his laptop signaling new email. But he had nothing to give right now.

Where was Angelika Aradi, and why was she so hard to find? He had one job. And for the life of him, he couldn't figure out what her next move would be.

The frustration built inside him. Scanning messages, scanning email, he wanted to put his fist through the computer screen.

And no Maguire. He was on his own again, roaming around, doing God-knows what for God-knows who, and he'd lost track of him in Bali. Now Aradi was back in Berlin, and just as he'd begun his tracking, she'd disappeared, as if in a puff of smoke.

It was all getting on his nerves.

He looked up at the cheap tropical isle poster and thought of everything he wanted to do, instead of sitting in the beige little world of public service. And failing his last assignment was not the way to go about it, he fumed, picking up the phone.

"Troost here. Interpol," he said into the phone. "I need to step up the information on Maguire. Have you gotten the latest report from the US?"

He listened.

"So they did get the FISA warrant on Aradi?" He suddenly relaxed. Now it was going to get a little easier. The Foreign Intelligence Surveillance Act allowed the US to monitor agents of foreign powers if the court deemed them worthy of a warrant. Should US citizens be tangentially caught up in conversations with monitored foreigners, it was permissable to surveille them, too. Now they could get everything on Aradi. And perhaps on Maguire.

"Send me everything you have? Great. Thank you. Thank you," he repeated, almost unwilling to hang up. He wanted to savor the news.

* * *

Stag was gritting his teeth by the time his feet were on level ground again. His leg, torqued and twisted from balancing on the rock-face, throbbed like an SOB. Just above him, Mac was lowering himself on a solo device. Up top, Jake peered down, his white hair blending into the gray, overcast sky.

"You did fine!" Mac exclaimed, unclipping his carabineer.

"Yeah. Except going up's the hard part." Stag released his harness from the ropes. Then he walked to the end of the ledge where the truck had humped down after falling from the road decades ago.

"It's an old one, all right. Before '44 is what they say." Mac followed him. "Not all here. The bumpers and the passenger door were taken for scrap. After the war, I imagine. Nobody would bother unless they were desperate." He nodded to the climb back to the road.

"Have you ever heard what it was carrying?" Stag asked, touching the rusty side, then staring at his hand and wishing they'd thought to bring a Geiger counter.

"Naw. No stories I've ever heard. It did have a gun up top at one time though. It's long gone."

Stag stared through the rear doors, cracked open on wonky, rusted hinges. The truck bed was busted out as if eaten from underneath.

"Must've had something there at one time," he said.

"Yeah. Never seen a gas tank like that."

"Gas tank?" Stag asked.

"The kids were fooling around on the truck, and with the bed rusted out so bad, the tank fell out right beneath them."

Stag felt a strange electric current begin to hum through him. "What happened to it? It must've been a helluva tank, judging from the hole in the bed."

"Shit yeah. A big one. Went right over the edge there." Mac pointed to the edge of the cliff next to the truck.

Stag went to the edge, unsteady and reluctant. He didn't know what he would find, but instincts raged.

"Yep, went right over the edge. I figured it'd bounce right down into the lake, but it jammed itself into a crevice. See it? Right down there."

Both men peered over the steep edge.

There it was. A great big aluminum "tank," powdered with white rust, nestled in the crevice like a fallen chick from the nest.

A perfect ampoule of horror.

PART SIX

"I can pursue my enemies even from the tomb."
—Reinhard Heydrich to Hans Gisevius,
German Military Intelligence Officer

CHAPTER FORTY-SEVEN

"It DIDN'T HAVE a tail kit assembly. No fins. I didn't see any wires, but..." The words dwindled. Stag didn't have to see the wires to know. It was Trinity, Hiroshima, Nagasaki. Ready, aim, fire.

"Good God," Jake murmured, shaking his head. They sat in a heated outdoor cafe overlooking the Königssee. Tourists mingled beneath the torchieres, laughing.

"It must've been too far to get a crane in to remove it. If the 'tank' wasn't recognizable as ordnance, the military just left it to rot. "

"Thinking all along it was useless."

Stag rubbed his eyes.

"How's your leg?" Jake looked at him sympathetically.

Stag snorted. No more needed to be said on that. He'd been lucky to get his ass up from the mountain.

"You know Mac's going to wonder about what we were looking for. We've got to call the authorities," Jake said.

"I know. I just don't know who. We can't just walk in off the street with this. They'll think we're crazy and have us hauled off. But something has to be done quickly. No telling what Tarnhelm knows." He looked around, paranoid.

"I could call up some old colleagues—"

"Take too long."

"Dare we trust the man on the card Aradi gave you?"

Stag quelled that idea with just a look.

"Interpol. That's where to begin." Troost had left a slew of messages asking him to call him, but he hadn't gotten them till he had returned to Berlin and was able to safely turn the Maguirephone on and place the old SIM card into it.

But now, in a new location, he would use a fresh GoFone. With the tracking on iCloud, he wasn't taking any chances.

"Should we take a stroll then?" Jake asked meaningfully. There was no thinking about this kind of phone call anywhere near people or buildings. Just in case.

"Yeah. Let's take a stroll."

*　*　*

Troost saw the strange number come up on his phone. Immediately he answered it. "Troost here."

"I need to talk."

"Mr. Maguire? Yes. Of course. Of course."

"Not on the phone. In private."

"All right. Shall I meet you or do you want to come in?"

"Meet me tomorrow. First thing. At Kehlsteinhaus."

"*Kehlsteinhaus?*" Troost wondered if he'd heard correctly.

"Yes. Do you know it?"

Troost barely knew what to say. It was such an absurd question. "There's no private road going there, Mr. Maguire. It's a two-hour hike from the town of Berchtesgaden."

"You can take a bus from the Document Center."

"Yes, yes, I know that, but may I ask, why there? Are you in Berlin? Surely there are better—"

"I'm traveling, but I can be there at ten tomorrow morning."

"I see."

"It's been opened for the spring. I don't expect it will be crowded."

"I suppose I shall meet you there, then."

Maguire ended the call.

Slowly, Troost put down his phone.

Kehlsteinhaus. *Kehlsteinhaus.* That was crazy. If Maguire wanted Interpol to meet him in such a strange place, there must be news. Shrugging off his surprise, he picked up his phone. It was time to inform the higher-ups that there was movement.

He looked at the sad poster of the palm tree and suddenly felt like whistling. Maybe he was going to retire there, after all.

* * *

Stag put his phone in his parka pocket and looked at Jake.

"He's coming?"

Stag nodded.

"Should we trust him?"

"I don't know." He pulled out the card that Angelika Aradi had given him. For a moment he stared at it, then out at the snow-covered mountains and the beautiful thawed emerald Königssee. He had to go to the authorities, but Tarnhelm made it very difficult to know which ones to trust. Aradi worked for Tarnhelm, that much was certain, but her remarks on the plane from Bali were hard to shake off: *I don't want my daughter in Tarnhelm's world.*

Maybe she meant it. Maybe not. But how could he take the chance?

He shoved the card back in his pocket. Jake motioned to head back. It was going to be another eventful day tomorrow, no doubt. Stag followed him, his mind on the meeting in the morning.

Kehlsteinhaus. Few relics remained of Hitler's Berchtesgaden retreat. Martin Borman had had Kehlsteinhaus—or as it was more
famously known in English, the Eagle's Nest—built for Hitler's fiftieth birthday. Mussolini even supplied the red marble fireplace
mantel for it. It was perched on a high ridge of a mountain so precarious twelve men died trying to build it under Albert Speer's
direction.

Hitler only visited it fourteen times.

It was a fitting place for the end—or the beginning—of World
War III.

CHAPTER FORTY-EIGHT

ANGELIKA WATCHED THE men get into the Porsche and drive out of the park. She followed behind in a staid BMW, not bothering to pass the tourist buses in order to keep up; she would find them anyway. She had them on her tracking, and they were headed to the Hotel Edelweiss. She would meet them there.

The mountains were brute indigo hulks as she slalomed the curves in the road. Her phone released an encrypted ping. She looked down at the message.

The time was running out. The buyers were getting anxious. Worse, Portier was losing patience.

She pulled into the valet area. It was time she and Stag Maguire have one final talk.

* * *

Stag couldn't say he was surprised to see her. Given the terrible timing of what they'd just found on that mountain, he was stunned to see her, horrified, afraid, yes. Surprised, not really. She had tricks that he just couldn't know about.

She sat waiting for him in the bar, her red coat tossed on a chair, her blond hair like a beacon. He took note that she was drinking white wine. He himself was going to order a scotch; he sure as fuck needed one.

"Ah, Ms. Aradi," he said, slipping into the banquette next to her. He ordered his scotch neat, then said, "There is no GPS on me."

"No."

"Then how do you keep finding me?"

"The human heart is a source of electromagnetism with its own unique pattern. It can be detected if you have the right scientific instruments. Expensive technology—not many have access to it— but once we've captured your particular signal, we can find you, if you're not too far away."

"That explains the gaps."

"It's cutting edge and extremely costly to implement, and like everything else, not perfect. We can't always use it. Best to have multiple technologies." She sipped her wine. "This is your second trip to the Königssee. Something have your attention?"

"Perhaps."

"Tomorrow this entire area will be crawling with Tarnhelm people. Have you thought of giving my friend a call?"

He wondered if she'd really been unable to track him to the mountain where the bomb lay. If he was alive, it seemed the only answer.

His scotch arrived, and he wanted to gulp it the hell down.

"There are a lot of people who want to get their hands on this thing," he said, putting down his empty glass.

"Stag—"

He interrupted. "You haven't told Tarnhelm you're following me, have you?"

She didn't answer.

"You're going rogue."

"I've always been rogue. My father was a Hungarian Catholic who married a Bosnian Muslim. Do you think this helped him in the genocide in Srebrenica? He was rounded up as Muslim and murdered." She paused. "This taught me that stereotypes are useful when you are trying to sell something. It's a scary thought, isn't it? The same techniques they use to sell you Oreos can sell you on mass murder."

"Tarnhelm's business is deciding who to murder, and who to sell the murder to." He motioned to the bartender for another. "Glad we got that straight. I mean, why go rogue if you've embraced the business model?"

"I've told you. This is about more than myself and Tarnhelm."

"Yes," he snarled. "This is about an entire section of the world going up in a mushroom cloud. Not to mention the politics and retaliation that will follow."

"Which is why I'm trying to save my daughter." She seemed to tamp down her emotions by fingering the hole in her sweater. She was wearing a beautiful black and white ski sweater with woven leather buttons that looked like it was out of the fifties. Of course, it was moth-eaten.

He watched her worry the little moth-hole. Her clothes were intentional. They needed *kintsukoroi*: golden repair. The Japanese would take a broken piece of pottery and mix the glue with gold dust. The vase or bowl would be an altogether new and beautiful object when it was fixed. But there was no golden repair on her. She was raw and abused in a strangely elegant way. It was such an honest reflection, it was hard to look away.

"I can take you to meet with someone in Berlin." She picked up her wine glass and took a sip. "Perhaps a discussion in the right circles will change your mind."

"Tarnhelm has the wherewithal to manufacture a 'meeting' in NATO or wherever they wish."

"Yes. Yes, they do. Which is why you have to find someone to trust who can get the information into the right hands."

"Give me one reason to trust you."

She said nothing. She simply stared at the hand that was slung around her wine glass. Slowly she moved her hand to his and touched him.

The quiet gesture strangely aroused him. Her vulnerability moved him, and the fear he felt around her was a raw aphrodisiac.

If Tarnhelm got their hands on Heydrich's weapon, the world was going to become a battlefield. It was now a time of war even though most didn't know it yet, and there was one universal comfort people took in a time of war.

She wasn't going to kill him yet. He still had information she wanted. All she was going to do was try to convince him.

Right then and there, on the cusp of Armageddon, he decided to let her try.

CHAPTER FORTY-NINE

STAG LAY IN bed in the pre-dawn light, listening to the breathing next to him. He'd had his final nightmare of Holly. He'd hit the wall. There was no more in him to dream after that last one.

The image of Holly burned in his psyche. She was lying in a deep pool of spreading red. The green, twin-tailed Starbucks siren smiled above her, luring her to her death, and luring all the rest of them into madness.

Last night he'd relived every final moment. There were no poignant last words, no declarations of undying love. Instead, all she'd whimpered was, "Please, God, I need some water. I've got to have some water." She repeated these words, blind to him, blind to her wounds, blind even to her dying, until she slipped away and her hand ceased its grip on his.

He didn't know it at the time, but when you bleed to death, your body and mind become obsessed with a search for liquids. It was not uncommon to find crime scenes slathered in blood with the inexplicable blood-smeared plastic gallon of milk sitting out on the counter. In death throes, the victim had gone to the refrigerator before calling 911.

There were many things he learned that day. Now he wondered if he was finally going to put his grief and horror over Holly aside, only to immerse himself with a new one.

He rose quietly, unsure whether she was awake or not. Last night opened questions he couldn't answer. But now he had to head to Kehlsteinhaus. All other questions would have to wait.

He and Jake met in the lobby. They reached Kehlsteinhaus from the *Dokumentation Obersalzberg*. The center was described as a place of guided learning and remembrance, to reflect on the National Socialist past. Tourists could drench themselves in photos of Hitler's long demolished complex of the Berghof, then ride up to the Eagle's Nest, and have a bratwurst and a tour. It was to be noted that the only tours available were those booked through the Documentation Center. No private tours were allowed. The Bavarian government maintained scrupulous protection against those who would be attracted to the place, such as Nazi-sympathizers and Neo-Nazis.

Waiting for the bus that would take them up the mountain, Stag read about the history of the area. He thought it served as an ominous foreboding:

> According to legend, Emperor Frederick Barbarossa is asleep
> inside Mt. Untersberg until his resurrection. His beard is said
> to be growing longer and longer around a round table and to
> have grown round two times. Myth says that when the beard
> has grown three times around the table the end of the world
> has come.

When he and Jake stepped up to the bus to drive the hairpin turn of the road to the Eagle's Nest, both men were silent and grim, a foil to the strange atmosphere of happy, tacky tourists on holiday.

They arrived and stood in line for their turn at the elevator, the first real vestige of luxe National Socialism left in the complex. The elevator was accessed through a tunnel. The elevator was fitted with polished brass walls, Venetian mirrors, and green leather. A jarring contrast to the stone mountains all around.

As the elevator rose, Jake looked at him in the mirror-like wall. Stag met his gaze. Every nerve was on edge. In truth, Stag couldn't wait to hand over the information to Interpol. He wanted it off his conscience.

The doors opened to a sparsely-filled restaurant. The building had spectacular views of the surrounding peaks and valleys. Walking through it, Stag could even see the Königssee and the mountain where the Angel of Death lay.

They found Troost through a set of double doors. Walking down a few steps, Stag took note of the plaque. *The Eva Braun Room.*

"Mr. Maguire." Troost stood. He was alone in the room. "This is a strange meeting place. I certainly hope you have some information for me!"

He made the introduction to Jake.

"What have you got for me, eh? Have you seen Ms. Aradi?"

Along with Jake, Stag began the long, strange story of how they'd come to the Königssee in search of a bomb and how they were pretty sure they'd now found one. When he was through, he took Troost out the door to the old Sun Terrace. It was now enclosed with windows, so Stag wiped at one to get the clearest view. In the distance, the Königssee could be seen snaking through the mountains. He pointed out the peak over the lake where they believed the bomb lay.

"This is most incredible," Troost exclaimed, his face taking on lines with every new revelation.

"Yes. I think we need NATO or the German government to get here as soon as possible. We're very worried this might fall into the wrong hands," Jake said, the sound of a distant helicopter wafting in with the breeze.

Troost nodded soberly, then he began punching into his phone.

At that moment, Stag's own phone began to vibrate. Since Jake was standing next to him, he couldn't understand it. No one else knew the number.

But then, he remembered what he'd done last night. It wasn't a big leap to imagine a woman going through a man's things to take a look at his cell phone.

"Fuck," he said under his breath. It wasn't time to give in to loneliness and sex. It was time to save the fucking world. But human frailty won out again.

He dug his phone out. The helicopter grew louder.

Google HEYDRICH *GET OUT!!!*

He looked down at the text highlighted on his screen and his insides lurched. He eyed Troost who was still busy tapping into his phone. Nervously, Stag gave Jake a warning glance. While Troost was distracted, Stag went to Safari and punched in HEYDRICH.

He didn't even get to the Wikipedia page. He didn't have to. On the first page of the listings, in small print, he picked out the words.

President of the ICPC (now known as Interpol)

Stag slowly lowered his phone to show Jake.

Jake tapped on the first entry, a Modern Motion article by Gilead Amit:

From 1938 to 1945, Interpol, or the International Criminal Police Commission, as it was then known, became little more than an extension of the Nazi state; the organization whose sole mission is to make the world safer, ruled from Berlin and was presided over by the very men responsible for planning and implementing the Holocaust.

Although speculation is rife concerning the extent to which different countries collaborated with Interpol during the war, it is hard to know anything for certain . . . the little anecdotal evidence that survives, however, is chilling enough . . . the

United States continued to exchange information with
Interpol until just three days before Pearl Harbor, and as late
as 1943, the ostensibly neutral Swiss government was still
paying its annual subscription . . . .

Following the end of the war—and Interpol President
Kaltenbrunner's execution at Nuremberg on the charge of
Crimes against Humanity—Interpol turned its back on its
past and began a slow and shaky journey towards
rehabilitation.

Stag could hear the helicopter getting closer and louder. What
seemed a benign background noise now seemed to grow into the
fury of a monster.

"Give me the phone, Troost," Stag said evenly, taking out the
P-83 and pointing it toward Troost.

"What is this all about?" Troost said, clearly unfazed by having
the gun pointed at him.

"Give me the phone." Stag grabbed it and handed it to Jake. He
also dug out the number on the card that the black man had given
to Harry before killing him. "Is this text to Switzerland?" he asked,
hoping Jake could match the country code.

Jake's hands began to shake. "It's not just Switzerland, it's the
same number."

Stag itched to pull the trigger on Troost.

"They know everything, Stag. Troost texted them. They know
where it is." Jake's voice cracked.

The helicopter landed in a patch of thinning snow just up
the mountain. Interpol men dressed like commandos began to
stream out.

All they needed was a Tarnhelm badge on their shirtfronts, Stag
thought.

"It's useless. Put down the gun," Troost said, nodding to the commandos who jogged toward the Eagle's Nest. Cries could be heard in the main dining room as people grew alarmed at the invasion.

"They're earlier than I'd hoped," Troost said.

You never hear the shot that kills you, Stag thought as Troost took the P-83 from his clutch.

"You still don't have the diary or my other evidence connecting Tarnhelm with that bomb and with the SD," Stag said to Troost who motioned them to the corner of the Sun Terrace. "That bomb is useless without us. Anything happens to us, the diary and all my other evidence goes to the authorities."

"Mr. Portier will decide what chances to take," Troost explained. "All I'm here to do is take my payment and retire to . . . where should I go . . . St. Kitts? The Seychelles? Whereever, just someplace warm and far away."

"That bomb's going to kill a lot of people," Jake implored.

"Yes," Troost agreed. "And were I a supervillain I might laugh right now, but I'm not. I feel bad about it. But it's them or me. I'm sick to death of it being me."

"How will you enjoy that island in nuclear winter?" Stag spat.

"There's no nuclear winter. Tarnhelm has assured me they'll be managing the entire episode. No one will know who acquired this bomb so there will be no retaliation. Which makes it much more valuable."

"You still need my evidence, and without my cooperation it goes out to every newspaper in the world. They'll know who ultimately got the bomb," Stag said.

"You have some value, Mr. Maguire, I don't deny that. But alas, your companion does not. As always, I've been sent to clean up the situation. I've been instructed to take out the collateral." He pointed the P-83 at Jake. The older man raised his shaking hands, unsure of what to do next. "Tell me," he asked him, "do you know the painting by David? *The Death of Marat*?"

Jake looked confused. He was about to answer, but there was no chance. Without warning, Troost put a bullet in his brain.

Stag screamed in outrage. Jake fell to the floor, DOA, the back of his head blown out.

"I'll fucking kill you!" Stag shouted. He rushed Troost and the P-83, numb to the consequences, on fire from his anger.

But this time, he did hear the shot, and it didn't kill him. Wrangling with Troost, the gun went off, the bullet burning the side of his skull. In a blind rage, he kept fighting, irrationally numb, until another shot rang out.

Troost fell backwards, a clean black hole through his forehead. Stunned, it took a moment for Stag to look behind him.

Angelika Aradi stood in the doorway to the Eva Braun Room, the Walther in her hand, the Interpol Security Police commandos streaming from either side onto the Sun Terrace.

As if on automatic, he raised a hand to the side of his head. Blood covered his hand; his head felt like a hot poker had been taken to it.

Then he fell to the floor. Blacked out.

CHAPTER FIFTY

STAG OPENED HIS eyes. He looked around at the sunny room, immaculately modern, white and clean. On the table next to him sat a clear vase of white roses, bursting with freshness.

He didn't know where the hell he was.

Sitting up, he tried to put a hand to his aching head, and he saw the IV stuck in his arm. He then registered the hospital bed he was lying in. Outside his room, he heard the squeal of gurney wheels and a voice speaking German.

"Ah, you're awake." The voice came from the doorway. There appeared a middle-aged man in a wrinkled trench. He introduced himself as James Duffy, NATO.

Stag gave him a blank stare, still trying to recall what had happened to him. He remembered his fight with Troost, and the searing pain to the side of his head. Then he remembered seeing Angelika. And then the black hole she'd put in Troost's forehead.

He lay back, trying to absorb the meaning of it. If Angelika shot Troost while he was texting Portier, then that meant she was a double agent.

"I want to offer my condolences in the loss of your friend," Duffy said.

Stag hesitated, still numb.

"I know you're in pain, Mr. Maguire. I would like to leave you alone. However, when we sent our agents into Kehlsteinhaus, we found Troost's phone. It was encrypted to erase all texts after sending them. We don't know what the scuffle was about, but we have a very good idea."

"Interpol . . . " was all Stag could manage.

"Yes. Sorry about that. Interpol has some very good agents. Excellent, in fact. Rarely are we bedeviled by an embedded holdout from an earlier ethos."

Stag took a deep breath, trying to reconcile all the new information.

"We have an urgent need for information. You see, our best agent works at Tarnhelm under Portier. She found out this morning from Portier that Troost was taking a meeting there with you. She wanted to make sure to interrupt it. However . . . we believe we may have come too late."

Angelika Aradi worked for NATO. And since these people had obviously saved his life, he had to trust them. There was no time to spare.

"There's a bomb. Heydrich's lost bomb. On the mountain above the Königssee. We'd just told Troost about it. We were hoping to retrieve it before Tarnhelm."

Duffy's face was hard. "I see."

"We've got to send machinery out there to get it. Contact Mac. He knows where it is. Here's his number." Stag looked around, not seeing his phone.

"Are you talking about the mountain climber, Killburn's the name? I'm sorry to tell you this, but he's dead. They found his body at the bottom of a cliff."

Stag squinted his eyes against the sunshine. It was suddenly killing his head. Without further thought, he untaped his arm and slid out the IV, grimacing.

"Take me there. I'll show you." Blood streamed from the IV wound. He hardly noticed. He slapped the old tape on it and went to the wardrobe to retrieve his clothes.

* * *

The helicopter flew right atop the bend in the road where the SD truck had accidentally gone off the cliffside in the spring of 1942. From the air, Stag could make out the scarring in the rock where the truck had fallen down the cliff in the snow and landed on the ledge. Below that was another scarring. Where a large object had rolled from the truck bottom farther down the mountain.

But the crevice where the object had been lodged was empty.

Duffy sat in the back, humped against the helicopter window. They were both wearing headsets. Both connected to the intercom, but no words were necessary. The bomb was gone. Tarnhelm had gotten there first.

Stag swallowed his bitterness. If he'd only known who to trust. If he'd only tried NATO first.

Hell, if he'd only Googled Heydrich.

The helicopter landed on the roadside above. They got out and surveyed the pylons still left behind where Tarnhelm's work crew had hurriedly lifted the bomb by sky crane and spirited it away.

NATO was on it. Stag had no doubt. But where the bomb was now and, more importantly, where it would end up was anybody's guess.

"You don't look too good," Duffy said, stepping up to him.

"You don't look too good yourself," Stag answered.

There was nothing more to say.

* * *

Stag was rushed to a NATO plane for a meeting in Berlin. Duffy sat across from him in the rumpled raincoat.

"Is she an assassin or not?" Stag asked, accepting the two Motrin the man mercifully held out to him. He was bleeding through his head bandage, but there wasn't time to care about it.

"We characterized her as such to keep her cover. We suspected a mole in Interpol for a while, only we could never quite identify him. It took you to bring Troost into the open. But no, she is Tarnhelm intelligence, and always has been. She grew up poor, her mother an outcast, her father caught in a Muslim genocide. But she was bright and street-savvy, and Portier grew to trust her more than anyone. He was instrumental in her daughter's recovery. And she grew to trust him."

"What made her flip?"

Duffy thought for a moment. "Time to fly straight, I imagine. Her daughter's been given a second chance and I suspect she wants better things for her, if you forgive me the cheap sentiment."

"What does she do for NATO?" Stag wanted all the information he could get.

"She's an operative of what we call TWR, the NATO anti-genocide arm that was first developed specifically to fight nuclear threats. It now includes all others. It was meant to parallel the original White Rose first founded to fight Germany's National Socialists."

"The White Rose? You mean like in Sophie Scholl?"

"In her honor. We find we still have to focus on genocide. There were six million murdered Jews in the Holocaust. We thought we knew genocide after the Germans managed to mechanize it. But we fool ourselves. We don't have mass murder under control. There have been fifty-five million targeted peoples murdered since 1945." He shrugged. "And none of us have even used a nuclear device. It's the world's dirty secret. We kill those we don't like. En masse."

"Christ."

"People want to see themselves as good. But the truth is all people are bad. The only good ones fight it."

"I thought we'd gotten beyond the Holocaust."

Duffy sighed. "We're a species that needs groups and fears anything foreign. It is our biological necessity. But are we a school of fish moving in unison in the shallow waters or a school of piranha that scours the bones of our own? That we must decide one person at a time."

Stag knew about Sophie Scholl and the White Rose. It was an underground resistance group led by various students and a professor at the University of Munich. Sophie Scholl was twenty-one when she was beheaded after a Nazi show trial. Her judge had been Roland Freisler, one of the members of Heydrich's Wannsee Conference.

It never failed. All good things led back to Heydrich, he thought.

"I take it she didn't murder a NATO official?"

"No. Pure *deza*—what the Soviets called *dezinformatsiya*—disinformation on our part."

"Does Portier suspect?"

Duffy wearily shook his head. "We don't know. She took a terrible chance going to the Eagle's Nest. As I said, she worked intelligence for Tarnhelm for years before she flipped. Now she's our asset, not theirs, but they don't know that." He grew grim. "She's in a bad situation. Very precarious. Very. With that bomb out there, I don't need to tell you she is most vital."

"We have to figure out who they sell it to. They don't want it for themselves. They want it for a client."

"Yes, well, that list is pretty long. But we've already got a good idea who the top contenders are. Now we just have to interrupt the transfer." Duffy paused, looking uncomfortable. "On the face of it, our intelligence tells us the bomb is targeted to destroy an oligarch suburb of Moscow."

"The face of it? There's more?"

"Portier is planning to send out the documents of the strike to Moscow afterward. Proving it was a hired strike by the man in Washington. I don't need to tell you, the Russians will retaliate once those documents are seen in Moscow."

Stag went numb. Next it would be DC. Then it would be Moscow. And so on and so forth until they were just a black crumb whirling in space.

His nerves taut, he looked out the window. With stress numbing him, it was easy to just watch the ground go by below. They ducked through several mountain passes out of Berchtesgaden and headed north by northwest toward Munich. He thought about Jake and the guilt he felt over getting him involved. He was grateful that Angelika had taken the chance to save him, but he only wished the situation had been such to save them both. Now it seemed obvious that she was the shooter in the alley in Bali. While working for Tarnhelm and Portier, she'd also been watching out for him all along.

But no one could afford to think about personal safety any longer. Not while the bomb was out there, headed to parts unknown.

CHAPTER FIFTY-ONE

"IT'S A GRAVITY bomb," Sadler said in his library. "It has no guiding system, which accounts for the few number of wires on it, and no tail kit assembly. Needless to say, we will manage the operation from beginning to end."

"The only thing we care about is that the town is destroyed and nothing ever gets traced to us." The man from DC was back. Arriving with the same creepy smile and Brooks Brothers blazer, the Surrogate looked pleasantly malevolent. Like that inherited green wallpaper that you find out, too late, has been shedding copious amounts of arsenic.

As before, the Surrogate spent most of his time in the meeting looking at his phone.

And Sadler watched him, amazed. Hundreds of thousands were going to be affected by this meeting in his library, yet the man took it with all the seriousness of an inconvenient detail.

You had to love sociopaths. Fuck. They were chill. Sometimes, if he was honest with himself, he got weary being surrounded by them. Maybe because he held onto the small hope in his soul that he was just an outsider looking in.

"The money has been verified in our account in the Cook Islands. We now expect the deployment to occur in less than a week." Sadler was pleased to see the man pause.

"That quickly?"

"The bomb, for all its weathering, was in excellent condition. We upgraded a few things in the renovation. It's ready to go."

"And there will be no tracing it?"

"Of course, there will be tracing. We're renting a business jet, a Global 7000 for the range and the ability to handle the weight. Nothing unusual that hasn't headed to Barvikha in droves. We're installing the custom bomb door now."

"Who will they trace the rental to?"

"The Black Plague."

The crisp-blazered man smiled through his insincerity.

"Everyone loves a new villain," Sadler commented archly. *Especially if the yahoos can shiver in their trailers and look up to the autocracy to "keep them safe."* "It's a win/win for your man, isn't it?"

"But how will you keep the Russians from shooting the plane down after the bomb is dropped? They'll collect a lot of evidence then."

Sadler smiled. "What plane? The only reason for a lot of wires on this type of bomb is to slow the thing down long enough for the plane to get out of reach of the mushroom cloud. By dropping it with no guiding system, a gravity bomb doesn't give enough time to get out of the explosion. There won't even be an ash left of the plane."

The other man nodded. Then something occurred to him. "Was Heydrich planning on his own kamikazes? For this bomb?"

"If anyone in Nazi Germany could have engineered it, it would have been that man. We are talking about Heydrich here."

"Does the pilot know what he's dropping or are you just going to pull the wool over—"

"Mr. Portier has his own army. If I might remind you."

"I'd only heard of the *Muscle Men* as rumor."

"And it will stay that way."

"Yes. Yes." It was the first time the cold Surrogate looked intimidated. Another thought occurred to him. He paused. "Isn't the Global 7000 made by—"

"The business jet company named Bombardier?" Sadler stood to refill their glasses from the bar. "Yes. Ironic, isn't it?"

* * *

Stag looked over the satellite photographs of the bomb clinging to the crevice. Size could easily be determined against the cliff face. Details as small as the shadow of wires on one side of the bomb were now apparent. They had been hidden by the view up top.

"We have to conclude that alterations will have been made. We can't be sure what it will look like once this is done." Admiral Buckner US Navy now assigned to NATO as an OF-9 tapped on the table in frustration. They were seated in a hyper-secure room called a Sensitive Compartmented Information Facility or SCIF room. It was deep inside Devil's Mountain, *Teufelsberg,* a former man-made mountain that was built to hide a Nazi military technical college. The NSA had used the hilltop as a listening post during the Cold War, but now the top was abandoned, its buildings in ruins and covered with graffiti. Deep inside the mountain, however, was another world entirely; a reconstruction of mazes, vaults, and US Marines standing guard 24/7.

"It could be transported as a gigantic machine part—or a tank of helium—and therefore allowed on private aircraft." The engineer of the group looked sternly down at the pictures.

"We've gotten photos and warning memos out to all international airports." It was Duffy's turn to scan the photos. "But I think our best chance is the White Rose. They've got several people in

Tarnhelm. On-the-ground intelligence is what's going to save us here."

"Have you a list of prospective clients, at least? That will help us narrow down the focus," the admiral said.

"Here is the best we've been able to gather. Given the price of the bomb, it does eliminate several of them." An aide handed out the paper.

The admiral glanced at the list, unsurprised by the groups on it, until he came to the last one.

"Is this correct?" he asked, pointing to the sole name.

Duffy stared at him. "I'm afraid so."

"Goddamnit."

"Yes, limiting the damage on this is going to be difficult," Duffy said.

"Mutually Assured Destruction is what's going to happen." The admiral looked around the table at the few in the meeting. The only other American was Stag, and being introduced as a journalist didn't make the admiral warm to him. "We need boots on the ground immediately," he ordered.

"Not yet," Duffy commanded, clearly the man in control. "We've got to be patient and wait for the intelligence. We can't go flying off the handle now when the danger is so great—not only to our agents, but to the world."

"Patience is not my virtue," the admiral boomed.

Stag muttered under his breath, "Then you sure as hell don't want to be a journalist." He looked down at the bomb photo and wondered where Angelika was now. As much as he wanted to rush out and do something to protect her, some situations couldn't be taken by force, no matter how awful the circumstances.

Duffy turned to him. "Stag, you're the only man to have seen the bomb before it was taken off the mountain. We couldn't get every angle from space. Did you see anything we might be missing? Were there any irregularities or signage—anything that can help us identify the thing from SAT?"

"There was another who saw it. Mac Killbur—" Stag's words dwindled at the reminder. He'd forgotten. The man was dead.

Duffy's mouth formed a hard line. "Mac Killburn was found at the bottom of a mountain. 'Failure in the rope,' I think they said it was. Tarnhelm was very careful. There was another death in town: a Herr Professor Hoening who was found facedown over a US military manual that outlined the locations and procedures of decomissioning enemy ordnance. I doubt they'll determine his death was anything other than a heart attack."

Another *fuck you* from Tarnhelm, Stag thought bitterly. He turned back to the satellite photos. "The only thing I remember was a faint marking on the nose cone. I could be wrong. It could have been just scratches from the fall down the cliff."

"Can you describe it?" the admiral demanded.

"It was just scratches, really. Just scratches. Like a stick figure, I think."

"Runes?" Duffy asked.

"Maybe," Stag answered, scouring his memory to make sense of what he saw.

"Could they have looked like lightning bolts?" The admiral took a pen and paper and began slashing SS runes on them.

Stag rubbed his jaw. "No. More like a stick figure. You know. Like a kid makes of a man." He took the paper and drew a legless stick figure with the arms reaching skyward.

"What do you think, Duffy?" The admiral's expression grew taut.

"I think it is a rune." Duffy took the paper himself. He looked at it. "With the arms facing skyward, this is a *Lebensrune*, the life rune." He turned the paper upside down. "But depending on which way the figure faces, it has a totally different meaning."

"Enlighten us," said the admiral.

"With the arms facing down, it is the *Todesrune*." He looked at both men emphatically. "The SS death rune."

CHAPTER FIFTY-TWO

PORTIER STUDIED THE copy of the flight plan. The plane was going to be taking off from the Munich Oberpfaffenhofen Airport. It was an airport used exclusively for business aviation and private jets. Without commercial aircraft, the security measures were much lighter. As long as the paperwork was correct—or rather *looked* correct—there would be no problem with unusual and not-quite-identifiable cargo.

Now he only had to decide the final details. The development at Barvikha, called Sputnik Luxe, was toast even if the pilot was a little inaccurate in dropping the bomb. The flight plan, the names and background of the crew and pilot, would all be traced back to the Black Plague, another arm of Daesh. Their signature would be all over it, from the Koran "mistakenly" left behind in the pilot lounge, to the manufacture of grieving "relatives."

The client was certainly satisfied.

But if everyone thought he was now going to be serving clients, and taking their billions gratefully, when his piss dribbled out with excruciating pain ten times a day, they were all sadly mistaken.

At the scheduled hour an email with attachment would head to Moscow. Whoever was in control—and not unfortunate enough to be cavorting in their Barvikha mansion on the fateful hour—would be given photographic and written evidence of the order that came from their scheming loan-holder. It wouldn't take the Russians long to put it together that they'd been duped.

Washington would soon look like Sputnik Luxe and the surrounding moonscape of Barvikha, he surmised. And Sadler's precious and safe Potomac estate would look like Nagasaki.

It was hard to hide his glee.

That'd teach them. That'd teach every last one of those motherfuckers, he thought miserably as he went to his private bathroom in the never-ending agony.

CHAPTER FIFTY-THREE

"Stag, we've got to get the board to meet with you," Duffy said. "Tarnhelm doesn't want your evidence to appear. It would connect them to the bomb, to Heydrich, to the resurrected SD. Perhaps they'll be anxious to get that loose end tied up."

"They can spin the bad PR. They don't need me for anything other than to up their body count."

"If we could get the board, their chain of command might be interrupted," said the admiral.

"I'd like nothing more than to orchestrate another board meeting. Hell, I've been planning to orchestrate another meeting all along. They owe me money," Stag snorted. "But I can't think of a way to get them to meet me now. Perhaps if they thought there was another bomb . . ."

Duffy stared. The admiral stared.

Stag shrugged. "No, there's no second bomb that I know about."

"They don't know that." The admiral motioned to his aide. "If we can put together the evidence for a second bomb, perhaps they'll take the meeting."

"Maybe." Stag thought of the broken wall and closet in the apartment. With all Tarnhelm's obsessive need to keep the apartment intact as possible, they overlooked the obvious omission. Tunnel vision always has a terrible blind spot. "They know I have more information than they do. That apartment they've been keeping connects them to Heydrich. The bomb connects them to the SD."

"Contact them. We'll provide the *deza*. Tarnhelm is an information and security service. They're most afraid of what they don't know."

Stag nodded. "Sure. No problem. I've got my ticket to Bali now."

"Bali? Why the hell are you dragging this to Bali?" the admiral demanded.

"I like it in Bali," Stag offered obliquely. "Besides, Bali's not a target by anyone on this list. They may actually meet me if I go there."

"Plan your meeting. Maybe they'll sit on this bomb long enough for us to get a bead on its whereabouts." Duffy looked down at his phone.

The encryption read: *In Zug*.

"Our agent is back in the fold," Duffy said with some relief in his voice. "Now we'll wait for them to do their work."

Or her work, Stag thought, his mind on the bomb, and that hole in Angelika's sweater that needed golden repair.

*   *   *

Stag arrived in Berlin by NATO plane. He slipped quietly back into the Airbnb apartment he and Jake had left, all the while on edge, waiting to see if Tarnhelm would respond to his request. Waiting to see if the news crawl reported a horrific nuclear incident . . .

The apartment felt like he'd been there a lifetime ago instead of a couple of days. After the autopsy was completed, Jake's body would be sent back to his daughter in Wuttke, no questions answered, many, many questions asked. The daughter would collect it, never knowing the events that had cascaded since that night at Gerde's and the fateful fluttering of that white silk.

He looked down at his phone. A text had arrived. It was now time for a most important meeting.

* * *

Stag and Kronbauer were the only mourners in attendance at the grave in the old Dorotheenstadt Cemetery. Isolda's coffin was lowered into the ground as a rabbi read a prayer. Each man in turn took a shovel of earth and poured it on top of the wooden lid.

Kronbauer was the first to speak. "The local *chevra kadisha* was willing to prepare the body. But without further divulgences, I had no way to get her into Weißensee, the Jewish cemetery. I can't prove she was a Jew. I can't even prove that was her real name."

He looked down at the tombstone already to be placed.

It said:

Isolda Varrick
Never Forgotten

"How have you been able to hide her from Tarnhelm?" Stag asked.

Kronbauer snorted. "I've done everything I can. The wall has been repaired to exacting specifications, but one can never be sure what they know. They are masters at information control. And they know about everything, it seems."

Stag looked down at the tombstone. He thought of Harry, wondering what he would have made of this strange adventure he'd been on since his death. He would have taken Isolda's demise hard. The look into the mirror of his ancestry would have been a lot for him. Maybe it was best Harry was gone. A tender mercy.

Kronbauer swept his hand at the old graves. "But here, here she is in good company. Those of the Resistance are all around: Bonhoeffer and Dohnanyi have memorials here, and many of the failed 20 July 1944 assassination attempt on Hitler are buried here. They were shot by the SS in a park just down the way."

"I'm surprised there was room. The place looks full."

"It is full. This is my family plot you see here."

Stag finally saw the names on the graves alongside Isolda.

"That one there?" Kronbauer pointed to the grave beside her. "He was my grandfather. Her *mausebär.*"

"He was SD. She was a Jew. Is it right that he should be next to her?"

Kronbauer's shoulders seemed to carry the weight of the world. "He was in love with her. And in the end, I believe, he grappled with salvation. Perhaps, if she can view her placement here as less than an insult than a plea for mercy, she may redeem him." He stared at his grandfather's grave for a long time. "You know, they say the past no longer exists. But that is not true. The past is a maze, and we are stuck in it."

He then began in German the Lutheran version of the Old Testament Priestly Blessing:

The Lord bless you and keep you;
The Lord make His face shine upon you,
And be gracious to you;
The Lord lift up His countenance upon you,
And give you peace.

"And give you peace," Stag repeated, his heart heavy with thoughts of the past. And now, the future.

PART SEVEN

Beware the fury of a patient man.

—John Dryden

CHAPTER FIFTY-FOUR

HE TOOK THE long way back through the Tiergarten. It didn't take her long to find him. The light was cold and snow had begun to fall, making the dreary, pre-springtime park appear suddenly fairytale-like. Few people were around during the workday, so when Stag saw her, in her scarlet coat and pale blue gloves, she was impossible not to notice.

"Beautiful, is it not?" she said, stopping a few feet in front of him.

"Yes."

A long silence ensued. Finally, he said, "Aren't you taking a chance here? If Tarnhelm—"

"Portier sends his greetings."

"Ah. Today you must be the messenger, not the assassin."

"He wants to talk about the second bomb. And about what you found in the closet at 12A."

"Ah, so he knows. Not to be petty but there is the rest of the money he owes me." He arched one brow.

She almost smiled. "He would like to make the payment and discuss further negotiations."

Stag nodded. "You know with the price of this bomb, I think I undervalued it."

"They are watching me."

"Yes."

"Shall I tell him you will meet him in Zurich?"

"He'll meet me in Bali, in my own time."

"The bomb's new owner is American. I thought you should know."

"They told me about NATO's White Rose. Will TWR be able to stop it?"

Her face went hard. "Portier is very ill. He wants to see the world burn."

"But you have your daughter . . ."

"My daughter is being held at his home, Eisschloss."

Stag felt the punch to his heart. "He suspects."

"Yes."

"You can choose the world or your daughter."

"For me, there is no world without her."

"He demands suicide missions from everyone, doesn't he?" His fury rose. "Why not just kill the bastard?"

"It won't stop the company. They need to be exposed. This is why I have to play both sides."

"I want more than to just expose the company. I want them, each and every one personally. After Jake and Harry—"

"We must stop this bomb. And the only way to do that is to let Portier feel he still has all the control."

"Yes."

"We're looking for any flight plan over Barvikha, but . . ." Her words dwindled. She started again. "I believe he has additional plans."

"Why do you think that?"

"I've been able to intercept his messages. He's been in touch with Moscow lately. And he hates Sadler. He doesn't care for DC and would love to see it on its knees. If Moscow believes the US was behind the Sputnik Luxe bombing, they will retaliate."

"And start World War III?"

"Any outcome is possible. Especially when a man is dying."

"Would my meeting with him delay the flight?"

"No."

"Plan the meeting anyway. That way he won't suspect."

"Portier needs to show the client he's dropping their five-billion-dollar bomb where he said he would. The leak of the flight plan to Moscow will be his signature."

"Does TWR know to watch for it?"

She nodded. Then looked nervously behind her. "I must go. I'll tell him you wish for the meeting as soon as possible, but the diary is in Bali."

"Yes."

"Stag."

He met her gaze.

"I . . . I like the man you are."

"Save your daughter. Save yourself. Maybe then we can save the world and get the hell out of it."

She tried to smile.

"Do you like Bali?" he asked. "I'm thinking of retiring there."

The smile finally came.

* * *

The crated "ball bearing" was slowly lifted by crane and placed on the flatbed of the truck. Men worked diligently to see to the straps holding it down. They signaled the all clear, and the truck took off toward the airport.

The Global 7000 was in the private hangar, ready to go. The cargo doors had been significantly widened, but the paperwork didn't show any of the modifications. As long as the doors closed properly, the ground crew would clear it for takeoff. It now just waited for its payload.

The hangar supervisor opened the doors for the Iveco flatbed, which trundled in slowly, crate intact.

"How are they going to make that fit?" the supervisor asked, eyeing the large crate and the new cargo doors.

"They've got a team. That's all I know." The Iveco driver jerked his head in the direction behind him.

"All right. Not my problem. But if it's not secure, the plane won't take off."

"It's a ball bearing. They've got engineers. They'll get it right."

The Iveco flatbed stopped next to the plane. By the time the driver had descended, there were armed men entering the plane hangar like they were readying for an assault on Entebbe.

"That's a lot of gun power for a ball bearing," the supervisor remarked.

"I told you they'd get it right."

The supervisor shrugged. He began ticking off items on his clipboard, and walked by the crate, which said only: *Contents FRAGILE*.

CHAPTER FIFTY-FIVE

BEFORE STAG COULD reach his apartment in the Sony Center, he was surrounded by five men in suits. One flashed a NATO badge as Duffy stepped forward, quickly escorting him to a black sedan. In no time, he was back in the SCIF room deep inside Teufelsberg.

"The admiral says it's urgent." Duffy raised his eyebrows.

Stag settled in.

The admiral and a middle-aged woman in a dark suit came into the room, each looking grim. The woman identified herself as a NEST engineer. NEST was the Nuclear Emergency Support Team run by the US Department of Energy National Nuclear Security Administration, the NNSA. Stag was getting familiar with so many things he had not even known existed.

Aides placed several photographs on the large conference table.

"I need you to look at these, Mr. Maguire," said the admiral. "Pay particular attention to the nose cone. These are the best our *deza* team could produce. Is this like what you saw on the mountain?"

Stag studied the photos. Some were grainy and black and white, others were color close-ups. "You've known about the bomb this whole time?" he said after finishing his examination.

"What makes you say that?" the admiral commanded.

"Well, obviously this is the bomb I saw. See? Here is the *Todesrune*." Stag pointed to it in the photograph.

"These are pure fiction. We took our best artisans and re-created only what you've told us."

"Wow. Then these are not photos of the thing I saw in Königssee? Your team does amazing work."

"We have no choice if we're to convince them there really might be two bombs," Duffy interjected.

The woman in the dark suit said, "If the Katanga deposit was as rich as rumor said it was, it would be as cheap to make two bombs as it would to make one. That is a logic you can use."

"But where am I to tell them this second bomb is right now?"

"Tell them these photos were taken at an ammo dump during the war. Perhaps the Soviet Union."

Stag shook his head. "They'll never believe that. If the Soviets had had this bomb, they'd have had nuclear know-how long before 1949, and they would not have been quiet about it."

"Tell them these photos were taken contemporary to Heydrich." Speculate the bomb was sold on the black market mistaken as a conventional weapon. Tell them only you know how to retrieve it.

"Won't they wonder if another bomb is out there, why it hasn't been used?"

The woman spoke up. "You give them two possibilities. They either don't know what they have, or they do know what they have and are holding it. Either way, you can get your hands on it."

"Or," Stag quipped cynically, "a third possibility: It was destroyed long ago and people are unwittingly living around a nuclear waste site. And if they believe that scenario, I will be utterly useless to them." He looked over the pictures again. It wasn't going to be easy to convince Tarnhelm.

"Gentleman," Duffy announced. "We've got our first bit of news."

The men looked up.

Duffy held out his phone. The text on the screen said: *Bombardier.*

* * *

Eisschloss was her least favorite place to visit. Not that it wasn't beautiful, Angelika thought, her eyes taking in the budding trees and greening slopes of mountains around her and the azure blue of Lake Zug just lapping at the stone patio they were now seated on. But it was just a beautiful trap. Every time she was compelled to visit, she wondered if Eisschloss would be her last vision on earth.

Now, the atmosphere at the schloss was as thick as coagulated blood. Her message had been sent to the numbers station. If they got to the airport in time, no one would ever know the world had teetered on the brink. If they didn't, there was only worse to come. In Washington in particular.

"I need you and Genevieve here with me for the foreseeable future," Portier said, wrapped in a paisley silk robe, a blanket over his knees. He was looking every bit the invalid he had seemingly become, but she knew it was deceptive. Portier might still be hiding the fact he was dying, but he would be plotting until his last breath.

"Mother! Come here!" Genevieve ran up from the lake, her hands cupped together. "It's a baby frog!" she said, letting her mother peek at her captive.

Angelika patted the child's most precious hair that was like Angelika's murdered father's. Bitter chocolate. "Make sure you let him go back to his home when you are through looking at him."

Portier watched as Genevieve went back down to the edge of the lake. He took a moment, then said, "You must stay with me. It's safe for both of you here. We don't know what will happen."

Oh, but you do, she thought. "Of course. We will stay as long as you desire."

"I would desire more affection. You have always been a cold one."

Her skin crawling, Angelika placed her hand over his. His trembled coolly. "It's my nature. Forgive me."

"When I get over this flu, I shall take you both to the Maldives. We shall swim in the warm, clear water and forget the world exists in its entirety."

"Heaven," she said with a smile, but inside, all she could think about was here they were, having tea on the patio, while the world was about to burn in all hell.

CHAPTER FIFTY-SIX

RIKHARDSSON WAS THE first to speak. "He's fucking with us. There are no more bombs." He addressed the last remaining board of directors of Tarnhelm. They'd all flown into Zurich for an emergency meeting, Rikhardsson, Sadler, and Zellner, the Canadian. Portier was on the flat screen, streaming from Zug.

"Agreed," Sadler chimed in. "There aren't any more bombs."

"But what if there is one more?" Zellner tapped at the photographs Maguire had sent. "These photographs matching with the rune are most upsetting. What if he's correct and can lead us to it? We should meet one more time to be sure."

"Another bomb would be useful, not to mention extremely profitable after our 'event.' I want you to go and meet him," Portier said from the screen.

Rikhardsson looked uncomfortable. "He insists on the entire board. I'm afraid—"

"I'll go. This flu will be over soon and so will Maguire."

Portier's will was admirable, but Rikhardsson wasn't convinced. "He's not worth—"

"I will go."

It was final. Zellner and Rikhardsson looked grim. Sadler looked delighted.

"By the way, Henry," Portier said, "I've a project for you in DC. I want you to head there ASAP, and stay there while I arrange everything."

Sadler couldn't have looked more willing and able. "You know Potomac's the only place I want to be."

Portier seemed to smirk beneath all the gray lines of illness. "Yes. Yes, I do."

* * *

"We've been looking at all the private Bombardiers being flown out of Germany and Switzerland. There's nothing so far," Duffy informed the admiral.

"How many have been altered?" the admiral asked.

"Pretty much all of them. They're intercontinental business jets. Nothing but money to customize them."

"What you're looking for is an altered Bombardier making a trip to Moscow, is that it?" Stag asked.

"Exactly," the admiral said. "But there are lots of trips to Moscow by private plane each day. We won't have much time to act between the discovery of the nexus of the altered plane and the flight plan. We're very worried it might take off before we can stop it." He paused. "Once it's airborne, I don't have to tell you we have the ability to shoot it down. But it will make an environmental mess of horrific proportions."

Duffy rubbed at the weariness on his face. "We're standing by in real time, waiting for whatever information the numbers station can convey. We have to balance our agent's ability to stay alive long enough to release the information with the delay of it getting to us. Very frustrating."

"Why can't they just shut down all airports till we get our hands on this thing?" Stag asked.

"We have medivac planes, planes carrying vital medicines and organs, not to mention a complete business shutdown. All based on what? The idea that someone might—might—have gotten a nuclear device? Preposterous. Particularly since any shutdown would be blocked at the highest levels of the government, as we know now."

It was Stag's turn to rub his weary face. "The waiting is excruciating."

"Yes," Duffy agreed. "But think of the poor fools in the path of this monster. Just going about their day."

CHAPTER FIFTY-SEVEN

INSIDE TEUFELSBERG, THE news stared at Stag from headlines of the day's *Berliner Zeitung*:

Employee of high-end building found dead atop Quadriga.

Attack of the Vikings?

Numbly Stag picked up the abandoned paper left in the coffee room outside the SCIF and read about Einhar Kronbauer's gruesome death. To others, it seemed like a sick joke. To Stag, it bore all the trademarks of a Tarnhelm hit.

Kronbauer must have been taken from his workplace. Escaping detection from the cameras of the Dresdenhof and the Pariserplatz, he'd been tied to one of the Quadriga horses and murdered. His back was cut open, and while still alive, his attackers had pulled out his lungs to lie like angel wings, paralleling the wings of the chariot driver behind him, the figure of Eirene, the goddess of peace.

Parallels aside, it was not hard to see the Tarnhelm footprint. Pulling the lungs out and laying them on the victim's back like wings was a Viking mode of death.

It was called the Blood Eagle.

He shoved the newspaper aside and resisted the impulse to beat his fists against the concrete wall till they bled.

CHAPTER FIFTY-EIGHT

THE GAZEBO WAS built at the end of a dock that jutted from Eisschloss out into Lake Zug. Portier liked to take cocktails there but, it was still too cold to do that. Now he was on the phone, an encrypted and secure line used only by him. While he spoke, Angelika played quietly with Genevieve who was making a big deal of putting on "lipstick" from a plastic toy shaped like a lipstick. The child's purse was emptied of its toy contents: a pink plastic Hello Kitty cell phone, matching plastic key and key chain, a comb shaped like a bow.

"Shall we feed the swans?" Angelika asked, grabbing a roll from the tea tray.

Genevieve was eager to go along.

"Aren't you going to take your purse?" Angelika asked with a smile.

Responsibly, Genevieve picked up all her purse's contents and placed them in her plastic Hello Kitty purse.

"The second it leaves 'O,' I want to know." Portier hung up. His assistant placed documents in from of him, diverting his attention.

'O' was Oberpfaffenhofen. An educated guess on Angelika's part, but the airport was private and near Munich. Convenient when one was transporting a bomb from the Königssee.

"I'm ready," Genevieve announced rather imperiously.

"You sure? You didn't forget anything?"

The little girl clutched the pink plastic purse now bulging with her accessories. She ran ahead, the purse flapping on her arm.

Angelika nodded to Portier who acknowledged her with a glance.

When they got to the gazebo, they lounged on the cushioned chairs. Angelika enticed the swans with pieces of a roll. Genevieve laughed with delight as more of them arrived by wing, spraying them with icy droplets.

She handed the roll to Genevieve and took the chair farthest away from the lake. Beneath the gazebo, satellite surveillance was impossible. While she had no doubt there were at least two boats training cameras on them, there was no way to see what she was up to behind Genevieve's chair.

She watched her daughter and laughed, all the while stealthily pulling out the Hello Kitty phone. Built into it was all the circuitry of a real phone, but because it had to pass the weight test as a useless child's plastic toy, it had an extremely limited battery. She had just enough power to get out a last text.

Taking a paperclip from her pocket, she stuck the end into a tiny hole in the toy phone. Nothing indicated it was turned on but a very faint vibration.

Watching her daughter while typing the encrypted message onto the phone's big purple keypad, she laughed and played the doting mother, all the while sending out the word *Oberpfaffenhofen* over and over again to the numbers station that would signal Duffy.

"Mama! Come here! A black one!" Genevieve pointed to the group that had gathered at the end of the dock. Angelika slid the toy phone back in the toy purse. There was no need to turn it off. It was dead. The battery had little more use. Her desperation with this last message had surely drained it.

Now it was indeed a useless child's plaything.

* * *

In the NATO helicopter, Duffy barked into the phone while Stag clutched and unclutched the armrests. They were tearing across the 57 kilometers from Munich Airport to Oberpfaffenhofen. Intelligence on the ground had a flight scheduled to depart for Moscow in fifteen minutes with a parts payload that could serve cover as their bomb. All the paperwork was filed. Everything was completely good to go. The thought of it made his stomach lurch more than the helicopter ride.

"We need to see that flight plan," the admiral shouted into his headpiece.

In seconds, it was forwarded. He stared down at his device and pointed to Duffy how the flight path deviated slightly to put it over Barvikha on its approach.

Duffy's phone binged incessantly. He looked at it. "They say the co-pilot just emailed the flight plan to an IP address in Zurich."

"Portier's going to let the Russians know exactly who was behind this." The admiral released an extraordinary string of epithets. "We've got to hope like hell this intelligence isn't wrong. Who knows what the fuck the Russians will do if they think the US is behind this? Washington will be Hiroshima."

The helicopter landed. Behind it were four more. Several private jets were in the sky, having already taken off. A string of others awaited their turn.

"Which one is it?" the admiral barked.

"I think the Global 7000 is that one there," Duffy answered.

"We've got a NATO threat on the Global 7000 here on the tarmac," the admiral screamed into his headgear. "Tell the tower to take it back to the hangar. Now."

By now, several Oberpfaffenhofen airport security cars, lights flashing, sirens wailing, were racing up to them.

On the tarmac, the next plane in the queue went to the end of the runway. The Global 7000 was next.

Airport security jumped from their vehicles and ran toward the group of helicopters descending. Their faces were white. Clearly, they'd never experienced such an assault on their little airport before.

"Get that plane back to the hangar. On orders of NATO," the admiral boomed across the tarmac, gesturing wildly at the Global 7000.

Frantically the security men shouted into their radios, trying to gain insight into what was happening.

In the distance, the plane ahead took off, leaving the runway clear for the Global 7000.

"Goddamnit." The admiral watched as the plane moved to the end of the runway.

"Sir?" the helicopter pilot queried.

The admiral nodded.

Without warning, they were airborne again, rocking furiously until the pilot set the helicopter down between the runway and the Global 7000.

Chaos erupted on the radio as the tower began having to deal with all the planes in the queue behind it.

"Pull it to the hangar!" the admiral shouted into his headset like a rabid dog.

Airport security chased them out to the tarmac. The Global 7000 didn't move. Other NATO helicopters set down behind it. A show of force.

Suddenly, without warning, the Global 7000 jerked right onto the grass next to the tarmac. It made another hard turn and, skirting the helicopter, rolled back onto the runway, gaining speed with every spin of the wheels.

"Go!" the admiral bellowed.

Stag fought the G-force as their helicopter took off and flew overhead of the speeding airplane. In the tilt-a-hurl, Stag was only vaguely aware that the other NATO helicopters were swooping in on the plane also, each like a small black cricket trying to take down a grasshopper. After they reached maximum forward speed, Stag looked down at the plane below them, screaming to get airborne.

"Land this motherfucker! Do it! Now!" the admiral shouted to the pilot.

Inching away from the plane, the helicopter sped to the end of the runway and planted like an Olympiad coming off the double bar.

Stag shut his eyes at the roaring plane bulleting toward them. He wasn't a genius at math, but with momentum and forward speed, he saw no room to stop the plane before it hit them. His every nerve was on fire.

A scream of burning tires added to the cacophony of helicopter blades and screaming men. Its flaps up, the plane tried to turn away, but it was too late. The plane spun around and around but the forward momentum couldn't be stopped. The Bombardier careened toward their helicopter like a spinning top of annihilation, carrying the prescient doom of fuel and sparking metal.

In a split second, the pilot threw the helicopter into violent ascent. Stag slammed against his harness and they were airborne, the helicopter's rotors clawing at the air to get away. With barely inches to spare, the plane passed beneath them, skidding far into the grass next to the runaway. The helicopter lurched in the gale of wind as the Bombardier passed below.

Like a swarming bunch of predators, the NATO helicopters one by one landed next to the sliding plane, hopping around it until it finally came to a dead halt.

Sirens filled the air as fire trucks and police began streaming down the runway toward them. Stag looked over and Duffy was wearing his lunch all over the front of his suit. It had been a wild ride. Duffy lamely patted at himself with a handkerchief.

Stag barely could keep his own lunch down.

"Fuck," was all he could whisper.

CHAPTER FIFTY-NINE

WHEN STAG FINALLY had the consciousness to look around him again, they were drowning in a sea of police and fire vehicles. Two more NATO helicopters had arrived. All were focused on the plane.

But there was nothing. No movement, no opening doors, no white flag nor waving gun from the cockpit.

While the admiral was consumed by shouting into his radio, Duffy unlatched his safety harness and walked to the front of the helicopter to stare at the plane.

After a long assessment, Duffy said, "Admiral, I believe it's safe to open the plane door. You'll have to blow it open, I'm afraid."

The admiral put down the cockpit radio. "You know, I'm not looking forward to using explosives on *that* particular plane."

Duffy sighed. "Very prudent, but a controlled explosion is necessary. My guess is Portier used his Muscle Men for this flight. Just for this very scenario."

The admiral gave him a long, pointed stare. Then, as if accepting Duffy's logic, he barked into the radio, "Blow the door."

Duffy went back and sat down. Stag looked at the plane. They were so close they could see the rivets in the tailpiece.

"I sure as hell hope those pilots don't do anything stupid. If the bomb's aboard, they can always make the case they were duped as to the payload." Stag's fingers dug into the already worn-out armrests.

"It's Tarnhelm. They won't be coming out."

"What makes you say that?"

"Because they have their own army. The *muselmänner*."

"Muslims?" Stag asked, interpreting the German.

"No. The term goes back to Auschwitz. The *muselmann* was the walking dead; those concentration camp inmates too skeletal, too sick to keep living, though beaten and compelled to walk till they expired on their feet. They were referred to as Muslims because of the way they would fall to their knees and crash forward as they died. Gallows humor. Portier employs an army of them."

"I'm still not getting it—you mean those guys in the plane—"

"They are dead. Suicide. Probably the old reliable cyanide capsule. Portier acquires his 'army' by buying off the terminally ill to go on suicide missions. He calls them his *Muscle Men*. It's his little Auschwitz joke, you see?"

Stag sat back, absorbing this new information. Every time he thought he understood this modern SD, he was thrown another curve. Another jacked-up, fucked-up, twisted, revolting curve.

Outside, the explosives unit drew back from the plane door. They ducked and covered, and with a loud boom, the plane door was open.

Duffy watched as the first men entered the plane, automatic weapons full bore. It didn't take long to assess.

The admiral listened on his headset.

He pulled it off and looked at Duffy. "Muscle Men. As we suspected. All four are dead." He looked at Stag. With unnecessary formality, he said, "Mr. Maguire. Will you do me the honor of accompanying me into that plane to identify the weapon?"

* * *

Portier stared down at the screen. He was better that evening. After his interferon treatment, he'd dressed in a suit and asked Angelika to meet him for dinner. She had a particularly beautiful black dress. The silk had "shattered" with random shredding that was unique to aging silk. But this dress had shattered in the most exquisite manner. Vintage Mainbocher, he thought. Really sublime. He'd requested she wear it and ordered his best bottle of Krug from the cellar.

All was looking up. Until the notice that the plane had been stopped.

It wasn't the money. It wasn't the fear of being caught. Of that, he was certain there was no risk. The legal churning of an accusation like that would take years to resolve itself. It would take more time than he had. So no worries.

But now, Sadler was relaxing in his Potomac estate, master of all he surveyed. The chaos he'd so deserved was held in check. Washington continued its slog through the swamp undeterred.

The news took the charm out of the day.

And that irritating flea, Maguire, was still underground and claiming there were two bombs.

His fuckery had unraveled into even more fuckery.

But Luc Portier was alive and feeling better. Perhaps the interferon was the magic bullet he needed. Perhaps it was just another sign that he had more to do, and now more days to do it.

A knock came at the door. Angelika was there, just as he imagined her, his own special beauty, gowned in black silk rags.

He raised a champagne glass. "To a wonderful evening, my dear."

He tried to imagine she looked pleased.

CHAPTER SIXTY

STAG WAS READY to go to Bali. When he finally dragged himself back to the apartment in the Sony Center, he checked his messages. There it was. Yes, indeed. Portier, Sadler, Rikhardsson, and Zellner were willing to buy first-class tickets on the Bali Singapore Airlines flight. Once in the sky, he would get his final payment, and cut a deal for the "second" bomb, assuring them of his secret knowledge with the pictures comparing the *Todesrunes*.

"Portier has said he will be there. With his prostate problems, I don't think I should delay," Stag told Duffy when he met him for coffee the next morning.

"I don't need to tell you how dangerous this is—your having discussions with him. Let's not kid ourselves. You're poking the beast. We haven't been able to trace a goddamned thing about this bomb back to Tarnhelm except for what you've told us. They'll be happy to see you gone."

Stag nodded. "I've made plans. I want to finish what I started."

"All to write a series of articles that NATO will probably ban you from publishing?"

"I have my own grudge."

Duffy rubbed his jaw. "Is there anything we can do?"

Stag studied him. Finally, he said, "No, but I think there's something I can do for you."

* * *

Portier looked down at the confidential report sent by courier. There it was in black and white, a full dossier of who was involved in Tarnhelm's fail at Oberpfaffenhofen: NATO. Interpol. Maguire.

He crumpled the news and watched it burn. Deep inside he felt only a mild antipathy. Certainly, he had nothing to fear. Tracing any of the mess back to Tarnhelm would be near impossible with the Muscle Men involved. Plus, once the bomb was in NATO hands, it would be disassembled and rendered neutral. No surprises waking up to find he was breathing the fallout from Munich or Prague.

Of course, Tarnhelm would have to repay the money. But there was always more money. What there wasn't was more time. Tick tock. Tick tock. It was driving him mad.

Outside his office, he watched Genevieve play on the docks, once more feeding the swans. He and the little girl had shared much. Her cancer fight had moved him. Now he was her compatriot. A warrior like she was.

But he was losing his war.

There was little denying it. He knew he had a rally or two left, but after that, he would be done. He would take to his bed and cease to be.

The notion astounded him. It didn't seem possible to no longer *be*. He was a force in this world. He had fought and struggled to gain everything he had. But in spite of his outraged denials, deep down, he knew it was coming. He was reaching his end. And when he lay snuffed out, the rest of the world would continue to laugh and drink and be merry.

His gaze settled upon Angelika who handed the bits of bread to Genevieve, the wind off the lake whipping her hair seductively.

Because of his affliction, he would never know the joy of her. He would die never achieving intimacy with the one woman who utterly fascinated him. He would surrender his life and be forced to leave her to other men. The world, in fact, he would be forced to leave to other men.

With a quiet, deadly rage, he acknowledged he no longer had patience for ruined plans. He didn't give a fuck whether his bomb was sold and paid for. What he'd been counting on by that profitable blast to Barvikha was payback. When the bomb was detonated, he was going to send out the information in the documents he now held in his hands. That opportunity was gone now. Yes, he might have the chance at another bomb, but he doubted it. The best he could do now was create the chaos and instability he felt inside, and spread it like burning napalm across the world.

He looked down at the papers. They were meant to be destroyed after his perusal. But he had not destroyed them. It was the flight plan of the Global 7000 over Barvikha. Also, the specifications of the bomb, and the new bomb door placed in the belly of the craft.

There was also the printout of a payment from a Cypriot bank account from a certain company that had a very renowned family name.

It wouldn't take a rocket scientist to put the facts together.

He thought of the Russian president glaring at these documents, infuriated that his beloved oligarchs had been annihilated by a more furious American greed. Portier had been counting on the Russian president's one surefire reaction: retaliation. Right where it would hurt. Washington, DC. And the best, most delicious part? Sadler's beloved Potomac would become nothing but a ruined, abandoned suburb of Chernobyl.

Apre-moi, le deluge.

Portier was going to send the documents. Potomac might stand,

Russian presidents might use discretion, but that vulgar asshole in DC would be ground into borscht and caviar by a smarter, more nefarious foe once "Vlad" was informed of the rat he had in his cage.

He would think of another fitting end for Sadler later.

It wasn't what Portier had planned, but it offered cold satisfaction, at least.

He summoned his personal high-security courier back to his office. Placing the documents in a sealed pouch, he handed them over, and said, "Three hours to Moscow. See that the president gets these tonight. I want top anonymity on this and top priority."

The courier, well trained, nodded.

"Tell him this is courtesy of 'a friend.'"

"Yes, sir."

Portier watched the courier exit. He could now enjoy the day with Angelika and Vieve. His last damned trip to Bali was tomorrow.

Then he would be done.

CHAPTER SIXTY-ONE

STAG ARRIVED IN Bali the day before. He was now ready for his trip to Singapore. The taunting alligator briefcase from Wuhan was at his side, his safety deposit box had been emptied out, and everything was now stowed. He was going to make his last and final sale.

He'd instructed Portier and the board to meet him at the Singapore Airlines lounge in Bali an hour before boarding. He wanted to show them the letters. They'd agreed. Portier more grudgingly than before. But still willing.

The thought of Angelika and her daughter gnawed at him. She was on the inside and anything he could do to help her would just put her in greater danger. Portier would bring her with him to Singapore. There, at least, she would have less security than at the house in Zug.

He studied the Wuhan briefcase. It was beautiful. As well made as the finest Parisian leather goods. He felt smarter just holding it in his hands. No wonder Portier was glued to his.

He put it in a black duffel bag, unzipped, and got into the cab for the airport. The day in Bali was breezy and clear. Perfect day for flying the short job to Singapore.

"Airport," he said to the cab driver.

He sat back and watched the slums appear on his trip to Denpasar.

* * *

The courier presented the sealed pouch to the president in private. Russian to the core, the president sat behind a gold-ormolu desk with a desk set of Fabergé, no doubt a gift from a grateful oligarch who bought it from the shop, *A La Vielle Russie*, on Fifth Avenue. Of course, it had landed there in New York after it was pawned from the last revolution.

The Russian Circle of Life.

Dismissing the courier, he slit open the pouch with a pair of malachite-handled scissors.

He looked down at the papers, reading them once, twice, three times. And in different order. After digesting their meaning, he held a long, enraged silence.

Then he picked up the phone to call his generals. He ordered the highest defense condition that was one step down from a full-out nuclear strike. The Russian equivalent of DEFCON 2.

In Russian, it was officially called: *Danger of War*.

* * *

Stag's newest GoFone went off. It was the direct line to Duffy.

"He bought tickets for Angelika and the girl. He's not meeting them in Singapore. They're here with him in Bali." Duffy's voice came through loud and clear.

Stag frowned. He rubbed his jaw in frustration. "I'll scrap it then."

"You do that and your death wish will be fulfilled. They'll take their chances and see you dead first."

He wanted to punch something. The best-laid plans . . . "I'll play it out. If I can warn her off the plane, then I'll go forward. If not, I'm scrapping."

"We won't have a second opportunity." Duffy's voice was deadly serious. "There's no good evidence on Tarnhelm for trying to sell the bomb. They'll continue as always if we do nothing."

"If Angelika and Genevieve are going on the plane, I'm scrapping. Got it?" he said with more ferocity than necessary.

"Got it," Duffy conceded. "Stag?"

"Yeah."

"Try and get out of this alive?"

* * *

The Bali SilverKris Lounge was empty of patrons when Stag got there. The only thing to do after Portier and the rest of the board arrived was head through security and get on the plane to Singapore, but somehow, some way, he had to make sure Angelika and her daughter didn't go with them. He was stumped as to how. He'd never been great at improvising. His writing career bound him to research and study, not winging it, but now, with this whole adventure, he was a Ph-fuckin-D at it.

Portier, looking gray, arrived alongside Rikhardsson. Both men balefully took seats and accepted champagne from the obsequious Singapore Airlines hostess. Right behind them, Angelika, holding Genevieve's hand, accepted champagne also. Leaving the men to their business, she and Genevieve went to the windows to watch the planes.

The Singapore Airlines SilverKris Lounge was a separate room from the Premiere Lounge used by other airlines. It was exclusive, but small. Stag watched from his perch by the bar while Portier took a chair, placing the infamous Hermès briefcase on the floor. Stag went over and took the seat beside him and made a show of unzipping the ungainly black duffel and clawing though the contents to get at a pad of paper and pen. After knocking Portier's alligator case several times, Stag tucked the duffel alongside it in the floor space between the two men's seats.

"Sorry," Stag said, accepting his own champagne with relish. He sure as fuck wasn't going to drink it, but let them figure that out, he thought.

Portier refused to even look at him.

Sadler and Zellner entered shortly and took seats in the opposite cluster of chairs.

No one said a word.

Then the fuss came. Portier stood and demanded anxiously where the restroom was. He grabbed his briefcase and followed the hostess to the set of Balinese-carved teak doors to the rear.

Stag looked at his watch, wishing that he'd had the nuts to buy the fake Tourbillon also. Anything to irritate Portier.

They had fifty minutes to go.

Anxiously, he looked down at his notebook and began scribbling some notes. If he kept busy, it might take his mind off the death stares of the men surrounding him. When he decided to take a break, he stepped toward the set of floor-to-ceiling windows where Angelika and Genevieve were.

They didn't speak a word. Stag held his notebook to his chest, making sure she could see his large block letters.

DO NOT GET ON THAT PLANE.

His only reassurance that she got the message was a slight nod, then she took Genevieve's hand and walked away.

Portier was back, in an even more foul temper than before. He glared at Stag when he made a show of moving his black duffel in the narrow space between their chairs to make room for the Hermès. He further glared when Stag bumped the case with his duffel when he re-wedged it into the narrow space between them.

But Portier didn't have long to focus on Stag. It took less than ten minutes before the pressing need to empty his bladder came over him once more. Prostate's revenge.

Portier stood, angry and distracted, looking for his briefcase.

Stag handed it to him. Ironic courtesy. From the young to the old. From the living to the dead.

Portier snatched it away and fled to the Bali-carved doors.

Stag shrugged and turned back to fiddling with his untouched champagne. A long time passed in silence. Finally, Stag excused himself. Mumbling that he would give Portier the ultimate courtesy and leave him alone to use the SilverKris men's room in private, he announced he would use the public john down in the terminal. He grabbed up his duffel and departed. He was back in the lounge before Portier returned from his trial in the private restroom.

Stag could almost feel sorry for him. Portier's normally cool brow was beaded with sweat. His face was even more gray.

Almost sorry for him. Almost.

Their hostess announced their flight was ready to board and that they would be escorted through security.

Stag stood, clutching his duffel.

He didn't look at Angelika.

A private staircase led down to the security lines at the gates. First class had its own security line—streamlined and obsequious for the privileged few. Each ticket holder had his own personnel. Stag's was waiting for him, ready to take his carry-on with white-gloved hands, while the Tarnhelm passengers were escorted next in line.

Stag placed the duffel on the conveyer belt.

Immediately, his duffel caused suspicion. His nerves on fire, he watched as he was tagged for extra security and two men took him aside to hand-examine his belongings.

Behind him, he heard Angelika's voice. "I forgot my makeup case in the lounge upstairs."

"Let them get it for you." Portier referenced the overflow of Singapore Airlines attendants for the first-class passengers.

"Oh, they won't know where it is. I won't be a minute. Come along, Vieve." She held out her hand to the little girl.

"Leave Genevieve with me," Portier said. "They can get her settled, and we'll meet you on the plane."

If Angelika had any reluctance, she hid it with an iron will. She looked back at Genvieve pointedly, then turned to go up the stairs.

"But I have to go to the bathroom! *Now!*" the little girl mewled.

"Come along then, but we have to hurry," Angelika said, again holding out her hand.

Genevieve ran up to her. Angelika threw Portier a look that said, "Kids!" and they quickly disappeared up the stairs to the lounge.

Stag felt a tremor of relief surge through him. He wouldn't put it past Angelika to have trained Genevieve to do that should they ever be separated. Now one big problem was solved.

Exasperated, Portier handed his briefcase to the white-gloved attendant who carefully placed it on the conveyor belt.

The two German shepherds at the regular security line began barking. Curious, two security guards walked the dog up to the first-class line. The dogs grew frantic at Portier's briefcase.

Portier was taken aside.

A uniformed security officer asked Portier to open the case. He placed his code into the locks and opened it.

The dogs barked furiously when the guards began pointing to the contents of the briefcase. It was twenty pounds of cocaine, just enough to mimic the weight of a lead lining in another custom briefcase made by Hermès of finest American alligator.

When the guard shoved the Ziploc bag in Portier's face, Stag got a glimpse of dawning on Rikhardsson's eyes.

It was the same gauche Ziploc bag Stag had apologized for on their initial meeting. When he'd passed the silk strip around to the board, high in the air on the original Singapore Airlines flight. It was the same bag he was careful not to touch as he allowed them to slip it into the manila envelope. So now all their fingerprints were on it. And Portier was traveling on the same tickets they were.

Stag finished with his security check and began to walk toward the jetway. He paused under the big red sign that greeted visitors to Bali:

WELCOME TO INDONESIA!
DEATH PENALTY FOR DRUG TRAFFICKERS!

All along, Stag knew he'd need a bigger force than Tarnhelm to take the bastards down, and he alone was no match for it. But a little research and some thought, and he realized he'd found one. If the Indonesian government had told the Australians, their closest and most powerful neighbor, to take a hike in order to punish the Bali 9 according to their laws, then Stag didn't give Portier and the gang on his ticket much chance. Sure, their money might vacate a death penalty for them, but he didn't count on it. Not when they might serve as an example. The one thing the majority-Muslim Indonesia was sincere about was drugs on their soil. Besides, even if they could battle the government, they would all be stuck in Indonesia's infamous Hotel K prison for years. It was a *de facto* death sentence for Portier.

It had all gone true to plan. The Wuhan case was beautiful. Exact. And made to his specifications, detailed right down to the high security locks that whatever, no matter what code was put into it, the case would open.

When Stag had gotten downstairs to the public restroom on that last moment before the flight, Duffy had been there to receive

Portier's precious briefcase. More than once, Stag was sure someone had seen him switch the cases during the handoff, but no one noticed a cheap black duffel. They were the black holes of the earthbound. Stag had left the duffel conveniently unzipped next to the Hermès in the obscured space between the seats. When Portier was anxious to go to his next trip to the bathroom, it was easy enough to reach down and hand Portier the Wuhan case. After he had left, Stag stashed the Hermès inside the duffel. In order to be the first through security and maximally distance himself from the clusterfuck that was going to ensue when security got their hands on Portier's goods, Stag had needed to get rid of the Hermès, so before the flight he'd handed it to Duffy underneath the stall of the public restroom, all by designated plan, and then went back upstairs to the lounge.

Now it was done. NATO would find the contents of the briefcase immeasurably useful.

And he would get the story of a lifetime for a journalist.

He thought of Duffy waiting for him now in the limousine at the entrance to the airport. Stag took the duffel that now held nothing more than an iPad and some clothes, and swung it to his side. He exited security and walked slowly away from the fray as security officials and police went running by. Angelika would surely be in Duffy's car by now, waiting for him with Genevieve, grateful she had not been caught up in Portier's security check.

Angelika Aradi. The mystery woman. The sphinx. The woman who wore her travails like art. He'd had sex with her, and she'd saved his life. Wasn't it now maybe time for a first date?

He didn't know if she'd want to. After all, there was going to be no second twenty-five-million-dollar payment. And being the bum he was—though he knew Holly forgave him—he could honestly say he blew his entire Settlement on cocaine.

But, broke and crippled as he was, he was going to take the chance and ask her out anyway. Hell, why not? He'd persisted when Holly had turned him down. And that had been the best thing he'd ever done, no matter how it had ended. And there was one thing everyone had to know about him by now.

He was a determined gimp.

AUTHOR'S NOTE

Reinhard Tristan Eugen Heydrich (1904–1942) was a main architect of the Holocaust. In his short life, he was the active agent behind the Jewish pogrom known as Kristallnacht; he was the instrumental machine behind the Night of the Long Knives whereby the assassination of Ernst Röhm led to the rise of the elite of the Reich: the SS. He created the *Einsatzgruppen* to follow behind the German army and shoot political enemies—even including women with their babies in arms—because first and foremost the political enemies of the Reich were Jews.

By 1941, before the introduction of death camps, half a million Jews had been exterminated by Heydrich's *Einsatzgruppen*—it was called the Holocaust of Bullets. Under Himmler, Heydrich formed the SD, the *Sicherheitsdeints*, which provided intelligence to the SS and the Reich. All the German security services were united in one unit called the RSHA, the Reich Main Security Service, of which Heydrich became the Director. The RSHA included the Gestapo and the ICPC, now known as Interpol. Heydrich chaired the Wannsee Conference, which streamlined the process that moved Jews to the east for extermination. His organizational skills and attention to minutiae struck fear into even Hitler himself, who wondered what secrets Heydrich might know about him and in the end use against him to gain power.

He was known as the Hangman, the Blond Beast, the Young Evil God of Death, but while his nicknames were terrorizing, he had a human side. He came from a musical family and was enormously talented at the violin, so much so that his plaintive music could being tears to his eyes and the eyes of his audience. He was secretly derisive of Himmler's descent into occultism. He, himself, had silly ideas at times, such as the development of an SS brothel where he could scheme to collect secrets from the clients. He was so enamored of spy novels, he once asked his subordinates to refer to him as *C*, perhaps referring to the habit within the British Navel Intelligence Division to refer to their chief as such, a practice that long preceded the Ian Fleming novels. Foibles aside, however, he was powerful, intelligent, and supremely destructive—personally instrumental in the murder of some twelve million souls.

Much has been written about Heydrich's assassination in Prague, but the man himself remains a sphynx. Even so, his thinking and directorship is alive and well today in many groups and individuals throughout the world. As George C. Browder wrote in *Hitler's Enforcers*, the SD was to "remain a flexible instrument for all eventualities." There is certainly a history of this. Interpol flourished under Heydrich's Gestapo and has now spent decades trying to rid itself of its Nazi past. SS Officer Paul Dickopf was its president till 1972, and while Interpol was aware of his Nazi rank, they disregarded it as his work record with the SD was "incomplete."

Of course it was.

Heydrich's methods of intelligence gathering included keeping individual cards on persons until he accumulated thousands of them. In order to keep track of Jews and other undesirables in the Third Reich, this progressed to the hiring of IBM and its punch-card system. We may not know all the persons that Heydrich saw murdered, but we do have a pretty good idea of how many thanks to his exactitude. He haunts to this day. As he told Hans Gisevius, the German diplomat and military intelligence officer, "I can pursue my enemies even from the tomb." I don't think he was lying.

ACKNOWLEDGEMENTS

As Sinclair Lewis wrote in *It Can't Happen Here*, "Under a tyranny, most friends are a liability. One quarter of them turn 'reasonable' and become your enemies, one quarter are afraid to speak, and one quarter are killed and you die with them. But the blessed final quarter keep you alive." He would know. He was married to Dorothy Thompson who was the first American journalist to be expelled from Nazi Germany in 1934.

I would like to thank that quarter of friends in my life. To Pam, Barry, and Thomas Ahearn, for the best family a girl could have; for Bekye Faragson, my big sister whom I love so much; always to Suzie Jagger Richards, eternally gorgeous inside and out; and, last but not least, to Donni Young and Corinne Cloud, my rock when I needed one. Also to my homegirlz: To Vonnie Lynn Sox (I'll always be your Dogg!); to Julia Sotcilina who proved to me that the Russian and American sense of humor is exactly the same; to Ashley Turner Clinton who wears the same social justice armor as I do; and lastly, to the artist Lovetta Clark, the bravest, kindest, most amazing person I've ever met.

To those who've made my path to writing this book infinitely easier: To Marie Dufour Goodwin; Halvor Mikel Halvorson;

Bettymae Cronheim; Tommy Lyons; Monique Muñoz; and, to the fabulous doyenne of the family, Anna Peterson Delson.

Lastly, with love forever and ever, to my two boys, Thomas Young Roberson III and Richard John Lafayette Roberson. I'm grateful every day for you both.